THE MUSIC TEACHER

ADRIANA GUYTON

Published by AG Publishing Australia
www.adrianaguyton.com

ISBN 978 -0-9943087-4-0

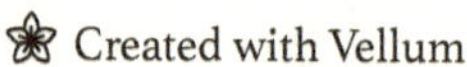 Created with Vellum

~

If music be the food of love, play on

William Shakespeare

1
———

PATRICK

Something cold and moist touching his outstretched hand dragged him from a deep and dreamless sleep. His fingers found the wiry coat of his dog Finn. Patrick lay still, his eyes adjusting reluctantly to the sunlight forcing its way through every gap above, below and between the slats of the bedroom shutters. A jumble of drunken memory fragments slowly assembled themselves in his mind - pleasure and guilt, acknowledging what his sixth sense had been preparing him for: the realisation he was not alone in bed.

How could he have allowed this to happen? He glanced across at the sleeping beauty beside him. He never brought a woman home. Never. *Well, he sure as hell had now.* As he lay chastising himself for his stupidity and lack of control, his throbbing headache seemed to intensify and pick up tempo, like a mad little drummer inside his head thump, thump thumping out a punishing rhythm.

His senses overwhelmed by the waft of stale beer and sex, he pulled himself up in bed and tried to focus on the room. It was a mess; clothes and shoes littered the floor, and an array of empty glasses sat on the chest of drawers - witness to the heavy night they'd had.

A handbag was hanging from a chair, gaping like a half-open

mouth, hinting at the hidden assortment of essentials that women daren't leave behind on a night out. The *just in case I need a toothbrush. Just in case I need tampons, combs, brushes, makeup, mirrors, vodka miniatures, wet wipes*, etc. The list was endless.

The intruding rays of sunlight continued to force their way through and around the shutters, casting golden shadows on the walls, highlighting tiny dust motes as they danced and floated through the air propelled by a gentle breeze coming from the open window in the en suite.

His eyes came to rest on Erika sleeping peacefully beside him, her long blonde hair fanned out across the pillow. Memories of the undeniable desire and passionate sex they'd enjoyed only compounded the feeling of shabby wretchedness Patrick felt. He couldn't undo what had already been done, but somehow he needed to extract himself from this situation and ensure Erika was safely escorted to a cab and sent on her way.

She woke at his touch, her blue eyes radiant in the morning light and her full mouth working its way into a lazy smile. She reached her hand out and pulled him down to her breasts, ready and eager to have more of him.

What a sight; what a beautiful woman. He knew what his body wanted, what any man would want, but it wasn't going to happen. He pulled back, taking both her hands in his, smiling at her gently.

'Sorry, I need to get up and showered. I have to get to the studio. I need to get moving. Shall I call you a cab?'

'Um...okay. I thought we might have enjoyed breakfast together?' She'd raised herself up on one elbow, the look of disappointment evident.

'I'm really sorry. I have a lot on today. Do you want to shower first?'

'Why not save water and shower together?' The lustful look she gave him was almost his undoing. He could so easily have pushed her back down amongst the covers and made love to her once more.

'I won't be long,' he said, leaping from the bed, almost tripping over Finn in his haste. 'I'll sort a cab out as soon as I'm out of the shower.' He knew he was being ruthless, a selfish bastard in her eyes, and it felt so much worse because he couldn't hide from the truth that he knew he was at fault. He should never have brought her back and couldn't remember why he had.

After stepping out of the shower, he glanced at his reflection in the mirror as he quickly towelled himself dry. He still looked like shite—clean shite maybe—but it wasn't hard to figure out how he'd spent the night. His phone beeped a reminder message.

'Fuck, fuck, fuck. Jesus and Mary! I'm going to be late for an appointment,' he shouted, his voice echoing around the bathroom.

Erika was still lying in bed when he came out, towel wrapped around his waist, his hair wet and tousled. Tripping over shoes and clothes scattered on the floor, he pulled open the top drawer in his chest of drawers, almost knocking over the empty glasses perched precariously on the top. He found socks and pants before turning to the walk-in wardrobe to find a clean shirt and jeans.

'Bathroom is all yours, but can you hurry?' he called out over his shoulder. 'Sorry, I'm going to be late for an appointment.'

'You go. I can lock up if you like.'

Patrick almost fell over trying to pull on his jeans. *Like hell.* That wasn't going to happen. He would rather keep a parent waiting than have Erika making herself at home whilst waiting for his return.

He glanced at her as she made her way to the bathroom, her naked body taunting and tempting. God, she was gorgeous. He shook his head in an effort to provoke his thumping headache and blot out the thoughts challenging his resolve.

Buttoning up his shirt, he was relieved to hear the sound of the water running and hoped she wasn't one of those women who enjoyed an hour-long shower.

'Shite. This is not a good look,' Patrick mumbled to himself. Hamish had recommended him to a new parent and here he was, not artistic, cool, and professional but late, hungover, and hopefully not looking like he'd had a long night shagging his brains out. *Well done, Patrick. You sure know how to impress.*

Why didn't I just come home alone? Why couldn't I keep it in my trousers? He silently chided himself as he tried not to pull on unmatched socks and slipped his feet into shoes.

She was lovely—he knew that. It was part of the problem, made worse because she was the sister of one of his band members. He really didn't want to think about how Phil would react if he thought Patrick was treating his little sister with a lack of respect.

Patrick hadn't seen Erika in years until a month ago when she'd turned up at the club to hear her brother play. Her interest in Patrick had been obvious from the start and they'd laughed and joked together after the gig when the band retired to the bar for a few drinks.

He'd been taken with the beautiful woman sitting opposite him. He remembered she'd been cute as a young girl, but now she was quite the looker, her Swedish heritage highlighting a natural beauty with long blonde hair, high cheekbones, and bright blue eyes.

She'd reached out across the table to touch his hand when he'd offered to buy her another drink, and it had started from there.

Later, she'd told him of her recent separation. That should have been a warning, but he'd walked head-on into a whirlwind of drinks, dinner, and sex. Until last evening, it'd always been more convenient to end up at her apartment in Notting Hill, and that had suited Patrick just fine.

Patrick's imperfect memory of the previous night was failing to answer why they had made the much longer journey out of London to his place in Henley. Could it have been drunken largesse on his part, or had it been Erika's idea, charming her way past his defences to draw their relationship just a little closer on his home turf?

It had been a mistake. The whole thing had been a mistake. His mistake—he couldn't blame Erika—but he knew from the look of surprised disappointment on her face this morning that she was expecting more from him. It was not something he could give.

Before her, he hadn't been with a woman, not even for an evening out, in over six months. Erika had been a welcome—no, that sounded like such an insultingly insipid and patronising adjective—a delightful, sexy, and interesting interlude, but that's all it was, all it could be.

Regardless of how much he'd enjoyed her company, the light-hearted banter and great sex they'd shared over the past weeks, it would go no further. He wouldn't allow it.

His behaviour was shabby, and whilst it might have suited a younger man, it was hardly flattering at his age and a wave of shame rolled over him.

Looking around the room for his wallet and keys, he saw them lying between the glasses on the chest of drawers. *God, what a mess.* He'd have to clean this up as soon as he got back this evening. There was certainly no time to do it now.

'Shall we meet for supper tonight?' Erika was standing in front of him, a towel wrapped around her body, her hair damp from the shower and her face radiant. She looked like something from a Nordic shampoo ad, and he was once again reminded of how lovely she was, inside and out.

'No. I can't tonight or the rest of this week. I'm too busy with work.' He was going to have to let her down gently. He didn't do commitment. He didn't want any ties, but however much he tried to make that clear from the start, inevitably it ended like this with the woman wanting so much more than he was capable of giving.

He saw the look of confusion cross her face before she composed herself and smiled. A smile that failed to reach her blue eyes. She was still young with plenty of opportunities to meet someone else and fall in love, but it wasn't going to be him.

Erika turned away, busying herself with picking up her clothes and shoes from the floor. 'I'll be ready in a minute. Can you call a cab for me, please?'

Her tone was one of defeat, and he felt the same wretched feeling he always did, that somehow he'd led her on, made her feel she meant more to him. He never made promises or mad declarations of love, but still women misread his intentions, and that was surely down to him.

'Of course. I'm sorry, Erika. I just have to get to work.' He wouldn't say, *'Otherwise I would love to have stayed in bed all morning with you.*

Made love, read the papers, eaten breakfast together,' but that wasn't how Patrick rolled.

It was thoughtless of him to have spent time with her these past few weeks, unwittingly leading her to believe there could be something more. She was still getting over a separation, and there he was: Patrick Devlin at your service. No wonder she looked crestfallen when he'd turned down supper.

He'd been foolish to bring her back here to his apartment. He'd let his guard down last night, but it wouldn't happen again. This was his space and a place where he could relax, unwind, and enjoy being alone. He loved his own company. He loved his own things around him. A man of simple pleasures.

His collection of guitars, expensive art on the walls, and simple, elegant furniture and furnishings made his two-bedroomed Henley apartment a home and he loved it. His tastes were masculine but stylish. He'd not sought nor wanted a woman's influence in decorating when he'd first moved in.

He'd told his parents back in Ireland when he'd phoned them to say he'd finally found something worth buying that he wanted to live in it for a month or so before changing anything. He wanted to *feel* the spaces and believed then and only then would his instincts guide him to making the right choices for each room. That had been a successful plan.

This was a mess, and he'd have to sort it out quickly before he hurt her even more. He grabbed up his phone and quickly scrolled through his contact list to find the local cab company.

2

JACK
THREE DAYS PRIOR

It was the day of Jack's interview for the music academy. Mr Neeson collected Jack as arranged from St Julian's and drove him to the studio in Henley. Jack felt like he'd gone to bed last night as a 14-year-old boy doing 14-year-old boy stuff and woken up this morning as someone different, more grown up and being treated like he could really be a proper musician. That stirred something in him more awesome than he'd ever known.

Mr Neeson had not only been his music teacher at prep school, he'd been there for Jack when Jack's parents separated. Although Jack never felt comfortable talking about that time, he'd found it comforting to know Mr Neeson understood and didn't push him to discuss anything personal. Unlike some of the boys in his dorm when he'd still been at prep school – they had been really insensitive, annoying him with their nosy questions and thoughtless comments about whether or not Jack's dad had a girlfriend. Jack had complained to his mother at the time about how unfair it had all been.

'Are you excited, Jack? Do you feel you've prepared sufficiently?' Mr Neeson asked. They were driving in Mr Neeson's old car, not his wife's new one. But Jack liked the old Peugeot with its worn leather seats and old-fashioned dashboard. He cringed as Mr Neeson crunched the gearbox, unable to find third gear easily, and thought it might be better for the car if he got an automatic next time.

'She hasn't been out for a run in a while, so she's a bit rusty, as am I with the gear stick.' Jack smiled and wondered, not for the first time, why people referred to cars as *she* and not *he*. It was one of those conundrums that occupied Jack's mind occasionally. He liked the word *conundrum*. It was a new word he'd discovered. A good word to use to describe this particular little puzzle.

'I've been practising nonstop ever since you talked to me about meeting Mr Devlin. I'm so glad you did, because I'm really bored with the music lessons here. The teacher is nice, but there's no challenge for me.'

'Well, I'm sure Mr Devlin will be impressed with you, Jack. You just have to relax and play the way I know you can.'

'Yes, sir. I know this is a great opportunity. I don't want to blow it.'

'I'm sure you won't. I've every confidence in you.'

They parked in a side street on the outskirts of Henley, and Jack looked up at the tall stone building. *This is it. He'll either like me or he won't.*

Mr Neeson pressed the buzzer, and almost immediately Jack could hear a click and the door swung open slightly. They stepped inside to an entrance hall with a sweeping staircase that led up to the studio. Jack was clutching his drumsticks so hard his hand was hurting. He relaxed the white-knuckled grip and flexed his fingers in and out until he could feel the tension release.

He felt so nervous he feared he might throw up. It was only natural to be nervous, he'd been telling himself all the way there. He followed Mr Neeson up the stairs, and as they reached the top and stood on the landing, the door in front opened and Patrick Devlin stood smiling out at them both.

'Thanks for coming, Mish, and you must be Jack?' he said, extending his arm to shake Jack's hand. 'Pleased to meet you.'

'Nice to meet you, sir, and thank you for giving me the opportunity to audition.'

As they made their way further into the room, Jack glanced about. It had to be the coolest space he'd ever seen. The studio was huge, much bigger than he could have imagined. It had been divided up into spaces with room dividers. High ceilings punctured with skylights cast light patterns around the room and across the array of instruments which lined the walls.

Photographs and what looked like certificates hung in groups in every spare wall space. Large floor-to-ceiling windows ran across one side of the room, providing uninterrupted views of the Thames. Polished wooden floors glowed from beneath large rugs. The whole space was sophisticated and welcoming, and Jack's galloping heartbeat slowed to a trot. He immediately felt comfortable there.

Mr Neeson patted Jack on the back. 'You'll be fine. Just relax and remember you can do this.' He moved off behind a screen where Jack could hear him making what sounded like a drink. Pouring water, the sound of a switch clicking, and a cup being lifted from a shelf.

'Take a seat, Jack.' Mr Devlin said, pointing to two big leather chairs. 'So Mr Neeson tells me you're keen to step up to another level in music?'

'Yes, sir,' Jack responded, struggling to remain calm under this man's gaze. He was so unlike any music teacher Jack had met. With his collar-length hair, his designer stubble, dressed informally in jeans and a tee shirt, not the usual collar and tie, he wasn't the sort of teacher Jack was used to.

'Now, you don't need to call me *sir*. It makes me feel old.' He smiled at Jack. '*Mr Devlin* will be fine. At this academy, we take a different approach to music, probably not what you have been used to at school.'

'Yes, sir—I mean Mr Devlin.' Jack's heartbeat had increased a notch and was running at a canter. He wondered if he'd be capable of uttering anything other than *yes* and *no*. Finally meeting Mr Devlin in person was overwhelming for him, and he began to doubt his ability to impress someone so cool with his playing.

'I've devised a programme where musicians have the opportunity to learn multiple instruments. So far, it's been very successful. I've had a number of my more talented students go on to have very successful musical careers. Where do you see yourself in the future with music, Jack? Is it playing in a thrash metal band, conducting an orchestra, composing tunes for breakfast cereal adverts?'

The question took Jack totally by surprise as he'd sort of expected Mr Devlin to know what to teach him. He felt the increasing pressure of the seconds passing under Mr Devlin's penetrating gaze as he tried to work out what the best answer was meant to be. He so didn't want to say the wrong thing, and then he realised it was just a question, not a test, so he took a slow breath to steady his nerves before answering.

He looked down at his feet, hoping to find the right words to convey where his passion lay and whether by voicing this out loud it would ease the uncertainty he'd been struggling with for months. He'd not even shared this with his mother or Mr Neeson. It had evolved in his head, away from the risk of criticism or, even worse, puzzled disappointment. Now that he had the opportunity to articulate his dream, he hesitated before finding the courage to commit to where he saw himself in years ahead.

'Well, sir...I would really love to compose.' He looked up, expecting to see disappointment, but felt surging relief wash over him as he took in the face smiling back.

'For movies and TV series, that sort of thing. And maybe bands?' Emboldened by the smile from Mr Devlin, Jack relaxed a little.

'I think that's marvelous Jack. It's unusual for someone your age not to want to be in a band and perform, but I love that you see yourself beyond that.'

'It's not that being in a band wouldn't be cool, but it's not...it's not where my heart lies.' He thought he sounded lame using such an emotional expression and wondered if Mr Devlin would think of him as weird or sissy.

'I think that's incredibly mature and discerning of you.'

Jack had no idea what discerning meant, but assumed it was positive. He'd Google it that night when he was back at school.

'Have you thought of what instruments you would be interested to learn, ones that would enhance your musical knowledge enough to compose?'

'Well, I'd like to keep playing the drums. I love the drums, and you need percussion for composing. Piano, maybe strings, brass section?'

Jack looked across at Mr Devlin, hoping he had chosen the right combinations and he wouldn't seem ignorant and silly with his suggestions. He'd done a lot of research and felt he understood what was required.

'Excellent choice. We could start with piano, or probably a keyboard for practicality, then move on to brass. Do you know which woodwind instrument you would prefer to play?'

'I was thinking saxophone.'

'Interesting. And a good choice. It's an instrument that is required to be transposed when composing, which will give you a bit more of a technical challenge writing in different clefs compared to the piano. Woodwind instruments require a different part of the brain to operate. I think that would work well, with maybe later on, viola or violin. How would you feel about either of these for a string instrument?'

'Great. I like them all.' Jack sat back in the big chair stretching his legs out straight in front of him like he was unfolding from the inside out and releasing all the pent-up tension he'd been internalising since they drove out of the school gates. He realised that this man got him. He understood where Jack's mind was heading and didn't think it was uncool.

'So let's hear you play. I've set up the drum-kit for you. It's a vintage kit from the 60's, something you might not have played before. Mr Neeson said you were left-handed?'

'Yes, I am. Thank you. I've brought my own sticks.' Jack looked down and noticed his hands were sweating as he rose to walk across to the drum kit. He was tempted to wipe his wet palms on his school pants but could suddenly hear his mother's voice as though she were in the room. *Don't wipe your hands on your trousers, Jack. It makes marks I can't get out in the wash.*

He waited until he'd settled himself behind the drum kit and reached for the towel draped across the extra stool beside it. He wiped his hands thoroughly and began to play.

Jack knew this was his one opportunity. It was such an important audition, more important than when his mum had taken him for his interview to be accepted into St Julian's College. That had been more terrifying than important, even though it was important, as his mum kept pointing out endlessly. This senior college was perfect for him, the way Heathstone had been a perfect prep school, she'd said so often he'd wanted to shout that he knew all that. He wouldn't muck it up. He'd wanted to go to the school, he really did, and now in his second year, he knew he'd been right to believe it was the best school for him.

His mum had been right in suggesting they look at St Julian's as a first choice of senior college, but she shouldn't have nagged in the way she did. He knew it came from a place of caring, of love. But it was tiring and frustrating being told over and over as though he couldn't be trusted to remember just how important things could be.

Jack had spent time researching Mr Devlin, and he felt he knew quite a lot about him. He didn't want to disappoint with his performance or feel, despite Mr Neeson's recommendation, that he really wasn't quite ready for one-on-one tutoring at the music academy. The thought that he might not be accepted as a pupil had plagued his dreams, leaving him exhausted and grumpy in the mornings.

But now he was in this cool studio with its high ceilings and big windows and beautiful instruments, including a fabulous vintage drum kit, his nerves slowly dissipated, and he could feel the burn of confidence glowing brighter and brighter within him.

The moment his sticks hit the skin of the drum, he relaxed and let himself become immersed in the music. He played three pieces before Mr Devlin held his hand up signalling for him to stop.

'Would you like a glass of water, Jack?'

Jack declined the offer, despite his thirst. He suddenly felt so nervous he wasn't sure he could hold a glass steady and not drop it. And he thought, having only played three pieces, maybe Mr Devlin was going to let him down gently by explaining he needed to wait a few more years. A few more years before he could consider tackling the saxophone or piano or violin. Jack clasped his hands tightly together, waiting for Mr Devlin to say something.

'I enjoyed listening to you play, Jack. You're a talented young man. If you wish to strive to have a career in music, to compose as you indicated you would like to do, you need to understand the rhythm of other instruments. You need to feel how they sound, how you can embrace each and every tone that you make.'

'Yes, Mr Devlin, I understand that, I really do.' He knew he was sounding eager to please, like a kid seeking a teacher's favour, but his desperate need to be accepted was so much greater than trying to look and sound cool.

'Provided your parents agree, I would like to take you on as a pupil.'

'Really? Really? Thank you, Mr Devlin, that means so much to me. I won't let you down.' Jack was almost out of breath with excitement, so excited he didn't think to say it wouldn't be parents; it would be his mother.

'It's not me you need to be concerned about letting down, it's yourself. It's up to you, Jack, to put in the time, the practice, and the love for what you're doing.'

'Yes, sir—I mean Mr Devlin. This is what I want, what I need to become a better musician. I can't wait to start.'

In the car on the drive back to school, Jack was unusually quiet.

'You okay, Jack?' Mr Neeson asked. 'What's on your mind?'

'Mum. Do you think she'll agree to me having tutoring with Mr Devlin?'

'I can't see why she would say no. I realise there is a cost involved and you need to take that on board as well, Jack. But your mum wants the best for you always. Just keep that in mind.'

Jack mulled this over, knowing that what Mr Neeson had said was true. She did want the best for him in everything he did, whether it was sport, studies, or music. But he'd never wanted anything as much as he wanted this, and he was fully aware there was a cost involved without Mr Neeson having to remind him, and that made him feel anxious. Anxious that when his mother met Mr Devlin she wouldn't like him or wouldn't like his approach. It could be anything. She always said how it was important to have high standards, but he also understood she sometimes just didn't like someone, and once she made up her mind, it was very hard to change it.

He knew they didn't have a lot of money compared to some of the other boys' families, but surely they would have enough for this. Maybe they could ask his father for more maintenance, or whatever it was called. He'd overheard his mum talking about it with her friend Lizzie when she thought he couldn't hear them. Lizzie was his godmother and his mother's best friend from school days back when they lived in New Zealand.

Thinking of his father made him feel even more anxious. He really did not want his father involved in any decision around his music. In fact, thinking about it a bit more, he really didn't want him involved in anything he did.

Back at school, he was just in time for supper and quickly washed his hands and took his place at the long dining-room table.

'Where did you get too?' asked Dan. 'I was looking for you at break. The master said you were away at an interview. You applying for a job washing dishes in a cafe?' He laughed loudly at his own joke and immediately drew a scowl from the duty master.

'Funny, really funny. I was at a music audition, not an interview.'

'So did you pass or what?'

'Yes, I did, but it's up to my mum to decide if she'll let me do it.'

'Glad it's your mother and not mine. Mine wouldn't spend anything on extras. Your mum is way cool. Of course she'll say yes.' He patted Jack's back in the way one would comfort a nervous puppy.

Jack didn't respond, concentrating on eating his meal and wondering how quickly he could be excused so he could call his mother and let her know.

· · ·

LATER IN THE EVENING, after their homework time, Jack called his mother to tell her about his day.

'So how did it go? Did Mr Neeson take you? He told me he had a free period and would drive out to take you there and bring you back to school afterwards. Nothing went wrong, did it?'

'Yes, he did, and everything was fine. It was nice to have him there, supportive, and they know each other—the teachers, I mean. They went to university together.'

'Oh, right. Okay, so tell me what happened. I really want to hear about it.'

'It was great, Mum. I was really nervous to start with and I was frightened I'd make myself look stupid, but then I got in that special place when it's like you're sort of outside yourself, and I thought I played really well. And then he asked me if I wanted to be in a heavy metal band, and I told him the truth about wanting to compose music and that was the right answer, and then he said that he'd like to take me as one of his students. And, Mum, I really want to do this.'

He rushed on, almost stumbling over his words in an effort to get them out. 'I know it costs money, but I'll get a weekend job or something if we can't afford it.' That was ridiculous, and he knew it. He was fourteen, and he played sport after Saturday morning school, and then on Sundays he practised music. But it was all he could think of on the spur of the moment.

'Don't you worry about the money. It's a consideration, but it's how you feel that really counts. That's what's important. Of course, I'll need to meet Mr Devlin and talk things through with him. I'll arrange that as soon as I can.'

'Thanks, Mum. I won't let you down. I'll work as hard as I possibly can to make the most of this opportunity.'

'I know you will, Jack. I'm just worried you might overstretch yourself, but let's wait until I've spoken with Mr Devlin before we go getting ahead of ourselves.'

There it was. The caution, that *maybe.* Jack ended the phone call feeling a little crushed. He knew what this meant. His mum would have to *approve* of Mr Devlin, and she was tough to impress.

Since his father left, his mother had devoted all her free time to Jack. His school, his sports, his studies. He understood she wanted him to succeed to overcome what had happened in the past, but sometimes he felt suffocated by her love for him, her devotion. Sometimes he just wanted to see her kick back and relax, an expression Dan used and one Jack had liked and consequently adopted as his own.

His mum let him have school friends back to stay whenever he wanted and attended every sports match and school event in which he participated. He knew he was truly loved, but he was beginning to feel responsible for his mum's happiness, and the burden of that weighed on him heavily.

You're the man of the house, Jack; what do you think we should watch tonight on TV? You're the man of the house, Jack; what would you like for supper? You're the man of the house, Jack; you need to cut the grass for me.

He hadn't asked to be the man of the house. He'd felt so grown up when she used to say this, when he was younger and still in prep school. Now it just annoyed him. He wanted to be set free of the burden of responsibility. He was a fourteen-year-old boy. He just wanted to be a fourteen-year-old boy without all this grown-up pressure. He wasn't the man of the house.

The thought of broaching this subject with her was overwhelming. He knew she'd be hurt, confused that he felt this way. He didn't believe she would understand, and therefore there was little point trying to discuss it with her.

They'd always shared a close and open relationship. He knew this. But for reasons he couldn't define, he couldn't imagine having a conversation where he told her, however thoughtfully, to back off. *Kick back and relax, Mum.* That's what he wanted to say. *Find a life for yourself. Find friends. Find a boyfriend.*

All she ever did was work, organise Jack's life for him, and occasionally see Lizzie and Michael. Even then, she didn't seem to be spending much time with Lizzie and Michael anymore. He didn't believe anything had changed, like an argument or something, but she was spending more and more time either working at home over the weekend or organising Jack's social life, encouraging him to have boys back and to go off on bike rides or go to the movies. He didn't have much say in how he spent his spare time unless he shut his bedroom door and practised music.

JACK FELT SMOTHERED by all this love and attention and intensely guilty for not being more appreciative that she put him before herself in so many ways. He just wanted some breathing space to make his own choices, but he'd never share his feelings with anyone. To do so would be disloyal, and so he contained the burden within himself.

Well after lights out, Jack lay on his back looking at the ceiling, unable to sleep. He was thinking of the interview with Mr Devlin. He was such a cool dude—not what Jack had expected, despite all his Google research of him. He smiled, realising he was like his mother. She spent half her life, it seemed to Jack, Googling people, clients, potential employees, teachers. It was a long list, and he'd clearly caught the bug because he'd spent a serious amount of time Googling Mr Devlin. But even with all that knowledge and the pictures he'd seen online of him, he couldn't have known how intense he would be. How warm and encouraging he was.

It wasn't that Jack felt Mr Neeson wasn't warm and encouraging; it was just different. Mr Devlin had something else. He was passionate in a way Jack felt he himself was. He was so cool, funky with his hair longer and touching his collar and his designer stubble and dressed in jeans and a tee shirt he was so different from any other music teacher.

He wanted to shout out '*Yes, I'm in*' and punch the air, but he restrained himself just in time. He didn't need the rest of the dorm thinking he was dreaming out loud or want to get in trouble with the house master for waking them all up.

Jack recognised the passion both he and Mr Devlin shared, and that was intoxicating for him. He felt giddy lying there in his narrow boarding-house bed. Giddy with the excitement of what the academy could bring, what it would be like, and how it would feel to play another instrument other than his drums. He loved drumming with all his heart, but he'd longed to have a go at playing piano and saxophone.

His gaze had roamed around the studio, drinking in the atmosphere and checking out the instruments lined up against the walls. He couldn't wait to get started, and with that thought in mind, he finally drifted off to sleep.

3

JULIA

Julia arrived at the studio a few minutes ahead of time. She liked to be early, never late. She lifted the heavy brass door knocker designed in the shape of a Celtic knot and let it fall heavily against the door. It was then she saw there was a doorbell. She buzzed, but no one came and there appeared to be no sound from within. She buzzed again, but still no response.

She stood back from the doorway and looked at the building. It was a beautiful example of Georgian architecture, and she wondered if he owned it or leased it. Probably leased. It was a handsome and expensive multistorey property.

Checking her watch, she noted he was now five minutes late. She hated to be kept waiting. A woman who liked order and control and professionalism did not like to be kept waiting.

She wasn't at all sure if this tutor would be suitable for Jack, despite Hamish recommending him. She could rely on and trust Hamish. He'd been so kind and thoughtful following her separation, and he'd taken a special interest in Jack's progress as a musician. And so when Jack had voiced his concerns about the lack of challenge in his music classes, Julia had consulted Hamish, and now she was here, having agreed to the meeting, but Patrick Devlin seemed not to think it as important as she did.

That was a black mark against him. Jack didn't need another unreliable man in his life—his father had excelled in that department. She'd give it a few more minutes, then she would leave.

A minute later, she saw a tall figure almost running towards her with papers under his arm, keys jangling from his fingers. His collar-length hair was still wet, presumably from a shower, unless he'd being doing laps of the local pool. She presumed this must be him. This must be Patrick Devlin. No one else could look that desperate and ridiculous at this time of the morning.

She sighed. How could Hamish have thought this would work? If this man couldn't manage to be on time for a prospective new client, it didn't say much for his personal standards. *How irresponsible.* Having little social interaction outside work and her son's school, Julia found it easy to judge others' failures to manage the intricacies of everyday life. Even Michael, the husband of her best friend Lizzie, had commented about it recently.

'You need to get out a bit more, Julia, find a little more balance. You know what I mean, between work and, you know, social stuff. It's not good for you to be locked away every weekend like a hermit with only Jack for company. Have you thought of seeing someone, you know, a counsellor or psychotherapist to help you move on?'

Michael was a doctor—a GP, not a psychiatrist.

'Oh, thank you, Michael, for worrying about me, but I think I'd be the first one to know if I had a problem that I thought needed fixing.'

She'd bristled with indignation at his pointed comments. Of course she wasn't a hermit. How ridiculous. She saw people every day in her job. She saw people at school. She had Jack.

Hermits had no one; they were loners living in the woods. (She did have woods at the back of her cottage, but that didn't count). They lived on mountaintops or sometimes in inner-city apartments that they seldom left because they were maladjusted outcasts. They were solitary because people didn't want to hang out with them, and that clearly wasn't the case with Julia, who could have as many friends as she wanted but chose instead to have a little quiet time when away from the office.

She'd fumed silently at the perceived slight. Maybe it was Michael who had the problem, needing crowds of people around him to feel validated, whereas Julia was a stronger individual, and a mother.

'I'm so sorry to keep you waiting. I'm Patrick, and you must be Mrs Davis?' He didn't wait for an answer.

'Please come up.' Close up, she could smell stale alcohol on his breath; even the after-shave he was wearing couldn't conceal it. His hair was wet, as she'd first thought, but at least he appeared to be wearing clean clothes. A smart shirt and jacket with designer jeans.

Julia had perfected the art of quickly appraising someone from top to toe whilst appearing not to be obviously studying them. Reading people accurately was a necessary skill of her job as a lawyer.

She followed him up the stairs and waited while he fumbled through multiple keys to open the door ahead of them.

God, this is ridiculous. Does he work here or not? Was she really thinking of putting her son into the hands of this dithering unreliable man, however gifted he was meant to be as a musician and tutor?

She'd made up her mind before the key turned in the lock that it wouldn't be happening. She'd find someone else. Someone more suitable, more like Hamish. Calm, reliable, that's what Jack needed. Not this disorganised, man in front of her.

Patrick stepped aside to let her pass, and Julia walked into what could only have been described as a beautiful space. It was exactly as Jack had told her when they'd talked over the phone. In amongst his excitement at being accepted, he'd described the high ceilings, the floor-to-ceiling windows, all those beautiful instruments lined up against the wall like silent members of an orchestra. Certificates and photographs hung from the walls. She wanted to inspect them but didn't wish to convey interest.

Julia had a powerful urge to examine everything in detail for what it revealed about this man, although she would describe it to herself as her "inquisitive nature as required for the job".

The floors were polished English oak. She could smell a faint scent of wax, conjuring up a sudden memory of her father waxing and buffing beautiful furniture in his workshop as she sat on the stool he'd made for her and watched him labour.

Large Turkish rugs covered the floor, adding to the style and well-laid-out design, Julia thought. There was order and calm in this space, and she couldn't help but be impressed. It was not what she was expecting.

A door at the far side was shut, and she wondered what lay beyond that. Probably a room he kept for entertaining. He looked the type. The studio was such a contrast to her first impression of this man standing looking at her that it left her feeling slightly off balance, a tiny bit less certain about her spontaneous assessment of him downstairs.

Over the phone, Jack had also talked nonstop about Mr Devlin. 'Mr Devlin this' and 'Mr Devlin that.'

If she believed everything Jack had said, Patrick Devlin was right up there with God. Only God hadn't worked the seventh day, whereas, according to Jack, Mr Devlin probably had. Teenage boys were so impressionable.

'How do you know that?' she'd asked.

'Mr Neeson told me. Mr Devlin helps disadvantaged kids learn music, often on Sundays.'

Her thoughts were interrupted as she stopped staring around the room and turned to focus on what Patrick was saying.

'I really am terribly sorry to have kept you, but now you're here, let's talk about Jack. Please, take a seat.' He pointed to the two large leather club chairs. 'Can I make you a tea, coffee, water?'

'No, thank you. I don't have much time. I need to get back to my office.'

That was a lie; she had plenty of time. She'd booked out ninety minutes in her diary, and Maria would handle anything that was urgent.

She didn't want to let him off the hook so easily, keeping her waiting like that. It was so annoying and disrespectful to her. And the

Irish lilt to his voice was disarming. She wouldn't allow herself to be charmed into a cosy coffee with this man with his designer stubble and rakish good looks.

'I've met Jack, as you know, and heard him play. He's a delightful young man and talented. I think he would benefit greatly from the academy I run.'

He was staring intently at her, which she found quite unnerving. But she stared straight back at him, holding his gaze and forcing him to be the one to turn away from her scrutiny.

'So tell me, Mr Devlin—'

'Please, call me Patrick.'

She wouldn't call him any such thing, not today anyway. He was too familiar too quickly. Too smooth, and maybe a little patronising to think he could just charm her.

'As I was saying, how is this going to work, playing multiple instruments? I mean, Jack's already an accomplished drummer, so I wouldn't wish to see him lose his enthusiasm for drumming.'

'Jack will, of course, continue to play drums, but he will also learn piano, saxophone, and possibly a string instrument. But ultimately it will be up to Jack to decide which instruments he wishes to play. It really depends on where he sees himself musically in the future. Jack has a passion to explore the limits of his ability, do you not think?'

'I've only spoken with him briefly, and yes, he sounded enthusiastic.' This was a disingenuous statement, she knew, but Julia was not prepared to commit to this music academy until she learned more about Patrick Devlin.

'We'll start Jack on keyboards, probably for the first term, interspersed with drumming lessons and see where he sits switching between those two instruments. The next term we would introduce the saxophone, depending on how Jack feels and how he's handling learning multiple instruments.'

'Why do you want to take my son on as a pupil?'

Julia could see the question caught Patrick by surprise, halting his rhetoric mid flow. She'd noticed him intently looking into her eyes as he made his pitch and quietly enjoyed his discomfort as he tried to recompose himself before responding.

'Apart from the recommendation from Hamish, and my own appraisal of Jack's playing ability, I'm looking for hunger in a pupil. A passion for music—the big picture not just an instrument. That's what I see in your son, and it excites me to think how far that might take him.'

She nodded in acknowledgement. 'This is Jack's second year of senior college. He's got a heavy workload with study. A lot of change. You don't consider this might push him too far?'

'Honestly, no, I don't. But we can see how he manages in the first term and perhaps we can meet and discuss next steps at that time?'

'We'll see. I have a lot to consider before accepting.'

She stood and picked up her bag from beside the chair, getting ready to leave.

'Can I just say something?' She stopped when he spoke and turned to face him.

'Most parents are pushing their children and nagging me to work them harder. It's encouraging to meet a parent who's not pushy but still wants the best for their child.'

She stared back at him, not a flicker of emotion.

'Thank you. I'll be in touch and let you know my decision. I'll see myself out.'

Julia didn't want him following her down the stairs. She found him unsettling. She'd certainly be grilling Hamish, and of course she'd undertake an intense Googling operation that night. It was her speciality. She Googled everyone she didn't know, including clients. The information gathered always left her feeling more in control of a situation.

While she was driving, Julia decided to phone Hamish Neeson and find out more about this Patrick Devlin. What she'd seen today had left very mixed impressions, and she was having real doubts as to his suitability to teach Jack.

She was used to Hamish and his refined gentle manner, not this smooth talker with beer breath who thought he could charm Julia into flashing her credit card with his soft, lilting Irish accent and award-winning smile.

She wouldn't be won over that easily, and what's more, to be kept waiting in the street for nearly ten minutes was an insulting lack of consideration for others.

'Hamish, it's Julia Davis. How are you? Free to talk?'

'Yes, sure, I've got fifteen minutes before my next pupil. How can I help?'

'I met Patrick Devlin today.'

'Oh, great. I'm glad you were able to catch up. How did it go?'

'Can't say I was that impressed. Are you really sure he's the right tutor for Jack?'

SHE HEARD a sharp intake of breath and a long pause before Hamish spoke. 'I've known Patrick for many years, we were at university together.'

'I know. Jack told me. That aside, can you honestly say, hand on heart, that you believe he's suitable as Jack's tutor?'

'What does Jack think?'

'I haven't really had much time to talk with him, but he said his audition went well. Oh, and thank you for driving him there and taking him back to school. It was really kind of you.'

'No problem, Julia. I was happy to help.'

'I suppose Jack seemed to like Mr Devlin.' She knew she was being misleading with this remark. Jack had raved about him in a way she'd never heard him do before.

'He's very keen to learn multiple instruments. He thinks it will be *wicked*, but you know what boys can be like.'

Hamish laughed, lightening the tension between them. 'Patrick is not conventional. He's not like me. I'm nowhere near as talented. Patrick is a remarkable tutor, albeit a little unorthodox. Is that what you're worried about?'

'He turned up late, unshaven, though so many men think that's fashionable these days. He reeked of alcohol and really looked worse for wear. It's not impressive for a first- time interview and I'm not sure that he will set a good example for Jack.'

There was a slight pause again before Hamish responded, as though he were choosing his words very carefully.

'Look, he's a single Irish man who is an extraordinary musician and teacher. He works hard and sometimes plays hard, but I don't consider him unfit for tutoring Jack, and I certainly wouldn't have recommended him unless I truly believed that they were the right fit for one another.'

'Okay, I suppose that's a very clear endorsement. I do trust you, Hamish. It's just...well, you know the history, and I'm also a little concerned that he may push Jack too far too soon, especially as this is his second year of senior college. He has a lot on.'

'He won't do that, Julia. Despite the circumstances today, Patrick's a professional and he's got an amazing rapport with children. He just seems to connect with kids.'

'All right, well, I'll let him know we'll progress with the tutoring and review after the first term.'

'That sounds like a great plan. You won't be disappointed, Julia, I promise. I must go but call me if you have any further concerns. Always happy to talk, and that goes for Jack as well. Let him know he was my star pupil and I'm always happy to answer any queries he may have. Bye for now, Julia.'

'Bye, Hamish, and thanks for the reassurance.' She pressed the button on her handsfree ending the call.

'Hmmm, so this Patrick is a bit of a lad about town. Well, he didn't exactly look like a lad to me; had to be at least my age or possibly older. Hard to tell when you're looking at an obvious hangover.' Julia was talking aloud to herself as she drove back to the office. She valued Hamish's opinion and she would keep to her word and trial "Mr lad-about-town Devlin" for one term and then see.

Her real concern was for Jack and how he would handle this opportunity without dropping the ball on his academic schoolwork. Even the additional cost of it wasn't the real worry.

The last thing she wanted was for Jack to feel overwhelmed, but maybe she was underestimating how much he could handle where music was concerned, and she also had to acknowledge he was growing up. He still had a long way to go in his healing process, but when she thought back to when they'd first arrived in England and how far he'd come since starting at Heathstone Prep, the gratitude welled up inside her.

She would still check out Patrick Devlin online that night. There wasn't much you couldn't find out if you were determined. If he was that special, as Hamish had implied, then there should be plenty online about him. Interesting that he was still single, or maybe Hamish had meant divorced.

Either way, it was of no consequence to her. Jack was her priority, followed by her job. They were all she needed in her life and she was content with that choice, regardless of fatuous pop psychology comments about hermits.

4

____

JACK

Jack wanted this more than anything. The opportunity to be tutored by Patrick Devlin. It was a dream come true, provided his mother agreed, and he knew all too well what she could be like.

Music and his mother were the two loves of his life, but increasingly frequently he'd found they were competing with one another for his time, his dedication, and his love.

He didn't know how to raise this with his mum. He wasn't sure he had the words to explain, so he just had to hope that she would meet Mr Devlin and all would be well. But whilst hope was meant to spring eternal according to something he'd read, it didn't always deliver.

They were to meet up this morning, and Jack knew if his mum didn't like Mr Devlin, she wouldn't hesitate to say no to the additional private tutoring, and there would be no second chances.

He loved the drums with a passion, but the opportunity to learn multiple instruments would be his dream come true. Sometimes he felt that funny thing in his stomach, the one his mother said were flutters of excitement, but he knew it was nerves and she was trying to be kind. He didn't want to fail if he was given the opportunity.

Jack knew all too well what failure felt like. Failing exams at prep school before he started learning support had sucked. Even letting the memories into his head brought back the heavy feeling of humiliation and the breath being squeezed in his tightening chest.

Now that he was that much older, he could physically feel his confidence changing, growing inside of him. He desperately wanted to hang onto these new feelings and never let the old ones grip him again.

Jack found senior college to be very different from prep school and the boarding house at St Julian's was less formal than he was used to, but now in his second year he'd grown accustomed to the level of independence St Julian's offered the boys. It made him feel more grown up. *I am grown up...sort of*, he would tell himself. "Fourteen is a special time," his mother kept reminding him. A time of "change and new beginnings."

Jack thought what she really meant was hormones and all that stuff. He didn't spend too much time thinking about that. There were no girls at St Julian's anyway to make the boys get all stupid and show off in class, but he'd overheard whispered conversations after lights out in the boarding house that some boys watched porn. Jack couldn't figure out where or when they did this without the masters knowing.

He made up his mind as he walked to his first lesson that he'd call his mother that night as early as he could to see what she thought about the music academy. He hoped with all his heart she'd agree to him attending. Even thinking about it as he walked to class caused his tummy to flip.

When he imagined himself sitting in front of a piano, his long fingers moving precisely across the ebony and ivory keys, a feeling of joy would spread through him. He wondered what playing the saxophone would feel like, it was such a different instrument to drums.

So much to learn and so many completely different things to get his head around that the little demon of self-doubt would start to twist his insides with tendrils of fear. Maybe it would never be more than a dream.

He knew he wasn't in the little group of the brainiest boys in his year, so maybe all of this would just be too much for him and he'd be embarrassed all over again when he failed.

Even though he wanted this so much, maybe he should wait till he was a bit older instead of having all this challenge on top of his schoolwork.

He was pretty sure his mother would think that was sensible. His thoughts and emotions churned around swapping hopes and fears, what if he did and what if he didn't.

'Hey Jack. Jack Davis.'

Jack turned to see his friend Dan running across to meet him.

'Are you playing squash at lunch break?'

'Yes, I got picked for the team and I'll play in the first round and see how it goes. Are you?'

'Nah, didn't get picked.'

'Oh, sorry, Dan. That sucks. Did you want to play? Have you played before?'

'Only a little. I wasn't that good, but I'd like to keep trying.'

'Well, maybe you should ask the sports master to arrange some extra coaching.'

'Yeah, maybe. I'll see. Anyway, I'll catch you later, Jack. I've got science now. Where are you heading?'

'History.'

Dan pulled a face. 'Glad I'm not doing that first up.'

'I love history. Anyway, I better run, or I'll be late. See you later, Dan.'

Dan had been Jack's best friend since their first day at St Julian's when they were both new and nervous and just a little bit afraid of what lay ahead. They needn't have worried. St Julian's was a great school with dedicated teachers and plenty of opportunities for the boys to shine in whatever interested them outside their academic studies.

Dan and Jack had been put in the same room in the boarding house for their first year, and that had continued by choice into their second year.

Dan never came right out and said, but Jack got the feeling he didn't like being at home much. His mum and dad had busy jobs and they never came to see him play sport or talk with him on the phone at nights.

He lived up in London and could have been a weekday boarder like Jack was, but he was stuck in the boarding house all weekend. Dan had an older sister, though she was a "pain" - according to Dan. Jack wasn't sure why she was a pain, but apparently she just was.

Jack knew he was one of the lucky kids. His dad might not have been around, but his mum more than made up for that. She was the best, in Jack's eyes.

Jack tried not to think about his father. In the beginning, when his father had first left, it was hard, but Jack had been a lot younger then, and now "we've moved on," his mother kept telling him.

He knew it was her way of keeping dark thoughts away. He could see it on her face when she thought he wasn't watching. It still hurt her, and he wished she would find a way to let go, to be a bit more light-hearted about life again.

To think of his father only made Jack angry, and he'd been teaching himself to avoid thoughts of him. To not allow his mind to drift back to that time, especially at night alone in his bed in the boarding house where memories would surface.

The memories were too often ugly images of his mother, broken and bruised in bed in Lizzie's spare room. Jack could still recall how confused he felt seeing her and both understanding and not understanding all at the same time, and how wrong it had all felt in his head.

He knew what his father had done, what a bastard he was.

Playing the drums had helped Jack control the anger and frustration. He would play especially fast and hard and play it out, right out of his mind until the next time.

He'd never shared with his mother the anger that rose to the surface. He didn't want her to know how often that anger turned to a burning rage inside him. It would worry her if she knew, and she already did enough worrying, he thought.

He wished she wouldn't. He also wished she would find a hobby or something as well as work so she didn't spend all her spare time organising him.

Jack had heard his mother talking to Lizzie in the kitchen when they were visiting. He'd been playing on the computer with Michael upstairs and come down to get a drink and overheard their conversation.

'I worry how he'll be when he has his first sexual experience. Will he have flashbacks? Will he find it difficult?'

'I think you just need to wait that one out, Julia. You don't know how much healing he'll do between now and then.'

They'd stopped talking when they saw Jack standing in the doorway to the kitchen. He'd felt embarrassed and angry that his mother was talking to Lizzie about sex sometime in the future. It was dumb, and he wished he'd not heard. It made him feel like a freak, that somehow what happened to him had broken him for life and he'd never fully recover.

As Jack settled himself in class and opened up his books for his history lesson, he let the memories from the past drift away. He was older now and no different from any other fourteen-year-old boy.

Whilst accepting sex was not an experience likely to happen anytime soon—and first he'd need to get a girlfriend, which was even less likely to happen while his time was filled with lessons, sport, and music - he believed in his heart he would be fine.

5

———

PATRICK

'Oh, Patrick, my boy, that did not go well!' Patrick said aloud as he sat back down in his chair. He sighed heavily. That had been an interview from hell, and he wondered whether his lateness and dissipated appearance had caught up with him. This could be a pupil he would not get to teach, which would be a shame as he believed Jack was unusually talented.

He'd been impressed with him when they met. At fourteen, he was tall for his age, slim, with shoulders already starting to broaden. Thick dark hair like his mother's, fine features, and the same dazzling green eyes.

He'd nearly said how like her son she was, before thankfully stopping himself. She clearly didn't resemble a fourteen-year-old boy so the comment would have come across as either vacuous or clumsy flattery, and he couldn't imagine either going down too well. But there was no doubting he was his mother's son. No mention had been made of a Mr Davis by Jack or by Julia. He'd call Hamish later and find out more about mother and son.

The opportunity to teach gifted children multiple instruments gave Patrick an enormous sense of satisfaction. You could never tell at the beginning whether the customised programme of nurturing and then stretching a student's physical, sensory, and intellectual skills would result in a capable but undistinguished musician or one of those rare individuals whose talent soared beyond the ordinary.

In the past four years since he'd introduced his particular method, he'd watched several of his senior pupils go on to positions in major orchestras and finding themselves enjoying a serious career in music. That's what drove him to work the long hours he did.

He shouldn't have let his private life interfere with his work. It was stupid and disrespectful to a client, and he just knew this one set high expectations of behaviour for herself and others. He'd embarrassed himself by being worse for wear and rushing up the street towards her, stumbling and bumbling with keys and papers. No wonder she'd been pissed with him.

His mind drifted back to the point when he'd rounded the street corner and seen her standing there, head down, stabbing at her phone and tapping her foot impatiently. She was not what he'd been expecting. He didn't know what he'd been expecting, but certainly not this tall, willowy, dark-haired beauty. Even from a distance he could see she was startling.

Close up, she was even more beautiful, arresting. And those eyes, emerald green and cool, but not cold. There was a moment when she'd looked directly at him—only a flash, and if he hadn't been staring straight back at her, he would have missed it—a vulnerability, a pain. Then it was gone, and he was left with her cool, professional scrutiny making him feel like an insect under a microscope.

Patrick was seldom caught off guard, but he'd felt himself blushing beneath her evaluating gaze when they'd sat down to talk about Jack.

'Hello, Mish. It's Paddy. Have you got a moment, or are you in the middle of kid stuff?'

'No, all good, mate. Susan's just reading them a story, so I can relax for a few minutes. I understand you had an interview with Julia Davis this morning.'

'I most certainly did. What's up with her? She was a real ice queen. And before you chastise me, yes, I know I was late - bad form on my part - but, boy, did she let me know how pissed she was.'

'Well, the two of you didn't get off to the best of starts, but Julia is lovely, she really is. Just takes a bit of getting to know. And as for Jack, well, he was my star pupil, and I think he could really go places with someone like yourself guiding him.'

'I agree. He's ripe for nurturing into a sensational musician. I'll be interested to see how he goes, if she decides to give me the opportunity.'

'She will. Don't worry about that. But you will have to win her over. She'll review at the end of term.'

'It's a change from the usual pushy parents. I told her as much, but she didn't comment. Is there a Mr Davis?'

'Ah, now, Paddy, I can't be sharing confidential information about a parent. All I'll say is she's divorced. And don't be going and getting ideas.'

'Jesus, I don't think she'd be the slightest bit interested in me. Made that fairly clear today. But it's...well, I get a feeling there is more about this boy. Is there anything I should know? And no, I'm not asking you to break a confidence.'

'I really can't discuss it, Paddy, not even with you. Just see how it goes this term and don't keep her waiting again. She abhors being kept waiting, so she does.'

'I kinda worked that bit out for myself. Anyway, I'm grateful Mish, for the referral, and I'll keep you posted. Say hi to Susie and the girls from me.'

'Will do. Give me a call in a few weeks and come over for dinner?'

'I'll do that. Night.'

So there was something! He knew it. Patrick was seldom wrong when it came to reading people. He realised he would have to tread very carefully, acknowledging to himself he could be a clumsy arse at times.

He poured himself a red wine and sat down on the sofa, ready to catch the news before he picked a few chords out on his guitar.

Patrick needed the relaxation of playing to settle himself before bedtime. It always seemed to do the trick in giving him a good night's rest.

Erika had sent him a text message thanking him for the lovely evening and hoping they could meet up again when he had time. *God.* He inwardly sighed. He'd have to sort that out and quickly.

Phil wouldn't be best pleased if he hurt his little sister, even if it wasn't intentional, and Patrick couldn't blame him if he got angry. He wasn't best pleased with himself. He should have left her alone. But it had been Erika who came onto him, as he recalled, after the last set at a gig he'd played up in London, but he realised he should have left well enough alone and ignored her advances.

It should be an unwritten rule in the book of musicians, he thought. Little sisters of band members were off limits, especially if married or recently separated. Now he'd have to explain to Phil and Erika that he wasn't ready for a long-term relationship. He was too committed to full-time teaching and playing to give enough of himself to a serious romance. It wouldn't be fair to the other person. She'd understand, he thought. They normally did.

He could only hope Phil would also understand. He'd had his fair share of tears and narrow escapes himself with women, so maybe he'd think twice before being too judgemental about Patrick's behaviour? Well, he hoped they could put any issues to rest over a few beers.

Patrick clicked the remote, but the news both horrified and confused him. News presenter Chris Lowe in a sombre voice confirmed that - *"UK hostage, Ken Bigley has been beheaded by militants in Iraq."* Patrick wondered what the remainder of 2004 would bring. In June 60 years had marked D-Day. Now a different war was being fought - terrorism.

His stomach churning, Patrick flicked to another news channel and was just about to turn the television off when he saw a familiar face smile back at him from the TV screen. Groomed, bronzed and made up to perfection, the news presenter announced – *"Liam Brady, a high profile property mogul will be moving his business interests to*

Ireland. Born in County Cork, Brady has always maintained strong links back to his country of birth and now intends to invest heavily in commercial property in an attempt to boost the Irish economy".

PATRICK HAD a sudden image of their life back in Ireland. Teenagers sailing in the bay. Just Liam, Patrick, and Carrick, Patrick's younger brother. Patrick recalled that despite Liam never having sailed before, he was a natural, and he loved it.

They went out many times after that, right up until Liam had made a sudden departure from their school.

He had something about him, Liam did. A way, a...Patrick couldn't think of the right words to describe him. Something intangible.

He was good looking but didn't know it, or if he did, he certainly didn't bank on it making a difference. He was a kind, generous person. Hard for him coming into a school at the age he was. Their school. Their little Irish Protestant school in Baltimore, County Cork, where both Patrick's parents taught, making it difficult for his brother and himself to ever feel totally at ease, let alone get up to boyish pranks or kiss a girl behind the proverbial bike sheds.

Patrick remembered Liam's parents were sort of new freedom traveller types, always on the move, taking him around the country as new opportunities captured their attention.

When Liam left their school it was to pursue a better life in Dublin, or so they told him, but it wasn't better for Liam, and Patrick heard several years later that he had left home, making his way to London, hoping to catch a lucky break and make his fortune in the big city. And he had—spectacularly so, by all accounts.

He switched off the TV and went upstairs to play his guitar.

As he sat strumming with Liam still on his mind, he remembered the last time they met up. A few years ago, but at the time Patrick hadn't seen Liam since he left Baltimore. He was playing a gig in London, and at the end of the set Liam had walked across.

'It's Paddy, isn't it? Paddy Devlin, or am I mistaken?'

'No, it's me, and Holy Mother of Jesus, if it's not Liam Brady I'm looking at, is it?'

They'd both laughed and embraced, holding onto that embrace longer than was strictly manly by English standards. But they were Irishmen reunited. And neither of them gave a shite as people stared on.

Patrick's bandmates had teased him the next day, saying they'd seen the tabloid headlines: "Hysterical women jam the Samaritans' phone lines. Seen with his long-lost Irish lover last night in a London bar, Patrick admits. 'Yes, it's true. I'm gay' *Ha bloody ha!*

They'd sat drinking Guinness well into the small hours, reminiscing about days back in Ireland. Liam had spoken of Carrick and it was clear the two kept in regular contact.

Patrick's response had been guarded. He was unwilling to spoil the night discussing with Liam the pain and disgrace of the past. He didn't want that particular boil to be lanced and spew out its ugliness, tainting the evening.

He picked out a simple tune on his Gibson guitar, one he'd not played in ages and wondered if he should give Liam a call and wish him well. He had a way, Liam did, of putting people at ease and listening to them, really listening.

Talking with him that night into the wee small hours, it was hard for Patrick to imagine this man was a seriously wealthy, successful businessman. He was just Liam Brady, the new boy at school who'd charmed everyone with his easy Irish ways and a kindness that was often at odds with the way his parents treated him.

Patrick seldom allowed his thoughts to drift back to school days in Ireland. He visited his parents when he could, but otherwise he preferred to keep the door to his life back there securely fastened.

It was surprising, therefore, to find himself reminiscing. His mind wandered to a time they'd all gone out sailing, Liam, Carrick, and him. They'd had a wonderful day on a calm ocean, catching fish.

Lighting a fire on the beach to cook their catch over an old oven rack they stowed on board their boat.

Simple pleasures. Simple days before life had become complicated, but Liam had already left Baltimore by then and knew nothing of what would follow.

Carrick had gone on to become a successful property developer, not in the league of Liam, but Patrick always believed it had been the influence of Liam that had led him to surprise and disappoint his parents.

Carrick had finished his final year at school and announced that, contrary to expectations, he had decided against university. He believed that he had more of a gift for working with people and would just lose several years of hands-on experience if he went to university.

Knowing how much Carrick at eighteen years of age didn't know about the world, it was easy to see how his parents had attributed such recklessness to Liam's influence. That being said, property became Carrick's all-consuming passion, and he'd done okay, Patrick had to admit.

They seldom spoke, the brothers. Patrick told himself Carrick was always travelling, often abroad, so it was difficult to know when it might be convenient to phone him.

The outcome was for he and Carrick to exchange infrequent short functional emails usually about their parents and whether they would or wouldn't be meeting up for Christmas or their mother's birthday.

There had been occasions when Carrick was in London and would suddenly appear at a gig, and the brothers would catch up briefly after the show before parting once more.

Distance had developed when Patrick left home for university in Edinburgh with unresolved issues between them and subsequent unwillingness on both their parts to have an open and honest conversation about what had happened.

6

———

JULIA

Jack had been so excited to learn his mother had agreed to the additional private tutoring.

Despite Julia's misgivings over Patrick Devlin, which had been temporarily allayed by Hamish's reassurance, she wanted what was best for her son, and if this made him happy and he believed he could manage learning multiple instruments, then that was all that mattered. Weeks had flown by and she'd listened to Jack's enthusiasm for Patrick's teaching methods.

'Oh, Mum, it's just so cool. He works me hard, but I'm learning so much and loving the advanced stuff he's giving me for drums. And yes, I'm still playing drums; that's not going to stop. But, Mum, Mr Devlin really is the coolest teacher yet. Mr Neeson was great, but Mr Devlin is, like, out there.'

'Well, it certainly sounds like you've found a passion for another instrument. I'm glad for you, Jack. It's wonderful to hear you so excited. And how's your schoolwork coming on? You didn't seem to have much homework last weekend.'

'No, in second year we cover off a lot of extra stuff in the early evening. I think I'm doing okay with all my subjects. I'm not behind, if that's what you are worried about.'

'It's not that. It's more, well, you do need to make sure your academic work doesn't get left behind with all the time you're spending on music and sport, that's all I'm saying.'

Jack sighed. 'No,' he said, sounding impatient. 'I'm fine. I'm managing everything. You don't need to worry or start nagging me.'

'I'm not nagging. I'm merely pointing out you have to balance all of it.'

'I have to go now, Mum. We're having a movie night in the boarding house and it's about to start. Speak soon. Love you. Bye.' He rang off before Julia had a chance to say anything further.

'Mr Devlin's out there.' Hmm, he's certainly that. Probably out there a bit too much, judging by the look of him the first time we met!

After their first meeting she'd Googled Patrick Devlin and found a surprising amount of information online. It seemed he really was a gifted teacher and musician. He graduated from Edinburgh University before taking up a teaching role at Abingdon School, teaching both prep and senior pupils.

He then went on to set up his own music academy and introduced his unique teaching methods with amazing results. Julia read how he ran his academy from his Henley-on-Thames studio as well as playing in bands. He also donated his services freely to some public schools in London that had more challenging children who would never otherwise have had the chance to experience the gift of music through learning to play an instrument.

She then went on to read about his music career, the band he was a member of, and the university band he formed with Hamish Neeson.

It seemed they'd been a successful band touring Europe and the States, with several big hit albums to their name. They'd called themselves Platonic. They'd disbanded not long after they finished university, but there was no doubting the list of Patrick Devlin's accomplishments, Julia had to admit.

However, be that as it may, the internet was full of accolades people wrote about themselves and asked a friend to publish for them. Julia needed him to prove his methods and connection with

Jack resulting in his musical growth and that learning multiple instruments would not confuse or overload her son.

Julia wasn't easily impressed by qualifications alone. She needed to see evidence that the talk led to results.

7

———

JACK

'So, Jack, we'll start with piano today. You've done a lot of advanced work with drumming, and I'm pleased with your progress, but it's time now to start the basics of piano.'

Jack felt nervous, wanting desperately to impress Mr Devlin. He wasn't at all sure, faced with the piano in front of him, whether he'd be able to adapt to the technique, the scales, and everything else that went with mastering a big instrument. To divert his fears he found himself wondering how Mr Devlin and his mother were getting along since he started at the academy.

She never mentioned him, and he never spoke of her during lessons. Well, he wouldn't really anyway, Jack thought. They were there to work on Jack's musical skills. It was a serious subject. There was no time to chat about women. He brought his attention back to Mr Devlin.

'First lesson is about posture. You have to learn to sit at the piano in the correct way and ensure your upper arms and elbows hang loose by your sides. Keep your forearms parallel to each other.'

He smiled at Jack in a way that always made him feel warm inside. Not the way he felt when his mum smiled at him or cheered him on from the sidelines at sport. This was different. It was kind of...

man to man. Although Jack was fully aware he was not a man, not yet, and he was not in any hurry to get there, despite his mother's constant reminders that he was the *man of the house*. He wanted to enjoy being the age he was.

Mr Devlin's passion for music and his kindness made Jack feel special. Special in a way his own father never made him feel and more special than Mr Neeson had.

He'd been awake after lights out wondering about playing the piano and whether he would be able to master it. If he couldn't prove to Mr Devlin that he could do more than play the drums, then the chances that one day he'd become a composer weren't promising. These random thoughts plagued Jack.

AN HOUR LATER, Jack finished his first piano lesson. It was even better than he could have imagined. Mr Devlin had been pleased and had put his hand on Jack's shoulder just as he was leaving, something none of the other teachers did, but Mr Devlin did this every now and again when he wanted to emphasise something important.

'You're doing really well, Jack. Your drumming is superb for a young man your age, and now watching you work through those first scales, you have the potential to be a great pianist. But you'll have to practise. Just ten minutes a day is better than nothing. You have several pianos at school—do you think you can manage that?'

'Yes. I'm sure I can, except for the weekends. We don't have a piano at home.' He felt embarrassed saying that, as though he were betraying his mother in some way.

'Well, don't worry too much about the weekends, just don't overdo it during the week. Your fingers will suffer if you do, and as we progress, it might be worth considering a keyboard for home practice. Think about it. Talk to your mum.'

When Jack closed the door behind him and started on his walk back to the boarding house, he wondered how he would be able to convince his mother to buy a keyboard. It needn't be new; a second-hand one would do. He'd have to do more research on what features it would need: eighty-eight keys or sixty-one, portable obviously, different voices, a sequencer for composing, headphones for practising?

He pulled the hood of his jacket up over his head and thrust his hands into his pockets. The nights were drawing in and becoming much colder, but he enjoyed the opportunity to walk through the Henley streets back to school.

Alone with his thoughts and feeling more and more grown up at being granted permission to be out of school in the early evening without supervision.

He knew some boys would take advantage and go off somewhere for a smoke or to chat up girls. Jack had no thoughts of this. He would never betray the trust that his housemaster had given him, nor Mr Devlin and certainly not his mother. He walked straight to the academy each week and straight back, no deviations.

He'd phone his mum when he was back at the boarding house and tell her the latest news and maybe hint at getting a keyboard. She'd not been all that keen on him learning multiple instruments, but he knew he could do it without losing his skills with the drum kit. Drums would always be his first love.

He had told his mother that and believed she now felt better about his choices. He knew the academy fees were expensive, although she'd never told Jack exactly how much, but he knew it would be a lot and she would have to budget.

She was always budgeting. He remembered her saying "talent will far outweigh money." He kind of got what she meant, but he didn't want to let her down and feel she'd wasted money. But he also didn't want to lose this opportunity. Because it was the best thing that had ever happened to him. The best ever.

8

———

JULIA

Julia felt she'd been summoned, or at least that's how it had seemed. She was acutely aware that her thought process around Patrick Devlin could be a little irrational. She was overprotective where Jack was concerned. She knew this also.

Gradually, and it was only gradually, she'd allowed herself to believe he would be all right. That time and music would heal him. But anything outside their routine, Julia tended to go a little off-piste with her speculation that there were problems.

Jack had been privately tutored for the past three months, and now Patrick Devlin wanted her to attend his studio to hear Jack play. She cancelled the late afternoon appointments in her diary and headed out of the office to drive to Henley.

'I'm away now, Maria. On my mobile for anything urgent, otherwise see you tomorrow. Have a good evening.'

'Okay, thanks, Julia. You, too.'

Maria was her legal executive, and she had come to rely upon her skills heavily, from sorting out Julia's diary to interviewing clients or preparing court documents.

She read Julia's briefs and generally did anything and everything

46

Julia needed. She had inherited Maria when she started at Petrie's and took over heading up the family law department.

Thinking back to that time as she drove out of the car park made her smile. Maria had been frosty and offhand, and it wasn't until Julia had sat her down and asked some probing questions that she began to understand where Maria's hostility lay—never being given the opportunity to excel and having her opinion on a case seldom sought.

Eventually, Julia persuaded her to study for her legal executive exams, claiming budget from the firm to pay Maria's study fees. She'd never let her down, and Julia's belief in her had paid off in a myriad of ways. Maria was now a qualified legal executive and thrived on the opportunities Julia directed her way.

The traffic was heavy; the school run coinciding with tradespeople heading home made for slow going. At this rate she might be late herself this time. Heaven forbid that should happen. She was sure Mr Devlin would love to catch her out being late after the hard time she gave him at their first meeting.

Over the past months Jack had thrived not only with music but also his academic studies had continued to improve, and the changes in him were obvious.

A new-found confidence, a growing maturity, and something else, something she couldn't articulate. It was subtle, not obvious. She could sense things with her son.

It was there, this subtlety, but not enough for her to grasp hold of and give it a name, a title.

Jack practised every weekend when he came home from sport. Everything was "Mr Devlin this" and "Mr Devlin that." It was clear Jack idolised him.

She didn't have a problem with that. Did she? She questioned herself frequently on this subject.

Jack had loved being tutored by Hamish, and Hamish was a lovely man - kind, understanding, and a good tutor - but she'd never seen Jack worship him like he clearly worshipped Patrick Devlin.

Even though Julia had never seen them together in the studio—it would be her first time today - she could imagine Jack hanging on his every word. You only had to ask him one question about music and off he would go with a nonstop blow-by-blow account of all the Demi-God Devlin could do and say and play and...

Miraculously, she'd arrived on time, so absorbed in thoughts about Jack she could hardly remember the drive. Julia checked her makeup in the mirror, scolding her own reflection for worrying about what she looked like.

He's a music teacher. You're not going for a job interview or meeting with a top-drawer barrister.

Her internal dialogue spoke of standards and taking pride in oneself, all the while questioning the validity of such nonsense. Was she checking her appearance out of habit, or was there a subtle undertone of wishing to create an impression?

Patrick had emailed Julia regularly since Jack had started and spoken with her over the phone. Always reassuring and updating Jack's progress in detail. She'd come to enjoy the emails and phone calls. Something in his tone and certainly the timbre of his voice was attractive, she had to admit.

Was she really fussing over her appearance for Patrick or was it just plain, everyday vanity, wrapped up in a packaged labelled "standards needing to be upheld"? She could hear her mother saying that. When she was sober, she would often trot out silly clichés as though reciting from some *Manners for Ladies* book she'd read as a girl.

'One should always check one's appearance before leaving the home. After all, standards need to be upheld...'

Julia wasn't sure why she was thinking about her mother at this moment, she seldom entered her thoughts, although lately there had been times when Julia remembered small kindnesses.

They were rare and as unpredictable as an April wind in an English spring. But they were kindnesses freely given in the moment. And now, with the passing of many years, she found herself remembering more of the good than the bad.

She was also less inclined to keep polishing the pedestal she'd placed her father on after he died. She knew he would never have wanted to be placed above others, simply because he wouldn't ever have felt he deserved it. It had been her way of preserving him. Remembering only what she wished to and banishing the thoughts of fear, disappointment, confusion, and bewilderment that had troubled her as a young girl growing up.

She pressed the doorbell and heard the lock click open almost immediately. She walked through the door into the hallway and climbed the staircase to the first-floor studio. Almost as her foot touched the last stair, the door swung open, and she was surprised to see Hamish Neeson smiling back at her.

'Hamish. What a surprise to see you here.' They embraced briefly before Hamish explained he was playing bass to Patrick's lead.

'I think I've mentioned to you before Paddy and I used to play together at university?'

'Yes. I recall you saying.' She wouldn't add that she'd spent time reading up about Mr Patrick Devlin and all his amazing achievements, and Hamish had been part of that. But pride would not allow her to reveal the extent of her Googling activities.

'Well, I can't wait to hear this. How are you, Mr Devlin?' Julia turned her gaze to Patrick, who was standing to one side.

'I'm fine, thank you. Glad you could make it.'

'And Jack,' Julia said, moving further into the room to reach out and give him a quick hug. He was standing holding his drumsticks, which confused her for a minute because she thought he was going to be playing piano.

'You ready for this?' Julia beamed at him, thrilled to be there and keen to hear him play.

'Sure am. There is a seat over in the corner for you, Mum,' he said, pointing to the far side of the room.

She could see he was both excited and nervous, which in turn made her feel anxious on his behalf. Julia settled herself in the big leather chair she'd sat in the first time she'd been to the studio, and waited.

'I wanted you to hear this today for two reasons. Firstly, to see Jack's progression, and secondly, to reassure you that he's still getting plenty of drum playing and excelling with the piano as well.'

Patrick was looking directly at Julia, and she was determined to hold his gaze and ignore the tiny flutter of wings like a moth against the windows of her heart.

'It's a piece by The Ventures. The Shadows also did a version. "Walk Don't Run." It's the learning approach I've asked Jack to adopt.'

Patrick smiled at Julia the way he had the first morning they met. Fortunately, this time she wasn't angry with him, more a little puzzled at the piece of music he'd chosen.

'He needs to walk before he can run where music is concerned.' He glanced away towards Hamish.

'Anyway, I asked Hamish along to play the bass. It's important Jack understands the real work behind the harmony between musicians. I hope you enjoy it.' He turned to face Jack and reached for his guitar.

The Shadows or Ventures? Uh, not really what she was hoping to hear. She thought it would be something different, with Jack playing piano rather than drums. Not that she didn't love The Shadows, but she'd expected something...like what? Dramatic, classical?

She was feeling rather sceptical about this performance but smiled brightly at Jack. She didn't want him to pick up on her sense this was all heading towards an anticlimax.

9

———

PATRICK

'Thanks, Hamish. Catch up soon.' They embraced briefly the way men do when they feel self-conscious. In different circumstances neither of them would have felt uncomfortable but, under Julia Davis's cool scrutiny, they both hugged awkwardly, patting each other's backs as the elderly did when saying good night to a grandchild. Not like close Irish friends who shared so much history.

Patrick reached out his hand to Jack's shoulder as he walked around from the drum kit ready to head out the door.

'You did well, really well. Proud of you, I am.'

'Thank you, Mr Devlin. It was awesome. I've never played with two proper musicians before. It was like nothing I've ever done. Can't wait to do it again.'

His young face was flushed with excitement, and if it hadn't been politically incorrect to do so, Patrick would have hugged him.

'You better be off now before your house master comes looking.'

Jack hugged his mother and words were exchanged, but Patrick wasn't close enough to hear and turned away to avoid making them feel uncomfortable in his presence.

They were alone, just Julia and Patrick, and there was so much he wanted to say. So much he wanted to tell her about her son. About his talent. The excitement he felt inside every time he heard him play. He was gifted. Gifted in a way Patrick had not seen in a child this age. And he was his pupil. Patrick's to shape. Patrick's to challenge. And Patrick's to guide him to stardom. Which he was certain was within Jack's reach if he wanted it enough.

'So what did you think of that performance?'

'It was great, sort of 1960s surf sound. I loved it. Jack played so well.'

'No, you're not hearing my question. You're talking about the music. I'm asking about the musician. What I heard was Jack being so attentive to every nuance of what I was doing on the guitar, what Hamish was doing, as though we were one. He wasn't following me, he was absolutely holding the rhythm and the feel, absolutely rock solid. But he was completely connected to what we were doing and the feel of the changes. Do you understand how extraordinary that is? Jack's not just playing music, he's a true musician. In his heart.'

Patrick thumped his chest, so impassioned with getting the message across.

'If you'd seen as many children as I have who turn up and they do their lessons and they take their grades. They're all lovely, talented kids, but you put them with other musicians playing, particularly skilled adult musicians, they just can't hold it. They can't do their job, they forget their role in the band, and fail to remain completely aware of where everything is going. This is fantastic. What Jack has is something special, Julia.'

Shite, Patrick thought, his face filled with apprehension. He'd just called her Julia. A slip-up on his part. He might refer to her as Julia in his private thoughts, but not aloud when she was in the same room. He'd overstepped the mark.

Patrick knew he'd involuntarily given an impassioned speech that chided Julia for not understanding what she'd heard, but it was how he felt, how he lived as a musician, as a teacher. And he wasn't about to apologise for his enthusiasm and belief in this boy. In this son of hers.

When Patrick lifted his eyes to gauge her reaction, he was surprised to see tears, but not just that, something raw. An unmistakable vulnerability.

In that moment, that second before she blinked and the usual cool persona slipped back into place, he wanted to reach out and hold her. Tell her it was going to be all right. Jack was going to be a successful musician if that's what he wanted. He had the talent. It was up to him to take his gift and soar.

Later, when Julia had left and Patrick was alone in his studio, tidying up and putting things away, he thought about his reaction to Julia's emotion. He'd been frightened at the intensity of his feelings when he'd glimpsed her pain, that raw emotion, knowing that he'd be the last person she'd turn too. And she'd be right not to turn to him. He couldn't heal her pain. He couldn't heal his own.

10

JULIA

'Julia.' She glanced up to see Maria standing in front of her desk waving what appeared to be two tickets in her hand.

'Fancy coming to this with me?' She smiled in that slightly embarrassed way she had when she desperately wanted Julia to say yes but was preparing herself for a no.

'What is it?' Julia smiled back, hoping to reassure rather than interrogate.

'A show, up in London. For charity.' She quickly added, 'A children's charity, giving disadvantaged kids the opportunity to learn a musical instrument.'

'That sounds like a great cause. When is it?'

'Tomorrow night. Sorry it's short notice, but I thought with it being a children's charity event and all, that'd you'd like to come.'

She was twisting a strand of her hair, something she did when she was unsure of a reaction. Julia didn't wish to disappoint her, but children's charity or not, she seldom socialised during the week. If she was being honest, she seldom socialised.

'It's Irish music, so maybe not your thing? Just thought I'd offer a ticket to you first.'

Moving from foot to foot and twirling her hair around her finger only emphasised how vulnerable Maria could be. It was in direct contrast to the usually confident, outgoing person Julia knew.

Maria was a complex individual, Julia had discovered. Intensely loyal, bright, hard-working and sometimes vulnerable, like now.

'So it's up in London, you said?'

'Yes. It's a club up there, pretty cool place. I've been a few times.'

'Really? I didn't think you went to clubs, you sly dog?' Julia laughed. But it did surprise her.

She'd believed, obviously incorrectly, that Maria spent her nights and weekends at her flat in Maidenhead amidst her surprisingly diverse flatmates who, it appeared from snippets of conversation she'd heard, had nothing in common with Maria.

Julia couldn't quite fathom how that played out, how they forged a successful house-sharing relationship together, but it was a testament to Maria's nature that it did.

'What about your flatmates? Don't they want to go?'

'No.' She frowned. 'They're not into Irish music. Not surprising. They like that head-banging stuff with strobe lighting and party drugs.'

'Jesus. Really?' She'd said it matter-of-factly, as though she were referring to them enjoying scrapbooking for a hobby.

There was something in the way she was standing there, vulnerable and clearly hoping for a yes, that persuaded Julia to give in gracefully, whilst desperately wanting to find an excuse not to.

'I'd love to come. What time does it start? Will I have time to go home and change and feed the cat?'

'Yes, plenty of time.' Maria beamed back at Julia. 'It starts around 8 p.m. and runs until roughly 10 p.m., so not too late, but it is a Friday night, so you can sleep in Saturday.'

'How much do I owe you for the ticket?'

'Oh, nothing, Julia. It's a free ticket.'

'Rubbish. The whole point of charity events is to raise money. You must have paid for them. How much?'

'No. Well, yes, but it's my treat. I insist.' She hesitated, looking down to pick off an imaginary thread on her skirt. She looked up, and Julia could see she was struggling to keep her emotions in check.

'You've been incredibly good to me. Always encouraging and believing I could become a legal executive, and I've never really thanked you properly. So this is my thank-you.' A slow flush crept from her neck to her face.

'Oh, Maria, you've done the hard yards and qualified. I encouraged, but at the end of the day, it's been your perseverance that has landed you where you now are. Anyway, I insist I buy the drinks. Deal?'

'Deal. Shall we catch the train up together? I can catch it from Henley.'

'Sure, let's do that,' Julia responded.

Julia thought she'd probably regret saying yes, but clearly Maria wanted her to come, and maybe, just maybe it would be good for her to get out of the office, out of the house, and do something different.

She was too content being a homebody, using her work and her son as an excuse to shut the cottage door on the world, existing comfortably with little or no social life except when she hung out with Lizzie.

Lizzie was her best friend. They'd been friends since their school days back in New Zealand, and now they were both living in England, their lives were growing together again.

Lizzie would probably have enjoyed a night out listening to Irish music in London, but Julia sensed Maria wanted this night to be for the two of them, so wouldn't complicate matters by inviting Lizzie and her husband, Michael.

THEY ARRIVED at the club before eight o'clock and walked down the broad stairs that opened into a large seating area leading to a slightly raised stage neatly arranged with instruments and amplifiers, a PA system facing out from the front corners, and subtly lit by spotlights on low power.

'What will you have? My treat, remember.'

'Glass of bubbles, maybe? What are you having?'

'I feel like that, too. How about I buy a bottle? Cheaper that way and it's only a few glasses each.'

'If you're sure. That might be quite expensive.' Maria frowned before reaching for her purse.

'Nah, close that. You are not paying for this. We agreed.' Julia tut-tutted at her and walked up to the bar before Maria had a chance to argue.

Julia looked around as she waited to be served. It really was a great venue—big stage and plenty of space without feeling huge and unwelcoming. The ceilings were high and ornate, unlike so many pub and club venues in England that had low and beamed ceilings.

When she turned to look for Maria, champagne bottle and two glasses in hand, she saw she'd found a table for them near the stage.

'Here we go. Great table you've got. Who are all those ones for, do you think?' Julia asked, pointing at the row of tables in front with "Reserved" signs on them.

'The musicians, probably, and sponsors or maybe philanthropic guests?'

'Be interesting to see who turns up.'

Julia's steady hand poured two glasses of champagne and clinked glasses with Maria. 'Cheers. Here's to a great evening of music.'

'Do you know any of these musicians?' Maria asked, sliding the programme in front of Julia.

'Mary Black. I've listened to her music. Maura O'Connell, Sharon Shannon—'

At that point the MC walked out onto the stage, capturing the room's attention.

'Good evening, everyone. Thank you for coming. Shortly we'll be starting the evening's entertainment, and a reminder that all the musicians playing tonight are donating their services for free. So please give them a rousing applause when they come out. It's seldom we have so much talent on one stage for charity.'

'Wow, this place is really filling up now,' Maria said.

Julia glanced around, noticing dozens of people were queueing at the bar before weaving their way between tables to their seats whilst still more were filing down the stairs

The place was rapidly filling, and Julia was amazed at how many people the venue could seat.

'Ladies and gentlemen, please welcome to the stage The Voice of Ireland.'

The place exploded in a roar of approval as the musicians stepped out.

'Jesus,' Julia exclaimed and hoped only Maria had heard her.

Maria swung round, eyes wide with expectation. 'What? What's wrong?'

'Nothing. Sorry. Just surprised, that's all. The drummer is Jack's old music tutor, Hamish Neeson, and the lead guitarist, his new tutor, Patrick Devlin.'

'Nooooo. Oh my God, Julia, I didn't know Paddy Devlin was his new tutor. He's amazing. I've heard him play several times, well, both of them, actually.'

Maria could hardly contain her excitement and reached for the champagne bottle, quickly refilling her glass and Julia's as though knowing two musicians was worthy of a toast.

'I didn't realise you were such an avid fan of Irish music.' Julia found herself wanting to chatter away to avoid looking at the stage, wishing she'd read the bloody programme more carefully, therefore avoiding the shock of seeing them both.

'Yes. I love it, but none of my friends do, and not my mum and dad - they refer to it as "bog" music. Bog from the peat bogs, not bog as in toilet.'

'Um, got that. Bit harsh. Still, it's not everyone's cup of tea.'

'But you like it, don't you? I hope you didn't just say yes to tonight to humour me?' Maria looked crestfallen at the prospect that Julia might have accompanied her out of a sense of misplaced duty. Which was in part, true. She didn't like socialising particularly. It all seemed rather frivolous to Julia, and she didn't choose to squander money every Friday and Saturday night on clubs, bars, and restaurants like some of her staff seemed to do.

'Of course I do. My dad loved Irish music. I grew up with it, and I have Irish ancestors.' She heard Maria's sigh of relief.

'It's not all Paddy plays, though,' Maria gushed, unable to take her eyes off the stage. 'He plays in a really cool blues band here at this club, actually, and maybe a few other venues, but mainly here.'

'Really. Talented man, then?'

'Oh yes,' enthused Maria. 'He plays multiple instruments. And my God, Julia, you ought to hear his voice...' She was unable to keep talking as she watched the musicians tune their instruments.

Julia had learnt a lot about Patrick Devlin in the last few minutes, more to add to the personal data she was collecting following her Google searching. She watched and listened as they pinged, plucked, retuned and fiddled with guitar pedals and microphones.

When the final tuning had been completed, the MC welcomed Mary Black to the stage. Another roar erupted from the crowd as Mary approached the microphone, smiling at the audience before turning to the musicians and raising her arms in thanks.

'Our first song tonight is one I wrote some time ago now, a little number entitled "Vanities",' Mary said in her husky voice. She still looked amazing and must have been closer to sixty now than fifty Julia thought.

The music began with a guitar intro played by Patrick, or Paddy as everyone seemed to refer to him. But for Julia he would remain Patrick. It suited him, and that's what she would call him.

She found herself mesmerised by his hands, his fingers moving with such dexterity across the fretboard of his guitar.

When he glanced at Mary, she read a familiarity in the looks exchanged and wondered if they'd been lovers. The thought made her stomach contract in a way it had no right to be doing.

At the conclusion of the song, two handsome men seated at the table in front of Julia and Maria leapt to their feet and applauded loudly, calling out their appreciation before sitting again, smiling at each other in the way men did at a rugby match when their side had just scored a try. Such boyish enthusiasm made Julia smile.

11

PATRICK

Patrick hadn't expected such a big crowd when they came out on stage, and it thrilled him to know they would be raising a significant amount of money tonight for his charity. One that was so close to his heart.

He'd thought up the idea after seeing so many kids struggling in mainstream schools that had little time for music, let alone the funds to support a music department.

Patrick had helped awkward and often angry young children climb up out of their lives of poverty, neglect, and violence to become competent musicians, giving them the opportunity to overcome their sad start in life and become greater than the sum of their parents.

It wasn't always like that, of course. There were some children he just couldn't reach, too damaged from within for music to be their healing balm.

Patrick hadn't played with Mary Black for many years, but they were old friends and she'd taught him a lot about stage presence in his early days.

It wasn't until they were into the first song and Patrick looked out at the audience, giving them more attention and letting his eyes settle on faces, that he saw her—Julia Davis. She was with another woman at a table almost directly behind Liam Brady and Patrick's brother, Carrick, both of whom had surprised him by making the time to come tonight.

Seeing her looking back at him almost threw him off key. His fingers momentarily slowed as he registered that it was actually her. Why was she here? Did she know he was playing tonight?

Patrick viewed this venue as his club, not literally, but the place he liked to think of as his second home. The band he belonged to played there regularly and had done so for years. It was where he felt most at home performing, but tonight he felt uncharacteristically nervous.

Liam had watched Patrick perform before, and Carrick, well, Carrick hadn't been to a gig in a long time. He wasn't sure why his brother was here tonight but figured it was for the charity more than him.

But having Julia Davis sitting in the audience was unsettling, and Patrick needed to get his head into the right place, playing with these artists and the big line-up of musicians. He needed to give this gig his undivided attention.

They finished the song, and he glanced across at Hamish who was on drums. He raised his eyebrows and gave Patrick a look, indicating he'd seen Julia as well. That look had been a warning. But Patrick didn't need a warning. He wouldn't be going anywhere near this woman. She was way too dangerous for him.

More musicians came out on stage for the next few numbers, and Patrick immersed himself in the magic of Irish music again. He hadn't played this genre in ages, and so when the opportunity arose to put this night together for his charity, he'd elected to go for an Irish theme, knowing it was always popular and bound to draw a good crowd in London.

They'd take a break and then Maura O'Connell would make her appearance. Patrick hadn't seen Maura in many years, but she had a fine voice and the audience would love her, he was sure of that.

At the break, Hamish and Patrick joined Liam and Carrick at their table. Patrick made a point of keeping his back to Julia and not giving eye contact. Even so, she unsettled him in a way he couldn't fathom.

'Great sound, you guys,' Liam said as he stood to embrace Hamish and then Patrick.

'Don't know how you two do it, but you just keep getting better with age. What a line-up, Paddy. You must have pulled in a few favours to draw Mary Black and Maura O'Connell here tonight.'

'Old muso friends, Liam. We all look out for one another, especially we Irish.'

'Indeed we do, Paddy. What can I get you both? Guinness, beer, wine?'

'I'll just have a pint of Directors, please, Liam. Mish, what are you having?'

'Guinness for me, please. Thanks, Liam.'

'My pleasure. It's just so great to be here. To hear you play all these old tunes, ones that we knew when we were young.' Liam was beaming with pleasure, and Patrick was pleased that he'd made the time to come.

'And how are you, brother?' Carrick stood and gave him a hug, startling Patrick. It had been a long time since the two had embraced with any real affection.

'I'm glad you're here, really glad,' Patrick said.

PATRICK AND CARRICK'S relationship had been distant and sometimes hostile in a way that he believed should be foreign to brothers.

Patrick had let the mistakes of the past throw shadows across their future. When was it time to forgive and move on? Never, for some people, Patrick thought.

Knowing his brother must have given up whatever he'd been doing and whichever city he'd been in to come to London tonight, meant more to Patrick now than he could ever have imagined a few years ago. Previously he would have resented his presence. A reminder of the past and the hurt and pain Patrick believed Carrick had caused.

The brothers looked at each other and clinked glasses, and a softening and building of bridges had begun. Perhaps they would be able to move on from those dark days and become close again, like they had been as kids, Patrick thought.

He studied Carrick for a moment. He looked fine, handsome in fact, something he'd reluctantly had to admit a long time ago - Carrick was the better looking of the two and he was charming as well, and none of that had changed with the passing of time. If anything, it had enhanced.

'Come on, Mish, down that. We better get backstage. We'll see you two after the show—don't go running off anywhere. We'll be having a little Irish jig after. You need to both be there.'

He patted his brother on the back and left without looking at Julia. She'd probably think he was rude, but he couldn't handle the distraction of those green eyes shining out from that beautiful face.

12
______

JULIA

Julia was mesmerised by his playing. It was different from when he and Hamish had played "Walk Don't Run" with Jack. This was a whole new level of musicality, and if she'd harboured any remaining doubts about the choice of Jack's tutor, they had now dissolved, and she knew Patrick Devlin was exactly the music teacher Jack needed.

A wave of warmth mixed with relief washed over her in that moment of clarity.

'What shall we drink now, Julia? We seem to have polished off that bottle of bubbly.'

Maria was smiling at her, waving the empty bottle in her hand at the exact moment the tall handsome stranger from the table in front arrived at their table.

'Hello ladies. My friend Liam and I wondered if you would like to join us? You seem to be out of champagne, so I'm just in time.'

He had the kind of face that stopped you in your tracks, Julia thought as she felt herself blushing beneath his warm, steady gaze. Before Julia had time to decline, Maria had answered for them.

'We'd love to. Thank you.' Raising her eyebrows at Julia intimating there would be no argument. They would join the two men.

. . .

INTRODUCTIONS WERE MADE and the two seated themselves either side of Liam and Carrick. Julia couldn't help but stare at Liam, she was certain she'd seen him somewhere before, but couldn't place exactly where.

She was surprised at Maria's openness. She'd only ever socialised with Maria at work functions and in that environment she was quiet, demure almost to the point of stand-offish. In this environment, she was the caterpillar emerging from her chrysalis, a sociable butterfly.

'So what would you like to drink? I saw you had some champagne. Would you like another?'

'I have to drive later, so maybe something non-alcoholic for me would be great, thanks, Carrick.'

'Same for me. Anything non-alcoholic would be grand.'

'So, what brings you out tonight, a love of Irish music or are you involved with the charity?' Liam Brady directed his question to Julia.

'Both really. We love Irish music and the charity is an important one.'

'So it is. Paddy has done an amazing job tonight to draw a crowd like this.' They were interrupted with Carrick returning to the table with two non-alcoholic drinks in his hand.

'Carrick here is Paddy's younger brother, and an old friend from my school days back in Ireland.'

Julia was lost for words. *Patrick's brother.* Where Patrick was ruggedly good-looking, Carrick was more chiselled. They had the same build, tall, broad-shouldered, and slim hipped with long legs – that's where the similarities ended.

Carrick had warm dark chocolate eyes, but they were different to his brother's - the kind of eyes which drew you in and Julia could feel herself inexplicably drawn to this brother of Patricks.

13
____

CARRICK

When Carrick had noticed the two women sitting at the table behind them, he had been immediately captivated by Julia. Despite what people thought, particularly his brother, Carrick didn't date. He didn't want a relationship.

One-night stands were his usual practice, physically satisfying but too often leaving him feeling emotionally empty.

He tried to avoid putting himself in potential relationship positions. He found comfort in work and crafting the next deal. Like a cat stalking prey, and recently he had his business focus riveted on New Zealand as a property investment opportunity leaving no time for women.

He could hear the Kiwi intonation in her vowel sounds and watched as she pushed an errant strand of hair away from her face. The green eyes were enchanting, and he found himself looking at her in a way he hadn't looked at a woman in many years. Her voice was attractive. She was attractive. No, she was beautiful.

Carrick knew immediately that his brother would find Julia irresistible, and he would never stand in the way, even if he wanted to, which he told himself he didn't.

The damage from the past was not yet repaired, although being here tonight, Carrick hoped, would go some way to forging a closer relationship with his brother. But it took two, and he wasn't altogether sure Patrick wanted to rekindle what they once shared as brothers.

They had been so close. That was before Patrick went away to university and before all the pain and hurt had unfolded.

Carrick had been the younger kid tagging along when all three were young schoolboys back in Ireland. He'd been in awe of Liam, like so many others. But it was Patrick who had forged the close bond between them back then.

Patrick was closer to Liam's age, and they'd connected in a way Carrick had not seen his big brother do with anyone other than himself. There was no envy, just a need in Carrick to be accepted, to be as one with the two older boys. It seemed pathetic now as he looked back, his neediness to be accepted a flaw in his character.

The band was about to come back out, forcing Carrick's attention away from his contradictory thoughts and furtive glances at Julia Davis.

HE LOVED WATCHING PADDY PLAY. He was incredibly talented, and this charity event he'd organised meant such a lot, he would not have missed it, regardless of other commitments.

Carrick wasn't at all musical, much to the surprise of his otherwise musically talented family. Whether it was with tin whistles, drums, piano, or guitar, talent spanned the generations of the Devlin family.

His decision not to attend university, instead heading to London, had been a disappointment to his parents and, he had always believed, caused a deeper resentment on the part of his father that Carrick had rejected their wishes that he follow a traditional higher education.

Regardless of his success as a property developer, his parents had never truly embraced his choices. Despite their love and support for him, he knew deep down he was a disappointment.

He'd always been the backdrop to Paddy's musical talent and continuing success. And tonight's charity event would be yet another feather in the favoured son's very full hat.

They would never know of Carrick's philanthropic deeds. He had always felt that to talk of one's philanthropy was to betray the very principles of it being about the recipient, not the giver.

14

JULIA

Carrick turned to Julia. 'So you're a family court lawyer. Who is it you work for?'

'Petrie's in Maidenhead. You're unlikely to have heard of them if you're not in law,' Julia volunteered to save him feeling embarrassed.

Carrick bobbed his head with a bashful smile to acknowledge Julia's thoughtfulness.

'Have you always practised family law? Sorry, the last thing you need is to be talking shop tonight. I'm sure you ladies deserve a night off from law.' He smiled.

'We certainly do,' Julia said.' What do you do, Carrick?'

'I'm a property developer. Not on the same scale as Liam—far from it. But I make a living.'

Julia realised that's where she'd seen Liam before, on television. He was some sort of property tycoon in London.

'Don't believe that, Julia. He's very successful, just too modest for his own good,' Liam said, appearing beside Carrick and patting him on the back.

'Is that here in the UK or overseas?'

'Both. I've got investments here, France, Greece, Australia, and I'm about to move into New Zealand and see what I can do over there. I can hear a little touch of Kiwi in your accent.'

'Yes, although I've been out here for some time now.'

'Do you get back frequently? To home, I mean. New Zealand.'

'No. England is my home. I've never been back.' Julia wanted to change the subject. She didn't like talking about New Zealand. Too many dark memories and things she wouldn't wish to discuss in company such as this.

Sensing her discomfort, Maria came to her rescue and the subject swiftly moved off Julia and onto the night's entertainment.

Julia felt Maria reach out and squeeze her hand under the table. She really was the sweetest person, she thought. She might work in Julia's team, but she was much more to her than a work colleague.

'I haven't seen Paddy play in quite some time, but when I'm in London, if he's gigging, I try to get along.' Carrick announced.

'Do you play an instrument?' asked Julia.

'No. Not me, I'm afraid. I lucked out on inheriting any musical ability. He got both our shares.' He turned to Liam, pointedly changing the subject, leaving Julia with the distinct feeling that, like her, there was something in his past he didn't wish to discuss.

'Do you know Maura O'Connell, Liam?' Carrick asked, taking a large swallow of his beer.

'I've met her once or twice at functions in Ireland. She's a talented woman. I love her stuff. Speaking of which, they're coming back on stage.'

They watched as Patrick and Hamish walked out laughing together before being quickly joined by other musicians.

'Ladies and gentlemen, please welcome to the stage the one and only Maura O'Connell.' A loud cheer reverberated around the club, none more so than from Liam and Carrick.

'Thank you. Thank you all. It's a pleasure to be here, to be raising funds for such a worthy charity. When Paddy Devlin asked me to join you all this evening, I didn't hesitate for a moment. I know he's been working feverishly behind the scenes to make this night a success, and I'd like to take the opportunity before my first song to thank him for his dedication, love, and support to the children who benefit from his charitable work.'

She turned to Patrick and clapped, as did the entire audience, and Julia watched as Patrick smiled and nodded his head in appreciation.

To Julia's expert eye, he always looked so self-assured and confident at the times they'd met, but tonight she saw a more self-deprecating Patrick Devlin, and she felt a momentary doubt in the certainty with which she had categorised and judged him. A tiny hairline crack in her emotional stronghold.

Maura O'Connell had a deep richness to her voice. A voice you could fall into and be swept along by. She'd just finished singing "Living in These Troubled Times" and almost brought the house down.

'And now for my last song, "Summerfly". Thank you for coming tonight, and maybe I'll see you out in Nashville sometime.'

'She lives out there now,' Liam said. 'I watched her perform once. She's made quite a name for herself in the bluegrass scene.'

Julia noted that Patrick had changed to the slide guitar and Hamish had swapped out the drums for the double bass. They really were talented musicians and clearly loved playing together, she thought, smiling as she watched them quickly tune up before Maura settled herself in front of the microphone.

Julia had never heard the song before but found it beautifully haunting. She watched as Patrick lost himself in the music and the lyrics. If she hadn't been staring so intently at him, she might have missed the momentary emotion cross his face as fast as the blink of a camera shutter as it flicked across the lens and back. For a split second she saw pain, and then it was gone.

She immediately doubted herself, wondering if her imagination wrongly interpreted a trick of the light, but when she turned to face Carrick it was unmistakeable. Raw emotion etched in his face and telegraphed for her to see.

He turned suddenly and caught her staring. His eyes held hers, and Julia found herself wanting to reach out and take his hand.

Whatever it was, whatever had happened, he was hurting inside, making her want to lie down beside him and stroke away the pain.

How ridiculous. What is wrong with me? One minute I'm having funny little flutters watching Patrick, and now I'm wanting to reach out and comfort his brother. Too much bubbly, she thought, although that had been a while ago, but all the same, she didn't need *man* complications in her life, or men with complications. She did not need or want to get sucked into what was clearly some emotional issue between two brothers.

When the song ended, the audience applauded loudly once more, drowning out Maria's words.

'Sorry, what did you say?

'I said she's amazing. That was the best song of the night for me.' Maria's eyes were shining.

'Does that have some special significance for you, Maria?' Julia wondered if what she'd seen with Patrick and Carrick had merely been the emotional feelings some songs could evoke, especially if you were Irish.

'I guess it resonates with me in some macabre way.' She turned her gaze back to the stage.

The words to the song were heartfelt and probably haunting for some. Julia could imagine they would have a real impact if you'd had your heart broken.

15

PATRICK

Patrick knew he should be pleased. Well, he was pleased, of course he was. The night had been a huge success. A full house and an appreciative one. They'd be plenty of people who would put their hands in their pockets and give again for his charity before the evening ended, but somehow Maura O'Connell's "Summerfly" had struck a heart-wrenching chord with him, and not in a good way.

As he played, memories of the past flooded in and he found himself transported back to Baltimore. The smell of the ocean, the expanse of blue sky, and the feeling the world belonged to him. It was his to take. And take it he had. However much he'd justified it to himself over the following decades, convincing himself leaving for university would not change things, it had irreversibly.

He couldn't accept he'd played a part in the ending. He would never know what might have been, what could have been. He would only know the heartache and pain and the rage he'd felt after. All that rage had been directed at Carrick.

The band was taking a short break before the final instrumental song that belonged to Sharon Shannon, but tonight Patrick would be the one playing the button accordion.

He'd practised into the early hours over the past weeks to feel comfortable that he could pull it off. He hadn't played that instrument in a while, and it took time and patience to master the buttons. Sharon had made that instrument her own, and Patrick felt he was a poor substitute.

All the musicians would come out on stage to play the final instrumental piece called "Blackbird". It would round the night off on a high and happy note, and that's what Patrick needed most of all.

He wanted to feel happy, euphoric even, satisfied that all his hard work over the previous months had been worthwhile and his charity would benefit hugely from tonight's concert.

Patrick had been shocked to see Julia and her friend sitting at Liam and Carrick's table when the band came back on for the second half.

He'd tried to suppress the little ball of anger forming inside him. Did Carrick know her? Or was it Liam who knew her? And why should that matter to him? If truth be known, a spark of jealousy had ignited inside him. If asked, he would have been unable to define why he felt so conflicted.

He had no intention of going after Julia, but that spark of jealousy had been there, flickering away, and he'd felt it keenly.

As he tuned up, he'd glanced at his brother and seen the animated expression on his face as he talked to Julia. Playing "Summerfly" had almost been his downfall.

The haunting lyrics toyed with his emotions, allowing memories and feelings to rise to the surface after being buried for such a long time.

He'd glanced up from his slide guitar and detected his own pain reflected in Carrick's eyes. Carrick knew, just like Patrick, what this song meant to both of them, and in that moment Patrick felt nothing had changed. Nothing had healed. And yet earlier, when they were talking together, Patrick had felt the old warmth again.

The love and respect they'd once held for each other. The protective cloak Patrick had draped around himself and his little brother. It had all been there tonight, he knew it had, and he could not let one song snatch that away from him. They had to move on. They had to heal.

Carrick had donated generously to his charity tonight and he ought to be grateful, but instead he felt the warmth evaporating, leaving behind emptiness and disappointment.

IN THE MONTHS since his first meeting with Julia, Patrick thought there had been a softening in her attitude towards him, a meeting of minds. He'd found himself drawn to her in a perplexing way, and it both excited and troubled him.

He'd spent years carefully avoiding attachment. What did psychologists refer to it as? *Privation.* He didn't believe he fitted this description. He liked women and had no problem taking a woman out for a drink, dinner, and sometimes bed, although the latter had become less frequent as he got older.

It had been a long time since his heart had been claimed, and the memory brought so much sadness, regret, and—if he was honest—anger at Carrick and Carrick's part in it.

Patrick would never know if the path he'd chosen, to attend Edinburgh University instead of Dublin or London, would have made any difference, or whether music would have always come first, before love, before commitment.

He wanted to banish these thoughts before going back on stage for the final number. He wanted to feel the warmth that had surged through him when he and Carrick had talked during the break. He wanted that brotherly love back. He'd missed it more than he'd allowed himself to believe.

When the band started playing "Blackbird", the audience rose to their feet and clapped and called. Most of them knew this piece of music, and it was, as Patrick had hoped, a moment that lifted the evening to another level.

A celebration of fun, love, and passion for Irish music, banishing his earlier dark thoughts back to the far recesses of his mind where he'd kept them safely tucked away. But only temporarily. The past would revisit him, and he would be forced to face what he'd done, the part he'd played. The lies he'd told himself for decades could no longer be sustained by his anger and rage.

16

———

JACK

Jack lay awake in his boarding house bed. He was finding it annoyingly small now that his mother had bought him a queen-sized bed for his bedroom at home.

He'd nagged her about it for ages and finally she'd realised just how *important* it was and taken him out to Reading so he could choose for himself within a budget she'd given him.

He'd been so excited, but then found, faced with so many choices, he'd been unable to decide, and she'd had to do it. They'd laughed together as they'd both bounced up and down on the beds trying them out. Seeing his mother laughing and light-hearted had warmed him greatly.

He turned over on his side and noticed how scratchy the sheets were, so unlike the ones his mother had bought for his new bed along with a new duvet cover and two new pillows. I

t had made him feel so grown up, and for once she hadn't mentioned being *the man of the house*. Instead she'd gone on about one thousand thread count. He had no idea what she was talking about at the time, but now he knew better.

Now that he'd slept in his new bed with its new mattress and one thousand thread count sheets, he could feel the difference. Did that make him a sissy? No, he assured himself. It meant that he was getting better at appreciating fine things. Well, that's what his mum had told him, and he understood what she meant.

Jack was awake due to the growing knot of discontent inside him, and he needed to find a way of undoing it and setting himself free.

Tonight his mother was going out, and knowing that had made him feel a little easier, a little less overwhelmed by this tension inside him.

She never went anywhere, and he'd discovered Michael had said something to upset her. He didn't know exactly what, but he'd overheard her talking to Lizzie on the phone and it hadn't sounded like a happy conversation, not like they used to have.

This had saddened Jack hugely because for him it felt like he was now the absolute and only source of interaction for his mother apart from her work.

He didn't want to be the centre of his mother's universe. It was too big a space to fill. There were times recently when he found himself wishing he could stay at school over the weekend. He didn't want to go home to find his mother had organised with other kids' mothers to have their sons come over for supper or the movies or anything else that she could dream up.

He liked his friends, particularly Dan, but none of them were into music; they were his sporty friends.

Frequently, when they came to stay, they'd be out in the field playing rugby games or riding their bikes across the hiking tracks that weaved snake-like around the hillsides, or in the summer they'd play tennis, all of which he enjoyed. But sometimes, and this was becoming more and more frequent, he just wanted to be alone with his music and practise and not have to talk all the time and look after his guests or spend hours watching some stupid movie with his mother that she thought they'd both enjoy.

All he wanted to do was shut his bedroom door and play music and write musical scores the way Mr Devlin was teaching him to do.

His mother was going out with Maria, she'd said. He didn't know Maria. They'd never met, but he'd heard lots about her from his mum. They had tickets, she said, to a night of Irish music in London, and he'd wondered who might be playing. It was very unlikely that it would be a proper band like U2.

As he tossed and turned, unable to get comfortable and unable to stop his agitated thoughts, he wondered if he could talk to Mr Devlin about how he was feeling.

His mother wouldn't be happy about that, but what choice did he really have? He couldn't talk to her because he knew she'd be upset and hurt, and he didn't want to deal with her emotions on top of everything else.

It wasn't that he didn't care. Of course he did. He loved his mother deeply. It was just too much pressure to be a teenager with his own interests and schoolwork, and a son, and a *friend*, and *man of the house* and, and, well, everything in her life. That was what was weighing him down.

Could he talk with Mr Neeson? No, he couldn't. Mr Neeson knew his mum too well, and he didn't trust that he wouldn't tell her, and then of course there was Lizzie.

When he was young, he'd talked to Lizzie about all sorts of stuff, but he'd found as he got older that he couldn't trust Lizzie not to spill the beans, breaking a confidence because she knew best or wanted to fix things.

She was his mother's best friend, and he understood it wouldn't be easy for her to keep something big to herself, and that because of their friendship, her loyalties would be torn. He needed someone who would respect his confidence, so he couldn't tell Lizzie.

That left Mr Devlin. He had such a bond with him. He could feel it growing, an absolute trust that Mr Devlin understood what was right for him and wouldn't let him down.

The passion he shared with Mr Devlin for music often spilled over into conversations about school and lessons and silly kids who said stuff that was dumb and sometimes quite cruel.

Mr Devlin had listened and offered advice, and not in a teacher-pupil way but in a man-to-man way, making Jack feel supported and somehow a little taller and stronger for Mr Devlin's particular type of wisdom.

Yes, that's what he'd do. He'd talk to Mr Devlin. He could trust him. He knew he could, and with that thought in mind, he drifted off to sleep despite the scratchy sheets and the lumpy pillow.

17

JULIA

The night of music was over, so Julia and Maria made their excuses, despite protests from both Liam and Carrick to stay and enjoy the after-show party.

Julia could sense Maria wanting to stay, to be backstage with the band enjoying a drink and chattering excitedly about the music.

'You can stay if you want, but I need to get home. I've got Jack's sport tomorrow.'

'No, I'll come with you. I don't want to go home by myself at this time of night and nor should you.'

Julia smiled wryly to herself, feeling like the errant daughter being lectured by a mother about the perils of being out late at night.

They said their goodbyes and walked briskly to Paddington station. Maria kept up a steady babble of recollections about the night, but Julia's thoughts were concentrated on two brothers and her aching feet. She couldn't wait to be out of these boots. She'd not worn them in ages, and they were making her pay for being left in the wardrobe for so long.

Julia weighed up the differences between the two brothers. They were both so different and yet somehow alike.

Carrick had been attentive and well-mannered. She'd seen the look in his eyes when he'd come across to their table.

She was well aware of the interest men showed in her, but her tendency was to politely signal disinterest and only show visible irritation if someone persisted with pushing their interest upon her.

Tonight, however, whether it was because she'd not been out for such a long time and she'd drunk more glasses of bubbly in one sitting than she had in goodness knew how long, she'd felt light-hearted and a little excited at the attention.

A night out with grown-ups with wide-ranging but relaxed conversation, had been refreshing—liberating almost, Julia thought.

The realisation that her life had become work and Jack, or Jack and work was a little troubling as it was probably not the healthiest balance.

Plenty of parents had to dedicate their life to work and children out of necessity, but she had choices, and if she'd witnessed a friend behaving in this way, she'd probably have told them to think about their life balance – but isn't that what Michael had done? Only Julia had not welcomed Michael's observations – the hypocrisy of her thoughts was a matter she needed to address.

The night had been fun and the music amazing. And Carrick's attention had been welcome, but she hadn't spoken with Patrick at all. He'd made no effort to come over to say hello when they'd finished playing nor even caught her eye to nod acknowledgement across the room, and somehow that had left her feeling a bit miffed.

As the months had passed and she'd shared emails and phone calls with Patrick, she'd reluctantly had to admit that he was an amazing tutor and a gifted musician as well as being truly professional in his approach.

Hamish had been right to recommend him, and Julia couldn't imagine what Jack's musical life would have been like without the academy. More to the point, she didn't wish to think what would happen if he suddenly shut down the academy and left. Not that there had been any hint that was even remotely likely to happen, but Julia prided herself on being one step ahead so had a habit of worrying about the what-if's and maybes, even in the absence of a shred of evidence to suggest a problem.

'...don't you think, Julia?'

She realised Maria was looking at her, waiting for a response, but she hadn't heard a word she'd said.

'Sorry, what did you say?'

'Paddy Devlin, he's a remarkable musician. Playing the button accordion, that's quite something. And he's such a dish. Far too old for me, of course.' Suddenly realising what she had said, she looked at Julia, aghast. '

Not that I mean you're old. He's probably about your age. It's just that, well, I wouldn't go out with an older man.'

'Really? Why is that?' Julia parked the analysis of the two brothers and was all ears. Amused at Maria's ham-fisted attempt to recover from her thoughtless implication about "older people" like Julia.

'Well, there's a big age difference between my mum and dad, and I don't think it works that well.'

Julia watched Maria's face crease into a frown and wondered, not for the first time, what lay beneath Maria's usually bright and happy exterior. She sensed there was something, and she'd seen it tonight in Maria's eyes after that song, the one that seemed to affect so many people.

'I guess it depends on the individuals as to whether an age difference matters or not.' She thought back to her own marriage to Nick and how that age gap had caused difficulties at times. She changed the subject quickly, not wishing to dwell on her ex-husband.

'So what plans do you have for the weekend?'

'I'll go over and see mum and dad and then visit my gran. I do that most weekends. I spent a lot of time with her when I was young. She's very dear to me and getting on now. More frail than she used to be.'

'That's a lovely thing to do. I get the feeling you struggle a bit with your mum and dad, or have I read that wrong?'

Julia glanced across at Maria and saw the change, saw her eyes harden and her mouth tighten. Perhaps she shouldn't have raised it, especially given they'd enjoyed a lovely evening.

'My mum and dad mean well. At least, that's what I tell myself. It's just a battle holding onto my confidence when I'm around them. I left home as soon as I could. Does that sound selfish?'

'Not at all. You're just being honest about how you feel. Nothing wrong in that.'

They had reached the station, which was packed and noisy with home-goers. Six women making up a hen's party were staggering along the platform, the bride-to-be wearing a long trailing veil, a pink tutu and orange boots, and looking severely worse for wear, not unlike her friends. They were raucous and foul mouthed. Julia and Maria hurried on by, giving them a wide berth as they made their way to the far platform.

Settled side by side enjoying the warmth of the carriage, Maria asked Julia, 'What will you be doing over the weekend?'

'I'll be at sport and probably entertaining a house full of boys that Jack's invited.'

'Does Jack have friends over every weekend?'

'Almost. Crazy, really. He just loves the company. Understandable when you're an only child. And I don't mind. They're nice boys, friendly and well-mannered, and they make me laugh with their antics.'

'You're good to do that - having them around, I mean. I wasn't allowed friends to stay over when I was growing up.'

'That's sad. Why was that?'

'Don't know, really. When I was little,' Maria said, absently twirling a piece of her long red hair between her thumb and forefinger, 'I used to think it was because my mother was a bit shy and withdrawn so found it difficult to cope with too many children.

It wasn't until I was older that I realised neither of my parents actually like people that much, if at all, really. They have no friends, and the only people they allow in the house are elderly relatives who sit and drink tea and talk about *Coronation Street* like it's real or discuss whether they should wash their nets this week or leave it until next.'

'Oh dear,' Julia said. 'That can't have been fun growing up.'

'Hence why I left home as soon as I got a decent job that paid enough for me to afford to live elsewhere. I've only moved twice: once when I left home and went to a bedsit on my own, and then later, when I started at Petrie's. I found a houseshare and that's where I am still. Been there, must be eight years.'

'Eight years!' Julia was astounded. She couldn't imagine living in a houseshare for eight years.

'Don't you want to get a place of your own some day?'

'I'm saving. I've seen an apartment. Just a one-bedroom place.'

Maria looked across at Julia as though she were expecting her to say, *"One bedroom! No, don't be silly. You need at least two for it to be a proper house."*

But Julia was thinking how awfully sad it was for Maria and how lucky she and Jack were to be living in Hambleden in a beautiful cottage. They didn't own it, but the rent was affordable, and they had no fear of being asked to vacate as the property formed part of the Hambleden Estate, and that wasn't going to be sold anytime soon, if at all.

'I talked to Carrick about it tonight. Given he's a property developer, he said he might be able to find me a better deal than what I'm looking at. He said it was too much money for where it was and the size of it. Not that he's seen it, obviously, but I guess if you're in property all the time you know about these things. He took my number and said he'll call me during the week and let me know how to view and all that. Even offered to negotiate on my behalf if it helped me. He's so nice. Really easy to talk to.'

'Sounds like he was quite smitten with you.' Julia was fishing, taken aback at the mention of Carrick and how this revelation from Maria had churned her up inside.

'Don't be daft, Julia. It's you he had eyes for. Did you swap numbers?' She smiled at Julia, a twinkle in her eye.

'Anyway, he's too old for me. Oops, sorry! I've done it again, haven't I? I seem to be exceptionally good at putting my size 8's in my mouth this evening.'

Julia laughed. 'No, it's fine. I know what you mean and no, we did not swap numbers. I'm not looking for romance, not with a busy job and a teenage boy to occupy me full time.'

Julia swiftly changed the subject to a safer topic. She wasn't in the mood for discussing her love life or the lack of it.

The unexpected fact of her flip-flopping emotional state was disconcerting enough for one night without necessitating a full dissection.

18

PATRICK

Finn was curled up on the large dog cushion beside Patrick's bed, snoring softly, whilst Patrick lay spreadeagled in his king-size bed, unable to sleep. The night had been a huge success and they'd raised a large sum for his charity. He should have been thrilled, delighted, and he was for the charity but not so with his thoughts and feelings.

He'd watched Carrick with Julia. There was an obvious chemistry between them, and he'd felt a wave of unsolicited anger and, if he was being honest with himself, jealousy.

Over the past months as he'd emailed and phoned Julia about Jack's progress, their relationship had evolved from one of hostility on her part to a warmth, an understanding. A coming together of minds focused on one thing and one thing only, and that was Jack.

This boy was special. Patrick had known it from the start, and now he was convinced Julia's son could have whatever his heart desired where music was concerned if he worked hard enough and believed in himself and believed he could be successful.

.   .   .

WATCHING Carrick look at Julia had reminded him of how Carrick used to look at Katie, and those thoughts were real and powerful in his mind as though it were yesterday.

Earlier in the evening, when he'd first gone over to their table and he and Carrick had embraced each other with real affection, he'd thought that time had healed them both. That the passing of time had brought with it a maturity and an understanding that family mattered.

He was now questioning that belief as the flood of painful memories crowded his mind, fighting for space, for the opportunity to be reunited with their old friends betrayal, hurt, and anger.

Carrick had hungered after Katie in a way that, at first, had been amusing, but amusement had quickly turned to concern on Patrick's part.

In the beginning, Katie had been oblivious as only Katie could be. Her consuming focus had been on secrecy. She and Patrick should never be seen alone together. She could never allow her parents or any of her relatives to know she was sweet on Patrick Devlin. He was not one of them, a Catholic.

In her family's jaundiced eyes, he was a Protestant boy from a posh family and therefore belonging to a different world to someone like her, poor and uneducated. And everybody knew that no good came from mixing between worlds.

The poor and the uneducated always ended up being used and abused by the wealthy, and that was the way it had always been. Except she hadn't been uneducated. She wanted out, wanted something better for herself than helping her father on his fishing boat. She'd studied hard and was succeeding.

It had been their dream, hers and Patrick's, that as soon as he finished university, she'd go to London with him. They would finally be together as one, no more clandestine meetings. No more hiding. In London they would find the freedom to love openly and without prejudice.

. . .

Patrick believed no one knew of their relationship, but he had been naïve to think his brother wouldn't find out, wouldn't discover their special meeting place, wouldn't discover the depth of their union.

It had been easy at first. They attended different schools, had different interests and different friends, but as time progressed and the attraction between them grew, the secret had become more difficult to contain, harder to maintain the façade over their blossoming love.

The one shared interest they had was sailing. Most kids in Baltimore sailed. It was an integral part of their daily lives, and Katie had been no different. Her father's fishing business meant she'd learned to handle a boat from a young age, but sailing was not the same as a fishing boat or dinghy.

As Patrick lay recollecting thoughts from the past, an image of Katie, her beautiful face illuminated by the moon, emphasising her sheer joy at mastering the spinnaker and turning his yacht to head homeward, had filled his heart with love the like of which he'd never known before or since. Sailing in the dark had been their most dangerous and therefore thrilling secret.

He hadn't realised until he reached a hand up to his face that he was crying, hot tears of regret, sadness, and pain.

Pulling back the covers, he eased himself out of bed, stepping carefully across Finn's sleeping body. He filled a tumbler with ice and poured himself a Baileys, watching as the thick, creamy liqueur trickled over the glistening cubes.

Walking through to the lounge, he flicked the switch to the lamp and sat in his leather chair, savouring the sweet taste of cream, cocoa, and Irish whiskey.

He heard the soft pad of Finn's paws on the stairs, and then a wet nose pushed into his hand and intelligent eyes looked up at his master, sensing there was something wrong. The dog stretched and yawned before lying down across Patrick's feet.

Dawn was fast approaching, and Patrick still sat in his chair, his thoughts no clearer than when he'd been lying in bed hours before.

His glass sat empty on the side table next to him and Finn still lay across his feet, tethering him to the chair.

'Come on, boy. I need to get up. Maybe I'll take you for a walk.'

The word *walk* was something Finn understood, so he stretched out his legs and arched his back, his tail wagging. He looked at his master with enthusiasm.

Patrick climbed the stairs and found some warm clothes, dressing quickly before heading out the door into the chill air of a new dawn.

19

JULIA

Julia lay stretched out on the sofa, cocooned between fat cushions, reading a brief for court for the following week.

She'd risen from bed earlier than usual for a Saturday and lit the fire in the lounge before making herself a strong coffee and settling herself down to read.

She was finding it difficult to focus, to concentrate on the paper before her. Her thoughts returned again and again to the night's music and the conversations she'd shared with Maria, Liam, and Carrick.

The music had been thrilling with Patrick's musical talent on display for all to see. He was amazing; there was no question about that. But it was his brother, Carrick, who dominated Julia's thoughts this morning.

For the first time since her marriage had crumbled and fallen, she allowed herself to think that maybe, just maybe, happiness could be found again in the arms of a man. A new start.

Those thoughts had barely formed before being dismissed as ridiculous, out of the question. She would never date anyone while Jack was still so young. Perhaps when he was older. When he'd left school and was at university, maybe then. Maybe then she would allow herself to love again. To feel sexy, to make love to someone.

She steadfastly refused to allow herself time to think of sex or a relationship, successfully compartmentalising any thoughts of longing or hunger for affection, for physical contact with a man, for love.

CARRICK HAD DISCOVERED a vulnerability in that protective wall she'd built around herself and Jack. But it was nothing more than a momentary weakness in her defences. It had taken her by surprise but was not an open door for him to walk through and into her life.

Even if Maria was correct when she said Carrick had been very interested in her, Julia knew she would not allow anything to blossom and grow. Her focus was on Jack, and that was all that mattered.

Thinking of Jack reminded her she needed to look for a second-hand keyboard. She'd asked Hamish, and he'd offered to ask around and let her know. It couldn't be something too expensive, but Hamish had assured her he would be able to pick up something reasonably cheaply, and it would still be more than adequate for Jack's present needs.

SHE COULDN'T HAVE ENTERTAINED the idea of a keyboard if they'd still been in their first cottage. It was just too small, but two years ago they'd moved to this beautiful place.

It was another of the cottages owned by the Hambleden Estate for which Julia had been offered first refusal as a rental. She'd leapt at the opportunity, praying that the rent would be affordable. Lady Hambleden, aware of Julia's circumstances, had been kind and generous, agreeing to a figure that satisfied both parties provided Julia did all the legal work with the assured short-hold tenancy agreement.

That was the easy part. Furnishing a much bigger property was more of a concern and had kept Julia awake at night.

Her previous cottage had been a house-sitting arrangement with absentee tenants who were working in the United States.

They'd returned at short notice to pack their personal belongings, arranged for the tenancy to be moved into Julia's name, and offered her the large items of furniture, insisting it was too much cost and hassle to have them shipped across to America, but on the provision that she adopted their cat, Chino, on a permanent basis.

Jack had been thrilled. He loved Chino, and since Chino was getting older, it had seemed unfair to uproot the poor animal from his home. It all fell into place rather nicely with a few additional items of furniture coming from Lady Hambleden's barn, which was an Aladdin's cave of tasteful but surplus items.

Julia now had three bedrooms and two reception areas, one of which she had recently made into a music room for Jack.

They'd worked together finding some big beanbags in a second-hand shop, which Julia had cleaned and freshened up, along with some black-and-white photographs of some of Jack's favourite musicians that Lizzie had kindly bought and framed ready for Jack to hang in his new music space.

They'd transformed a plain sitting room into a cool space for Jack to practise his drums, with plenty of room for a keyboard and stool.

She'd not shared with Jack her conversation with Hamish about the keyboard. It was to be a surprise. She'd be able to pick it up herself and bring it home in her car if she put both seats down.

They'd had no success in finding anything suitable thus far, so she hoped their luck would change and Hamish could find something soon.

She pushed herself up from the sofa, leaving the brief sitting on the blanket chest. She'd come back to it later, she told herself. Another coffee was what she needed. A jolt of caffeine would sharpen her mind and stop her thoughts wandering off into directions she'd rather not go.

An hour later she was still sitting at the dining room table with an empty coffee cup, head resting on the palms of her hands as snippets of conversations drifted in and out of her thoughts.

'So how do you know my brother, or am I being too nosy?'

'Not at all,' Julia had replied. 'My son, Jack, is one of Patrick's pupils at the academy.'

'Wow. He must be an exceptional musician. I understand my brother accepts only the best.'

Julia had laughed. 'All parents like to think their children are talented in one way or another. I'm no different. Jack is talented, and despite my misgivings in the beginning, Patrick is a wonderful tutor. Jack is thriving.'

'Misgivings? What misgivings were they?'

'Oh...nothing really.' Julia felt trapped, unsure whether to say Patrick and she had not got off to the best of starts.

She wouldn't say she'd viewed his brother as a bit of a lad about town. That had all changed, anyway, so there was little point in mentioning it. She'd swiftly turned the subject back to Carrick and his property development plans for New Zealand.

When it was time to leave, Carrick escorted herself and Maria up the stairs and onto the street. Julia had thought he was about to ask her something then changed his mind, and then it was too late as she and Maria strode off together towards Paddington station. She hadn't looked back, despite being tempted to.

Her thoughts at the time had been a frothing buzz of emotion and elation, neither of which she'd felt in a long time, and she'd been caught unprepared for how to tame them, how to place them quickly and safely into a box with a lid and padlock.

She hadn't acted quickly enough and now they roamed free, slipping uninvited in and out of her conscious thoughts as they pleased.

Beneath the easy charm there was a tenderness and a curious shyness about Carrick. *Was it shyness?* she asked herself, drumming her fingers on the table. Or was it a quiet determination not to boast or draw attention to himself?

In some respects, Julia thought, he was a little like his friend Liam who she now knew to be a high profile and successful property devel-oper, but without the arrogance of so many successful businessmen.

Liam was warm, friendly, and handsome. But where Liam had an aura about him that commanded attention, Carrick was quiet and unassuming.

She really had to stop thinking about him. She had work to do before going up to the school to watch Jack's rugby game, so sitting there daydreaming was distracting her from more important things.

20

CARRICK

arrick had risen early, restless but still feeling jaded from the late night and too much alcohol. A run in the cold morning air, he thought, might help sharpen his focus and relieve him of the headache he was nursing. Well, that and a couple of painkillers and some coffee.

Standing outside on the street doing his stretches, Carrick looked up at his apartment block. It was the first sizeable deal he'd negotiated and, although that had been a long time ago and it was looking a bit tired, the block had proved lucrative.

It had remained fully tenanted since he purchased it, with one two-bedroomed unit kept for himself as a base when he flew into London or, like last night, when Liam needed somewhere less obvious than one of his own more ostentatious Docklands apartments to rest his head, so Bedford Street in Chiswick, whilst hardly the trendy end of town, was perfect for Liam to use when he needed it.

Liam's very public move back to Ireland which had the press hounding him at every opportunity was a source of concern for Carrick, and he worried how his friend was going to manage the next stage in finalising the withdrawal of his business interests in London.

They'd been close friends for years and regularly met up in London or France. Sometimes it would be to discuss business deals, but more often it was the joy of sailing together.

They both loved the freedom of the ocean, dancing over white-crested waves, slicing a path through the wind-whipped water as it slapped against the hull of their yacht.

The spray of salt water against their skin and the harsh cries of the birds startled by the crack of the mainsail as their boat took a deep breath and advanced over the waves at speed with Liam calling out, 'Trim the jib, Carrick. I want to get home today!' Images and sounds filled Carrick's thoughts as he started a slow jog towards the towpath.

When Carrick had left Ireland for London, Liam had been the first person he'd phoned, he needed to hear a friendly, encouraging voice for his head was filled with the words of his parents as he boarded the plan to London.

'If it doesn't work out, just come home. There's no shame in admitting failure.'

They'd expected him to fail, to come back to Ireland with his tail between his legs, admitting they were right all along and he should make plans to go to university. That Liam had been a distracting influence and all Carrick needed to do was settle down with more sensible ambitions, starting with applying for a university place.

Carrick had never willingly wished to hurt his parents, but by not following the academic path they had so patiently carved out for him, he'd left the safety and security of home feeling guilty and more than a little frightened that they just might have been right. He might not make it in London, but he at least wanted to try and make his own way, stride out upon his own path.

His parents had never understood his passion for property development. An architect, well, that would have been completely different. They would have happily accepted him studying for a career in architecture, but property development—how could that be considered a proper job, certainly not a career?

They loved him, Carrick knew that, but regardless of his success, they couldn't get past their perception that there was something disreputable about patching up old properties so that you could get tenants you'd be forever chasing for rent when you weren't getting repairs done. It wasn't a real job, a proper profession, not like Patrick.

Using his part of the inheritance left by his grandparents had also been a subject of debate, anger, and bitterness. They believed he should have used the money for something less risky and considered it disrespectful to the memory of his grandpappy and grandmammy, who had worked hard all their lives to be able to leave both boys a sizeable amount of money to "set themselves up", as it had been described in the Will.

Truth be told, Carrick had set himself up very well with his inheritance, but there was no point discussing that with his parents. They simply didn't understand his world.

CARRICK REACHED the towpath and increased his speed running alongside the river Thames as it snaked its way past houses and boats, but the path was wet and slippery underfoot, forcing him to slow his pace.

Up ahead he could see a man settling himself into a wooden chair on the deck of his narrowboat, a cup of steaming liquid in one hand and what were probably the weekend papers in the other.

As Carrick came alongside, he could see the British racing green paint had faded and the name *Just Me*, once painted in shiny black, was chipped in places and the *e* was missing. The man nodded in greeting as he ran past, his cup raised to his lips and the curl of steam floating like smoke in the still air.

· · ·

THE COLD that had seemed mild at first now numbed Carrick's face and extremities. What residual heat he had absorbed in the apartment had gone. It had been his buffer.

With each breath more heat rose in puffs of white vapour, and he found himself running faster to keep warm. Soon he would feel the sweat form on his undershirt, chafing his skin. The friction of cold outer and steaming hot inner made him long for the soothing comfort of a hot shower and strong, scalding coffee.

He ran past houseboats locked up for the winter, their owners probably far away enjoying Mediterranean sun.

Swans displayed their noble elegance, gliding across the Thames. A large male taking an early morning bath splashed his wings forcefully in the water, almost disappearing in the storm of millions of waterdrops before they fell into the sun's rays, reflected back like tiny crystals, sparkling and glittering.

Carrick's thoughts returned to Julia. He'd been surprised at how comfortable he'd felt chatting to her. She was beautiful, engaging, intelligent, and witty, the kind of woman that attracted him, but he would only allow himself to admire her from a distance. The distance was important where his brother was concerned.

He recognised the set of Patrick's mouth last night and the way his eyes flicked across to her, back and forth, back and forth, probably thinking that no one would notice, but Carrick had. He knew his brother and knew that look. The longing in Patrick's eyes.

Carrick had sensed a tension between his brother and Julia. He could almost see it, like a string across the room, taut and loose and taut again. He wondered why Julia appeared disinterested and yet he could feel the tension between them. He was sure of that.

CARRICK HADN'T ASKED for her number, despite the urgent desire within him to do so. He wouldn't pursue any woman that he believed Patrick was interested in. The last time they'd been smitten by the same woman, those desires had ended in heartache.

Carrick recognised in Patrick the need, the longing, the desire for

Julia. The very same emotions that pressed against the surface of his own heart, as they had done for years, lonely and unrequited.

WHEN CARRICK ARRIVED BACK at the apartment, he quietly let himself back in, unwilling to disturb Liam's sleep. He needn't have worried. As he headed down the narrow hallway to his bedroom to change, he could hear Liam's voice echoing through the closed bedroom door.

'No comment. Like I said, I've already provided a statement to the media. I'll not be commenting further. Goodbye.'

Carrick shut his bedroom door quietly, cutting off hearing any further conversation. The press never gave up, always looking for another angle and if they couldn't find it, they'd make something up.

Shivering with cold sweat clinging to his body, he quickly undressed and headed for the bathroom and a hot shower. By the time he'd showered and dressed, Carrick could hear Liam banging about in the kitchen.

'Good morning. You just got up?'

'No. I've been out for a run. What are you cooking up?'

'Porridge. You always said you liked my porridge, so I'm calling your bluff and making you some.' Liam smiled across at Carrick before turning back to continue stirring.

'No bull. I do love your porridge. There should be milk and maple syrup in the fridge.'

'Yes, indeed there is. Should only be a minute more and it'll be ready. How'd you enjoy last night, then? We were both a bit worse for wear when we fell into bed.'

'I know. Haven't had that many pints in a while, but it was a great night. Paddy's done well to raise as much money as he did. It'll be good for his charity.'

'Absolutely. I'd forgotten just how much I enjoy Irish music.' He laughed, turning to Carrick and holding out a bowl of steaming porridge.

'It's hard to trump a night of Irish music,' Carrick remarked, remembering back to the words of Maura O'Connell's "Summerfly" and the way Paddy had locked eyes with him. Reminding him, always, of the past, of that last night before Paddy had left for Edinburgh.

'You and Julia seemed to be getting along pretty well.' Liam looked across the table at Carrick, raising an eyebrow.

'She's lovely. It was nice to enjoy the conversation of an intelligent woman.'

'Jesus. You make it sound like you were having a chat with a librarian.' Liam shook his head and dipped his spoon into his porridge.

'No.' Carrick laughed. 'I'm just saying it's a change from, you know, stilted conversations with women in bars. Maybe I've just been on my own too long and find intelligent female company irresistible.'

'Rubbish. You've dated one or two lovely women. One was a doctor, as I recall. Admit it, Carrick, she's beautiful and you were a little smitten.'

'Maybe.' Carrick looked down, finding a sudden compelling interest in his plate of porridge. He wanted to end the conversation. He didn't want to admit to Liam that he couldn't pursue Julia because he believed Paddy had feelings for her.

'How are you doing with the switch across to Ireland?

'Nice change of subject, by the way, and in answer to your question, fine. There's a lot to plan, to implement - plus the press are banging at my door all the time, just had them on the phone as you came in. I'm not that interesting. He looked across to Carrick, his mood had changed and Carrick thought there was more going on that Liam had disclosed.

'What does Anna think of you moving your business interests to Ireland?' Anna was Liam's wife, although Carrick believed it was a marriage of convenience, business convenience. He'd met Anna a few times and never warmed to her.

'She's not best pleased, but it's my decision, not hers.' His tone was terse and Carrick knew his friend well enough to let the matter drop. If Liam wished to talk about it he would.

· · ·

Liam pulled his chair back from the table to carry his empty bowl to the sink before returning, resting his elbows on the table and clasping his hands together as though he were about to deliver a sermon.

'If you find a woman that you really love, you shouldn't hesitate to tell her so.'

Carrick wondered why Liam was preaching in this way and watched with dismay as he saw his friend fighting to control his emotions.

'It's difficult with Anna. She's not Irish for a start and doesn't understand why I want to *throw my hat in the ring with a bunch of Micks* or words to that affect.'

Carrick reached across and grabbed Liam's hand in his.

'It's not going to be easy or straight forward easing yourself away from your business interests in London, you know that I'm sure, but I'm here for you. You appreciate that, right? And so is Paddy. He cares about you just as much as I do.'

'I know. Thank you. I guess I hadn't bargained on there being so much acrimony from Anna and her father. He's been a right pain in the arse, so he has.'

Liam began drumming his fingers on the wooden surface before speaking again.

'Paddy talked to me for a long time last night. In the end, I think we were both so drunk neither of us knew what we were saying.'

Liam wiped his eyes with the back of his hand. 'But I remember enough to know that Paddy cares. He's always cared, right back to that first day at school in Baltimore. I was a fish out of water, but he made me feel special, wanted, included. He was good like that. I can see why this charity means so much to him. He has a way with children.'

Carrick sat watching his friend, troubled by Liam's uncharacter-istic display of emotions. He was a warm, vivacious and often outspoken friend, but seldom had Carrick ever seen him display such raw emotion.

'Back then, we might have thought we were grown up. We weren't. We were all just kids, doing kid stuff. When Paddy took us out sailing that first time —' Liam looked across at Carrick. 'Do you remember?'

Carrick nodded. Of course he remembered. He remembered every summer in Ireland.

'I thought I was going to pee myself with both excitement and fear. I'd never sailed before, but Paddy was patient, encouraging, and you were that little bit younger than us.' He laughed, recalling the memory.

'I remember he was so protective of you, his little brother. Making sure you had your life jacket properly fastened, and you, looking like you wanted to punch him in the face for babying you.'

Carrick smiled the memory of that day so clear in his mind.

'You sat at the stern like an orange beacon in your life jacket. I remember those days so well, and the older I get, the more they matter.' Liam sighed heavily.

'For years I've felt like I was always looking for the summer, that summer. My compass set for the Irish coast. Is it like that for you?'

Carrick nodded in agreement. 'I often find myself back there, in that boat, out on the ocean. I can recall all of it so very well.'

He remembered the good and the bad. Sadly, it was the bad that he'd allowed to dominate his adult life and deny him the possibility of love, of children - of a meaningful relationship.

LAST NIGHT he'd felt something stir within him, a shift. But today in the harsh light of a winter's morning he'd realised it was out of reach. She was out of reach. He wouldn't stand in Paddy's way if his brother was serious about this woman.

'There's something I want to raise with you,' Liam said, gazing steadily at Carrick.

'What's that, then?'

'You and Paddy. What's going on between you two? It's been like this for years. This tension, this, I don't know, anger maybe?'

'It's a long story.'

'Well, it's obviously an important one. You were so close, as I remember. What happened after I left? Must have been something. I can only assume a woman—that's normally the reason men fall out. Women or money?'

'You were right the first time. It was a woman. Well, not much more than a girl, really. We were all so very young.'

'Do you want another coffee and then you can tell me all about it?'

'Yes to the coffee. Undecided if I want to talk about it. It was such a long time ago…'

'Not so long, seeing that it's obviously still bothering the two of you.'

As Liam poured more coffee, Carrick wrestled with confiding in Liam or keeping all his pain and guilt locked up.

'Do you recall a girl called Katie Fitzpatrick?'

'Can't say I do. Should I?'

'No, probably not. She was a Catholic, went to a different school, ran with a different crowd.'

'And what, you started taking her out?'

'God no. I was only sixteen when I first met her; she was Paddy's age. It was Paddy—he fell in love with her.'

'And what about you, Carrick? Did you fall in love with her, too?'

Carrick looked up from his coffee. 'Yes, I did. Foolish, boyish love which felt so real at the time.'

'So what happened, then? Where is she now, this Katie?'

'She's dead. She drowned herself. Took her father's dinghy out to sea.'

'Jesus and Mary. That's not what I expected you to say.'

'The thing is, I should have seen it coming. I should have known, and I should have stopped her.'

'Be that as it may, you can't stop someone doing something if they really want to. You can't blame yourself for that, Carrick.'

'I knew she was depressed. When Paddy didn't come back for the first university break, she took that as a sign he wanted nothing more to do with her, that she'd only been a fling and he'd found someone more interesting, more suitable in Edinburgh.'

'And had he?'

'No. Not as far as I was aware. I think he just immersed himself in music and the excitement of university and being away from home. All of it was a distraction. A distraction from thinking about her and knowing there was nothing he could do immediately. They'd planned to take off to London together once he graduated, but that would have been years away.'

'I can see from Paddy's perspective the need to knuckle down and work hard at university. He'd earned the right to be there. She would have been a distraction. He would have always felt each time he returned home that the leaving would be that little bit harder.'

'She didn't view it like that. Him not returning that first break, that was a turning point for her in some way. A turning point to a very dark place. She told me she believed it was over with him. That the promises he'd made were all lies so he could sleep with her. That he'd never had any intention of taking her away from her miserable life in Baltimore to the excitement of London.'

'What do you think?'

'He loved her, but I think once he arrived in Edinburgh and saw a bigger world of musical opportunity, music became the greater love.'

'And what of your feelings towards her by then?'

'I realised, once I got to know her better as a friend, that she wasn't how I'd imagined, how I'd fantasised. I'd only spent time in her company on the yacht with Paddy. There, in that environment, she'd been wild, carefree, always laughing and smiling. Out on the water is where she felt she could be her true self.'

'You were only young. It's hard to understand our own feelings, let alone those of another.'

'Yes, but I also became very angry with her that she'd made such harsh accusations against Paddy. I knew my brother and I knew he would never have used her in that way deliberately. He was just so wrapped up in the excitement of it all that he behaved terribly, thoughtlessly towards her. It's so much harder for the one left behind, isn't it? So, you see, my harshness towards her probably contributed to her slipping away into a very dark place.'

Carrick took a long sip of his coffee before he continued.

'I'd seen her the day before she disappeared. She'd taken a nasty beating from her father. He was a terrible bastard of a man, and he laid into her mother and Katie regularly. Back then people turned a blind eye to domestic violence, especially families like theirs.'

'Was that the last you saw of her?'

'No. I was walking along the pier the next evening, and I looked across and heard the sound of an outboard motor. I thought she must have been going out to her father's fishing boat. I waved out, but she was too far away to see me. If I'd known what she was going to do, I'd have gone after her. It wasn't until the next day that I realised her father's boat was in dry dock being repaired.'

'Did they find her?'

'No, her body was never found, just the dinghy, her shoes, and a necklace, one her mother had given her for her eighteenth birthday. She was so excited. It was just a cheap necklace, nothing fancy. I remember thinking she deserved so much better, but her mother had given what she could afford, and Katie treasured that.' Carrick drained the last of his coffee and put the cup down on the table.

'I'd given her money for her birthday, money I'd saved up. It wasn't much, but I thought it might be a start, a way for her to make plans to leave and escape her home life. By that stage, I wanted her to go. I didn't want her waiting in Baltimore for Paddy to return. I'd decided in my seventeen-year-old wisdom, that she wasn't right for Paddy.'

He looked across at Liam anticipating a comment, but none was forthcoming.

'Her world was too small, and to be honest, I thought she was too broken by her home life. I thought she would only hold Paddy back, and I wanted so much, so passionately for Paddy to succeed in music so that he would become the amazing musician that he now is and our parents would be proud of him.'

'Do you think she ever would have left?'

'No. I think the need to try and protect her mother from the abuse of her father would have kept her tied to Baltimore. Once I got to know her, I realised she had little ambition. Oh, she talked a lot about a future, a future that was pure fantasy, but it probably kept her buoyant enough at the time to stop her dark thoughts taking over.

But it was the money I gave her that caused the beating. Her father came home and was ransacking the house looking for pennies to go back to the pub. He found the money, and when she wouldn't say how she got it, he assumed the worst and beat her. With the money gone and her faced with humiliation and despair, it must have been the worst moment for her.'

'Did Paddy not know how she was feeling?'

'No. They didn't see or speak to each other again after that last night before he left. They'd argued, and she'd run off.'

'Did she tell you they'd argued?'

'No. I was there.' Carrick felt acutely embarrassed, not wishing to share that he'd taken to being quite voyeuristic where Katie and Paddy were concerned. That night he'd been walking home from a friend's and in the distance he'd seen them enter the boat shed.

He'd gone down and stood on an empty fishing pot to look through the tiny window. He'd seen his brother holding out Katie's clothes to her as she lay naked on the blanket on the floor of the boat shed.

Startled by what he saw, Carrick toppled from the fishing pot before making a hasty retreat into the darkness, where he stood waiting. He'd heard his brother's voice raised in anger and Katie pleading.

It wasn't long before the door opened and Paddy had looked outside, and then Katie, with a coat draped about her shoulders, had run from the boat shed up onto the road and out of sight. Carrick had stayed hidden until he watched his brother lock the boat shed door and walk back home.

'You need to tell Paddy. He's your brother. You were so close as boys. Don't hang onto all this stuff. It was decades ago. Let it go.'

'It's not that simple, Liam. Paddy believes I was dating her after he left, that I was the cause of her suicide. Those were the rumours that filtered back to him and landed at his door in Edinburgh.'

'Well, you know that's not true, so tell him. Sit down and talk it out.'

CARRICK SAW Liam off at the airport. He was heading straight to Dublin. Carrick wondered how this was going to work for Liam. It was clear from their earlier conversation Anna was distinctly unhappy with Liam's decision to switch his business interests to Ireland and away from London. He didn't envy his friend having to deal with Anna and her father, Charles Willoughby.

They were an old family from old money and rumours had surfaced in recent years that Charles Willoughby's business dealings and the way in which the bank that he ran operated, were coming under scrutiny.

The serious fraud squad had been mentioned in the press, but Carrick knew this could all be speculation and exaggeration on the part of the media. He hoped Liam wouldn't get caught up in anything nasty.

AS HE LEFT Heathrow and drove back to his apartment, Carrick convinced himself that keeping relationships at arm's length was the only option if you wished to avoid heartache and he knew Julia Davis would mean heartache if he chose to pursue her.

21

PATRICK

Patrick walked briskly away from his apartment, taking the route towards the river. He loved living close to the Thames. It was his catharsis.

This morning he wished to purge the feelings of jealousy and pain that had made sleep elusive. A blanket of fog hung low over the river, making it seem eerie and mysterious.

A rowing eight were braving the elements, their boat slicing through the water, the sound of the cox calling stroke. They slipped from sight and silence fell as the fog sucked them in to its depths.

He was reminded of how much he used to love sailing. He'd not been on the water in years. Time was a factor, and the likelihood remote of any of his friends wanting to accompany him.

When he visited his parents, he would go out with his father, but visits back to Ireland were rare. He had too much happening in the UK to allow himself the time. That's what he told himself. Often enough to believe it.

Finn stopped and sniffed, pulling a little on his lead, desperate to get nearer the water's edge.

'Not today, mister. I'm in need of a coffee. Come on, boy. Let's go.'

Patrick gave a slight tug on the lead, and Finn trotted back alongside his master.

He was heading for his favourite café, and the smell of coffee and a freshly baked croissant was all he could think of. He felt famished. Having little sleep, hungover, and hungry, he quickened his pace.

When they reached the café, a tiny place huddled between imposing Georgian buildings with its royal blue paint glistening in the first rays of a watery winter sun, Patrick found to his dismay the doors were closed and the iron tables and chairs normally perched carefully on the uneven pavement were missing. Even in the winter, the owner always put out tables and chairs and sometimes an outdoor heater if it was especially cold.

A surge of disappointment washed through him, and he turned to leave when he heard a knock on the window. The owner, Louis, waved at him, gesturing for Patrick to come in.

'Bonjour, Patrick,' Louis called.

'Come in. Bring the dog. It's too cold to sit out today, even for you Irish. And it is still so early. With nobody about, I am not bothering with the outdoor tables today.'

He smiled at Patrick as he waved him inside.

'Bonjour, *Louis. J'ai besoin un café crème et un croissant. Comment allez-vous aujourd'hui?*'

'*Bien, merci. Je ne peux pas me plaindre. Et vous?*'

'*Je suis fatigué, Louis, tres fatigué.*'

'Very good, Patrick. Your French is coming on nicely. *Très bon.*'

He laughed and slapped Patrick on the back before returning to the kitchen from where Patrick could smell the aroma of the light buttery croissants, making him even hungrier. He smiled at Louis's comment. His French was improving, and he'd been trying very hard to increase his French vocabulary.

Patrick was mulling this over as his body thawed in the warmth of the café, and his senses came alive with the smell of freshly brewed coffee and the warm yeasty aroma of baking bread.

'Bon appétit, Patrick,' Louis announced as he placed his steaming coffee and croissant on the table in front of him. A tiny dish of raspberry jam was perched on the plate alongside a stick of butter.

The perfect breakfast, Patrick thought. He could see from the corner of his eye Finn sidling up to the table, his head held high, sniffing the air with an obvious look of appreciation and hunger in his eyes, hopeful there might be a crumb for him.

Patrick lingered over his breakfast, reluctant to leave the warmth of the café but knowing he had work waiting for him at the studio and he couldn't stay nestled in the cafe all morning, however tempting it might have been.

His thoughts returned to the evening before and Julia. He'd not been able to get her out of his mind. He'd watched how animated she'd appeared talking to Carrick and acknowledged his own feelings as those of jealousy tinged with anger.

Why had she been there anyway? Why last night of all nights? The night Carrick and Liam had turned up to support his charity. The timing couldn't have been worse.

On his second cup of coffee, he was about to put the cup to his mouth when a sharp blast of cold air made him look up. Coming through the door was Julia, dressed in a black coat with a red scarf and black jeans. Her hair down and her cheeks flushed from the fresh winter's air, she looked stunning.

Patrick almost dropped his cup, astonished to see her there in this little place, what he considered *his little French café*, so out of context.

It took him a moment to remember Jack had mentioned they lived at Hambleden, so it was probably natural for her to come into Henley, but of all the cafes she could have visited, what were the chances that she'd choose this one at the very same time that he was there?

He watched, astonished, as she headed for the counter, clearly oblivious to him sitting in the corner. As she approached, Louis appeared from the kitchen.

'Bonjour, Madam Julia, and how are you this cold winter's day?'

'Bonjour, Louis. Cold and in need of your pastries.' She smiled back at Louis, and Patrick's heart skipped a beat.

It was then that she turned and caught sight of Patrick. He watched as her expression registered astonishment before she composed herself.

'Good morning. This is a surprise seeing you here. Is that your dog?'

Patrick watched as her eyes settled on Finn and an expression of joy spread across her face. A couple of strides and she was at his table.

'May I? Pat him, I mean.'

'Of course. His name's Finn.'

'Oh, he's gorgeous, Patrick. So handsome, and what a beautiful coat.'

Patrick couldn't help but feel she was clearly more interested in his dog than him, but he'd take that. It was better than an uncomfortable greeting and a quick exit.

Finn, who was often quite reserved with people he didn't know, dipped his head and put a paw on her knee as she crouched down beside Patrick's chair to stroke him. She was so close Patrick could smell her perfume, warm and spicy.

'Ah, I see you two know each other. Would you like to join Monsieur Patrick, Julia?' Louis asked.

There was an awkward silence, leaving Louis looking from one to the other before a big grin spread across his face.

'Ma chérie, I will take that as a yes and bring you a coffee crème, just how you like it, and one of my croissants. *Oui?*'

'*Oui, Louis. Merci beaucoup.*'

'You speak French?' Patrick raised an eyebrow as he stood and pulled out a chair for Julia.

'No. I'm no linguist, but I try, and Louis loves that you try.'

She smiled, looking directly at Patrick, and his barren heart ached with a need he'd not felt in years.

22

JULIA

Julia looked up at the school as she locked her car and, once again, marvelled at how beautiful it was and how lucky they were that Jack had been accepted as a pupil of St Julian's following his time at Heathstone Prep.

The Gothic arched windows and doorways blended with brick, flint, and ancient sandstone, echoing centuries of history.

Like Heathstone, St Julian's College had a warmth about it. Not too big that pupils became anonymous figures scurrying to and fro across quadrangles and manicured lawns to classes and sporting activities, but large enough to offer a full and varied curriculum, particularly for the boys who were boarders.

Julia followed the path to the sports fields, taking the walkway flanked by hornbeam hedging leading to a herbaceous border that was stunning in spring and summer but now sad with the dieback of plants waiting for the first warm rays of spring sun to aid their burst into a new season.

Wet leaves left over from autumn winds clung to the path, making it slippery and forcing Julia to slow her pace.

She was deep in thought. Her morning had started early, and despite her best intentions, she'd not finished preparing the legal brief she'd been working on that needed to be ready for court on Monday.

Her thoughts had been hijacked first by Carrick Devlin and now by Patrick. It had been a shock to see him sitting in Louis's Café, and her first instinct had been to keep her distance, take her croissant, and make a polite but hasty retreat to the safety of the cottage.

Instead, she'd been distracted by the dog and then by the man, and now she couldn't clear her thoughts of him. When she sat down at the table, she'd noticed how tired and worn he looked. The charity event the evening before must have taken its toll, she'd thought.

He'd seemed tentative, even a little bit nervous, but that was silly. Why would he be nervous of her? They'd chatted for more than half an hour, and her heart had filled with joy when Patrick spoke of Jack.

'You know, Julia, he's an incredibly talented musician. I mean extraordinarily so.'

'Really? Thank you. Like most parents, I believe his talent is special, but I'm guilty of bias.'

She'd smiled at him, noticing how beautiful his eyes were. The colour of rich dark chocolate. Eyes that caressed, and for a moment he'd held her steadfast with his gaze, forcing her to be the first to look down at her coffee as she felt her cheeks redden.

She'd been stunned at how passionately Patrick had spoken of Jack and the intensity with which he'd conveyed his hopes and aspirations for her son. Even when Hamish had commented on Jack's exceptional musical ability, he'd not conveyed the promise of great things ahead in the way Patrick did, and she couldn't help but be warmed by this man's belief in her son.

As she turned the corner from the sheltered walkway, the winter wind howled through the gap in the hedging, making her duck her head and hunch her shoulders to brace herself against its cold fury.

Standing out on the sports field would be freezing, but the promise of hot tea and sandwiches at the conclusion of the game was always the carrot that teased and allowed her to believe the game would no sooner begin than it would end and the boys would tramp back to the shower block, faces elated with a win or saddened by defeat.

Julia joined a group of parents at one end of the field, lifting her hand briefly in greeting when she saw Jack looking across at her.

They were playing Abingdon today and they were a tough side, but Julia had every faith in St Julian's being able to pull off a win.

They were a strong side with some outstanding players, but it turned out she'd been optimistic to believe they could outplay the bigger, stronger Abingdon boys.

As the game drew to a close with a score of 14–10 to Abingdon, she watched with empathy as the St Julian's team left the field wearing their despondency like heavy cloaks upon their backs.

SHE NOTED the usual aggressively obnoxious parent who, by the time he had walked back to the reception room, would have perfected his analysis of the game in order to hold court over his unwilling audience throughout tea, criticising players, the referee, and poor tactical execution.

She hated the "win at all costs" mentality of some parents, which must put enormous pressure on their children, and he was a truly world-class bore.

Julia's approach was much more pragmatic. Winning was nice but losing was a life lesson opportunity. You either learned from the loss and were better prepared for next time, or you had a pity party, blamed anyone but yourself, and hoped the world would be nicer to you next time. Newsflash: It wouldn't be but, hey, you just carry on hoping instead of working for success!

Julia snapped herself out of the train of thought. God, that boring man got under her skin. She knew what it felt like when a court case didn't go her way, but it wasn't a place for the meek or the weak. It made you a stronger, keener lawyer or you realised it was time to find a new career.

· · ·

JACK WAS UNUSUALLY quiet on the ride home, and Julia found herself glancing across at him several times as she drove, wondering if it was just the loss of the game or something bigger worrying him.

When they arrived back at the cottage he went straight to his room and shut the door. *Teenagers.* All those hormones waging war on young bodies. She remembered her own teenage years. Times when she was filled with angst over the most trivial of matters. Spending hours in her room or at her Lizzie's house.

She looked back on those years with a sense of relief that she'd never have to revisit that time. She didn't envy Jack heading into puberty and knew she would have to tread thoughtfully when dealing with the inevitable mood swings and "Kevin moments", as she referred to the personality transformations once parodied by the comedian Harry Enfield's teenage character.

WHEN THEY SAT down to supper, Julia noticed Jack's mood had not lifted. 'What's up? Are you worried about something?'

'Nah...well, yes, a bit.' Jack stabbed at the chicken on his plate before putting it in his mouth.

'Do you want to share?'

'I don't think I can keep playing sport every weekend. It gives me no time for music, and that's more important to me, especially now I'm going to Mr Devlin.'

'You have Sundays. Is that not enough?'

'No. It's not or I wouldn't have said it,' he snapped back, then seeing his mother's startled expression, he added, 'Sorry, Mum. I didn't mean to be rude. I'm just feeling frustrated that I haven't enough time.'

'Do you want me to talk to the school?'

Jack looked across the table at her with the first sign of a smile.

'Would you? They won't like it, but maybe if you spoke to them and explained. I'll continue on until we break for Christmas. That way I'm not letting the team down.'

'I ran into Mr Devlin in Henley this morning. He spoke very highly of you.'

Jack flicked his head up from his plate and a broad smile creased his face. 'Did you talk with him? About me, I mean?'

'Yes, we did, actually. He's very pleased with your progress.'

'That's cool. I really want to do well. He's such a great teacher, I don't want to let him down or myself. This is so huge for me.'

'It is. But you don't want to get yourself all wound up about it. You're doing everything and more than is being asked of you. Just keep going and try not to wear yourself out worrying about stuff.'

'I do worry. It's a lot of money for you to pay.'

'That's my concern. Not yours. And by the way, it's not a problem, so put that out of your mind.'

She smiled across at him, hoping to alleviate his worries. The last thing she needed was Jack making himself sick with anxiety over juggling school, sport, music, and then worrying about how much the academy was costing.

She'd speak to the school as soon as possible, and if she had to, she'd insist he be released from sport. After talking with Patrick that morning, she'd been determined to give Jack every ounce of support she could to help him further his musical studies, and if that meant giving up sport, then she'd make that happen.

23

PATRICK

Despite the lack of sleep and the residue of a hangover that the coffee was trying to combat, Patrick had a bounce in his step as he walked through the streets of Henley towards his studio.

Julia had been different this morning—not just friendly, as she'd been over the past months, but more playful, more relaxed—and this made his heart soar despite his best efforts to stay grounded.

She was beautiful and funny and intelligent. How could one woman be wrapped up in so many adjectives? He didn't have an answer. He just knew she was special.

As he opened the door to his studio, he looked down at Finn. 'It's all right, boy. I have food in the fridge. You won't starve.' He bent to stroke the dog's head before closing the door behind him and climbing the stairs.

Finn would be happy there for hours, and it would be hours, Patrick wagered. He had a lot to do and a class to teach up in London the following day. It would be the last for the year, and he found himself wondering how many of those pupils would spend a sad, unfulfilling Christmas with families who neither wanted them nor cared about them.

Late in the afternoon, after Patrick had seen out the last of his pupils for the day, he took a call from Hamish.

'Hey, Paddy. Susan wants to know if you'd like to join us for supper tonight? I said you were probably out on a hot date.'

'No to you, and yes to Susan. That would be great. I'm famished. What time would you like me?'

'Say, 5:30ish? Susan thought you could read a story to the twins. Oh, and she asked if you would bring Finn. The girls want to see him.'

'Sure. I'm at the studio and Finn is with me, but I'll make tracks for home, freshen up, and be with you around 5:30.'

Privately, Patrick had anticipated strolling slowly back to his apartment, playing his guitar, and getting a takeaway for supper, generally getting in a relaxed mood and replaying every moment of his time with Julia that morning. But, being practical, Susan was a great cook and the twins were adorable so, all in all, the offer was too tempting to refuse.

It was roughly eight miles from Henley to Hamish and Susan's house on the outskirts of Marlow, so Patrick guessed he had plenty of time to finish up at the studio and walk back to his apartment, take a shower, and find a bottle of wine to take with him.

He thought perhaps he should pick up some flowers, but not from the local petrol station. Susan would be horrified and likely to tell him where to stick them if he couldn't do better than a petrol station.

He checked on his phone to locate the nearest florist and figured if he walked briskly, he'd make it in time before they closed, and he could offer the lady of the house something that didn't look like it had been stolen from a cemetery.

WHEN PATRICK HAD FINISHED READING several chapters of *Harry Potter and the Chamber of Secrets* to the twins and they'd both fussed and cuddled Finn, he rose from the chair nestled between both beds, kissed them each on the forehead twice before saying, 'enough now, or I'll wear my lips out', and bid them goodnight amid protests of "Just one more chapter. We love Harry Potter."

'Time for sleep now. Little girls need to get their beauty sleep or you won't grow up to be as pretty as your mother.'

They begrudgingly settled down as Patrick turned out their bedside lights, leaving the door open a fraction in case they needed to call out. He was sure they would. There was seldom a night that he'd been there for dinner when one or both had not ventured downstairs on the pretext of needing a drink of water or a last cuddle.

'Mish tells me last night was a roaring success. I'm sorry I couldn't make it; last-minute babysitter problems, I'm afraid.' Susan sighed.

'It's always a gamble with babysitters.' She handed Patrick the bottle of red he'd bought. 'You can do the honours, Paddy, and open that.'

'My pleasure. And yes, last night was great. We made a lot of money for the charity, way more than I'd expected. I haven't done a final tally yet, waiting on the bill from the club, although they said, since it was for charity, they'd give me a discount. But all the same, I believe we did well.'

'That's grand, it really is. What you do for those kiddies is amazing. Poor wee mites.'

'Some of them aren't so wee. I've got a real mix of ages from ten through to sixteen. But you're right. I was thinking earlier how many of them will have a bleak Christmas.'

'What you give them, Paddy, is a way out. A way towards a better future. That has to count for something,' Hamish said and took a sip of wine.

'This is good. You've got good taste, my friend—where wine is concerned anyway.' He grinned across the table and Susan elbowed him gently in the ribs.

'So, Paddy, Mish tells me a special lady was there last night watching you play?'

'Did he indeed?' Patrick raised an eyebrow at Hamish and tried to look puzzled.

'What I said was Julia Davis is a lovely lady and...well, maybe me old friend Paddy here is a tad smitten.'

Patrick could feel himself blush. He took a long sip of his wine, hoping to buy time to think. He wasn't ready for one of Susan's interrogations. She meant well and only wanted the best for him, and for her that meant him settling down with a good woman at his side.

'She is lovely. I grant you that, but I'm sure she's not the least bit interested in me.'

'Yeah. She did seem rather taken with Carrick. Well, at least that's the impression I got from up on stage.'

Patrick could feel his stomach tighten with Hamish's words. *So he'd seen it too.* It hadn't been his imagination.

'Don't take any notice of my potato-head husband. What Mish knows about romance you could fit on an Irish farthing, so you could. You should ask her out, Paddy. What's the worst that could happen? She says no. At least you'd know where you stand.'

'Hey, hey. You're charging ahead of yourself, Susan. I teach her son. Not sure it would be altogether proper to ask out his mother.'

'Don't be daft, Paddy. Is there a brain in that head of yours? If she doesn't feel it's appropriate, then she'll tell you so, won't she?'

'I don't want to put her in that position. Let's change the subject. Are the girls looking forward to Christmas in Ireland this year?'

'Nice save, Paddy.' Hamish laughed at his friend. 'Yes, they are. We've been Skyping both sets of grandparents. Not sure who is more excited: the twins or the oldies.'

'That's grand. They'll have a lovely time in Dublin. Cold, mind, but no worse than here.'

'I can't wait,' Susan said. 'I haven't seen my mammy and pappy for two years, apart from Skype, that is. And that's not the same as holding them close and sitting around a table with a roaring fire and chewing the fat, now is it?'

'No. You're right; it's not.' Patrick felt a pang of regret that he'd not made arrangements to go home to his parents this Christmas.

He was gigging with the band right up until Christmas Eve and then on New Year's Eve. The days in between made it too much of a rush to get across to Ireland and back again. That was his excuse to himself, but he knew he should be there. His parents were getting older, and he ought to be less selfish with his priorities. It had always been the Achilles heel in his life—putting music ahead of everything else.

Susan had cooked a delicious beef and Guinness pie with creamy mash and steamed greens. It was Patrick's favourite, and he was grateful that she'd gone to the trouble to invite him over knowing it would bring a smile to his face.

Thankfully, there was no more talk of Julia, and Patrick felt relieved he didn't have to endure anymore of Susan's matchmaking ideas.

After they said their goodbyes at the door, Hamish walked Patrick out to his car.

'Don't take any notice of Susan. I think you would be mad to ask Julia out. She's been through a lot...not sure she's ready for dating.'

'You her daddy now?' Patrick's relaxed mood changed in an instant. He didn't need Hamish telling him who he could date and who he couldn't. He'd work that out for himself.

'It's not that, Paddy. I know her. I know Jack. There's stuff, awful stuff. I just wouldn't want to see her get hurt.'

Patrick's flame of anger was extinguished as quickly as it had ignited. 'I know you're only looking out for her. For both of them. I wouldn't do anything that would hurt Julia or Jack. She'd not be a one-night stand Mish. She's worth so much more than that.'

Patrick had not wished his friend to see his conflict, the anguish and desire washing too and fro like a tide within him, but he couldn't hide the emotion in his voice and the look in his eyes, both of which he knew Hamish had seen and heard.

Hamish pulled him into a swift embrace. 'We want you to be happy, Paddy. We really do. Just tread carefully, that's all I'm asking.'

'I will Mish. I promise. Thank you for this evening; as always, it was great. Catch up during the week? I want to run something by you about music.'

'Okay, sure. I'll give you a call. Night, Paddy. Drive safely.'

His flash of anger at Hamish reminded him of the heated argument he'd had with Phil, over Erika, Phil's little sister. Phil had accused him of treating her shabbily the way he did all women. Patrick had been stung by the remark. He didn't treat women shabbily he just didn't do commitment and it was hardly his fault if they read more into dinner and sex.

Eventually Phil had calmed down after Patrick had let him have his say. They were musicians and couldn't afford personal matters to disrupt the band.

As the months went by Patrick learned Erika had met a financial planner and they seemed to be hitting it off. Patrick had been relieved when Phil had told him of Erika's latest love interest.

As Patrick drove back to his apartment with Finn sitting in the passenger seat beside him, he reflected on Susan's words and Hamish's warning. He was right. Hamish knew them. Knew them intimately, and whatever it was that had happened must have been awful for his friend to warn him off like that.

Patrick had no idea what had gone before in Julia and Jack's past, and he wasn't about to start asking questions. If Julia wanted to volunteer anything, then so be it, but he would not be doing the asking.

24

JACK

Jack was still awake, and it was past midnight. He'd been excited when his mother agreed to contact the school about sport. It would make all the difference to him if he could have a Saturday afternoon and all day Sunday for music and study.

He had been working on adapting a piece of music which he'd heard his mother play on the hi-fi from time to time by some guy called Grover Washington Junior. Jack had never heard of him, but the song, "Just the Two of Us", had keyboards and a lovely saxophone section.

He'd been working on composing his own version. He'd hoped to be able to finish it over the weekend and present it to Mr Devlin at next week's lesson.

He could imagine Mr Devlin singing the lyrics. He had that kind of husky, gravelly voice. The kind of voice his mother loved to listen to. Jack had listened to some YouTube clips of Paddy Devlin with his band, Soft Rock and Blues.

They performed a wide range of music covering several genres, and Jack felt sure this would be well within Mr Devlin's range. Well, he hoped it would be. He wanted to add in a guitar section, one that Mr Devlin could play.

It was a big undertaking, he knew, but the more he'd thought about it, the more he'd been determined to complete this task he'd set himself.

H E HADN'T MASTERED the new instruments himself yet, not enough to perform this piece, but Mr Devlin's band could if he composed it well enough.

He'd wondered earlier in the evening, when his mother had asked him at supper what was wrong, whether he should just have blurted it all out and told her not only did he not want to play sport but he was tired of her trying to organise all his time, or at least that's what it felt like. He'd only managed at the last minute to head her off from inviting back a bunch of boys for yet another weekend stay-over. He didn't have time for that. He didn't want to be playing outside or riding bikes or watching dumb movies. He just wanted to lock himself away in his music room and compose, practise, and practise some more.

H E FOUND composing took him to a peaceful, safe place the way playing music helped him to exorcise the feelings of anger and fear that still surfaced from time to time.

He found both composing and playing a perfect healing combination, so being distracted by other things and people was only compounding his growing frustration about how to raise the subject with his mother.

His thoughts moved to Mr Devlin. Could he tell him? Would he feel brave enough to say out loud what had happened? What had happened to him and to his mother? The thought made his tummy flip, and he knew it would still be some time before sleep would rescue him from these troubling thoughts.

. . .

JACK WAS LATE RISING. He'd not fallen asleep until nearly 1 a.m. and he knew when he woke that a decision had been made. He would be brave. He would talk to Mr Devlin. He could trust him. He knew he could and talking it out would surely be better than all these random thoughts cluttering his mind and preventing him from concentrating on anything.

He ate breakfast quickly and excused himself from the table. He put his dishes in the dishwasher and asked if there were any chores his mother wanted him to do, whilst hoping that she would say no as he needed every minute of the day to complete both study and the final touches to the music he'd arranged.

'No. You go off, do your thing. Don't leave your homework until last, though, will you?'

He'd wanted to leave it till last, but he knew himself well enough to know that if he didn't do it first, it wouldn't be done. Music would take over, as it frequently did, and his best intentions around study would come to nothing.

AFTER SUPPER, Jack packed his bags and sat in the car waiting as his mother locked the door to the cottage. As they drove, he kept up a steady stream of banal chatter.

He wanted to distract his mother from asking too many questions about his homework, which he had done, but he'd rushed some areas of English and maths, and she wouldn't be pleased about that. His chatter was also a distraction from his own thoughts. Would he really speak to Mr Devlin or not?

When he'd woken in the morning it had seemed like the right thing to do, but now he wondered if it would be a mistake, a burden to put on someone else, especially someone who was dedicated to teaching him. How would he go about raising the subject? How much would he divulge? And should he tell him about his father and what he did to his mother, or would that sound disloyal?

All these questions plagued Jack as he reached across to kiss his mother goodbye and grab his bag. He'd figure it out. He'd have to. It was becoming too big inside him to hold back, and he needed someone to talk to. He needed to share his concerns about his mother organising his life without understanding what he wanted and the pressure he felt that her world revolved around him. That made him feel bad because it would sound ungrateful, like he didn't appreciate her love, support, and protection of him.

He had to find the right words that would convey the frustration and pressure or else he was going to sound like some spoilt kid who didn't know how lucky he was when there were children in the world who didn't even have a musical instrument or a good school to go to.

It was a conundrum. Oh, how he loved that word because it was designed to mean exactly how he was feeling.

25

CARRICK

Following his weekend with Liam, Carrick had spent time in London seeing his lawyer and ensuring all his affairs were in order before he left for New Zealand.

He'd intended going out for a few weeks, but after the events of the charity evening, he'd thought time and distance would be a better option. He wouldn't stand in the way of his brother and any chance he might have of a relationship with Julia.

Whatever he believed he'd seen in his brother's eyes that night, and wherever that might lead, he couldn't be accused of ruining anything for Patrick if he wasn't there. In the intervening days since meeting Julia, he'd thought of little else. She plagued his thoughts to such an extent that even his lawyer had queried if something was wrong as his mind seemed to be on other matters.

It was embarrassing. He was hardly a schoolboy, but he found it difficult to concentrate, and frequently her face, her beautiful green eyes, and luxurious dark wavy hair would appear before him like a mirage.

More than once he'd thought of phoning her at work. He didn't have her mobile number, but he knew she worked at Petrie's and it would have been so easy to phone and speak with her.

No woman, not since his boyish love for Katie, had ever captured his attention or his heart in this way. It wasn't as though she resembled Katie in any way. Katie with the coal-black hair and blue eyes like the ocean, so full of life yet so damaged.

Julia was completely different—confident, witty, with a smile that could light up the room and those emerald green eyes that intoxicated him.

When she laughed, which had been often that night, the sound was bright and cheerful, reminding him of dandelions on an Irish summer's day, swaying in the breeze, carefree and pretty. This whole situation was turning him into a soppy Irish poet. It had to stop - and he had to leave.

He would spend the summer in New Zealand, which had its own appeal. Escaping the English winter and maybe enjoying sunshine and some sailing in New Zealand would help free him. He had plenty to do out there. A lot of miles to cover across both islands, exploring the best investment opportunities. He'd stop off in Australia and check on his property investments there as well.

The more he planned his trip, the more convinced he became that he would need to stay out that side of the world for several months at least. But before he left, he'd make a fleeting trip to Ireland to see his parents. He worried that they hardly saw either of their sons. Not that they ever complained, but he could hear it in his mother's voice when he phoned, the longing to see her boys.

A WEEK later Carrick was sitting in the living room of his parents' house beside a roaring fire. He loved the primal comfort of a proper log fire. He'd persuaded his parents to buy this property after they retired as schoolteachers and vacated the schoolhouse where he and Patrick had been raised. Now, years later, this felt like the family home. So much memorabilia reminded him of his youth.

The large model yacht sitting on the mantelpiece was an exact replica of the yacht his father had owned when they were children and on which both boys had learned to sail. Now his father was content to kayak on the saltwater lake of Lough Hyne, although he still owned a small sailboat, enough for him to handle alone yet big enough if he wanted company.

Carrick hoped the weather would clear sufficiently that they could venture out for a sail. It was something the pair would try to do, weather permitting, every time Carrick returned home. The memories of happy summer days, sheeting in and scooting off across the bay in their sailboat, were precious to both father and son.

'You probably won't have heard, but Kevin Fitzpatrick died a month or so back.' His mother made the announcement as they stood side by side at the kitchen sink, she washing and he drying. Carrick's father had retired to the living room to read the paper, leaving mother and son to talk.

'About time,' Carrick responded.

'That's hardly a Christian thing to say, Carrick.' His mother glanced at him, a frown creasing the still beautiful face. Age had been kind to her.

'He wasn't a Christian, Mammy, despite his Catholic beliefs. He beat his wife and daughter and made their lives a living hell, so good riddance to the man.'

Hearing the name Kevin Fitzpatrick had stirred up fire and hatred in Carrick. Feelings he thought were long buried had risen from the ashes with volcanic force, surprising even himself.

'That may be so, but it's not right to speak ill of the dead. I raised you better than that.'

'You raised me to be kind and loving, Mammy. Kevin Fitzpatrick was neither, and I'll not hold back in telling the truth of who he was, dead or not. What about Colleen? How is she?'

'Well it's sad, so it is. She's in a hospice. Cancer. Been lingering on for some time. Cruel it is, but God's way, no doubt.'

'Jesus. God's way be damned!' Carrick exclaimed. 'The poor woman deserves more than that from a God she so fervently believed in.'

'Don't get yourself so worked up, Carrick. I shouldn't have mentioned it. It's always been a sore point for you—the Fitzpatricks, I mean. And you're not alone with those sentiments. There was always talk about that family.' Carrick could see his mother wrestling with something further she wanted to say.

'You know, when you were young, after Patrick left for university, there was talk in the village that you and their daughter, Katie—was that her name? Well, anyway, at the time people talked that you were involved with her. I didn't think that could be possible. Where would you have had the opportunity to meet? You didn't even go to the same schools.'

'People talk, regardless of whether there is any truth or not. I knew Katie. Patrick and I both. She was a grand girl.'

Describing Katie, the girl both he and Patrick had loved, as *a grand girl* made her sound like some upper-class farmer's daughter who was a good old sort, not someone you would fall in love with. It saddened him to hear himself describe her in such terms, but the last thing he wanted or needed was his mother probing for information about a time that was best left in the past.

'You two all done out here? Thought I'd make us all a brew.' Carrick's father was standing in the doorway, looking from one to the other.

'I'll do it. You two go and sit down and put your feet up. You've been running after me all day.' Carrick smiled at both his parents, helping his mother out of her apron and shooing her out of the kitchen.

As he waited for the kettle to boil, he reflected on what his mother had told him. To the best of his knowledge there was no hospice in Baltimore. He'd have to find out where Colleen Fitzpatrick was, and he'd visit. He had too, for Katie's sake. She'd have wanted him to do that.

THE FOLLOWING DAY, Carrick made some phone calls and discovered Colleen Fitzpatrick was in a hospice in Cork an hour and a half's drive away. He'd visit her on the drive back to Dublin airport. That would arouse the least suspicion on the part of his parents. They wouldn't understand why he wanted to visit.

Saying goodbye was always hard, especially as Carrick could see his parents were ageing. They were both fit and active, but a little of the sparkle and enthusiasm was missing, and he couldn't help but feel this was in part due to them not having grandchildren to keep them young at heart—something he knew they'd longed for but were now resigned to the realisation that was unlikely to happen.

He watched in the rear-vision mirror as he drove down the drive, his father's arm about his mother, their hands held up waving, his mother's hand swiping a tear away.

He was glad he'd made the decision to visit before he left for New Zealand. It had been more than a year since he'd last been back, and from what his parents had said, Patrick hadn't been out to see them for even longer.

It was almost a four-hour journey back to Dublin, so Carrick had left plenty of time to stop off in Cork at the hospice.

NOTHING COULD HAVE PREPARED him for the shock of seeing Colleen after so many years. Where once there had been beauty, now only pain remained etched on her features and evident in the clawlike hands that reached out to him.

She resembled little more than a husk, and he wanted to cry out with frustration at the indignity of prolonging life in this cruel way. He was both surprised and grateful she recognised him and that the morphine drip hadn't robbed her of memory.

He sat on the chair beside her bed and wondered who else visited. Did she have anyone left who cared, who would visit? Or was she alone with the beeping machines and only her thoughts for company? Her voice when she spoke was raspy, and he had to bend closer to hear what she was telling him.

'I know you loved my little girl and you were kind to her. I've always been grateful for that. I couldn't protect her and I should have…' A small gasp escaped her, and Carrick found himself holding his breath, unsure whether he should ring for the nurse or wait.

'Sometimes the pain takes me by surprise.' A watery smile touched her parchment lips. She stretched her hand out to his and carried on. 'I knew. I always knew…about Patrick. They loved each other. It broke her heart when he left.'

'Hush now. That was a long time ago.' Carrick wanted her to stop. He didn't want to hear any more. He knew the story all too well.

'She shouldn't have gone out that night. I don't know why she did, do you?'

Carrick thought he knew, but he wouldn't tell a dying woman that her daughter believed her future was bleak and her own life worthless.

As Carrick left the hospice, a nurse stopped and asked if he was a relative.

'No. An old family friend.'

'Will you be back? It's just she has no visitors, and we find it helps, you know, with the pain and coping with the long days.'

'I'm afraid I'm heading back to London today. I'm sorry she doesn't have anyone.' He wanted to be gone, far away. Away from the bleakness of approaching death and the eyes that had looked into his, so like Katie's.

He shouldn't have come, he berated himself as he drove out of the car park. He should have left well enough alone rather than stir up the past, but in his heart, he knew that was guilt talking. Katie had been let down too many times in her life, and however difficult it had been, he knew that visiting had been the right thing to do.

ARRIVING BACK IN LONDON, he drove straight to his house in Lymington. It was the place he escaped to when life became too much. It was a place of private reflection few knew he owned and even fewer were invited too.

The property, accessed by double electric timber gates, was

secluded, surrounded by woodland, making it an ideal location to retreat to.

Carrick set his bags down on the kitchen floor, grateful that his housekeeper had turned on the central heating and stocked the fridge with the bare necessities of milk, butter, bread and some fresh ham.

He made himself a sandwich and a coffee and sat down at the dining room table. He was tired. It had been a long and stressful day, and all he wanted was a hot shower and a good night's sleep. Tomorrow he would have to finalise a few business matters before confirming his flights to New Zealand, including whether he would schedule a short visit to Australia on the way out or the way back.

Hours later he woke from a dream, soaking in sweat with his heart racing. He'd been walking along the pier in Baltimore, immersed in his own thoughts, when the sound of an outboard motor had cut through his preoccupation.

Lifting his head towards the bay in search of the source of the sound, he had seen Katie in her father's dinghy angling away from the mooring. He'd waved out to her, but she was too far away to see, and he'd watched as she manoeuvred the dinghy further out beyond the safety of the harbour into the open sea.

It was a recurring dream but not one he'd experienced in several years. Being back in Ireland and seeing Colleen had forced buried memories to surface once more, and he wondered, not for the first time, whether Liam was right in urging him to talk to Paddy, to tell him everything. Explain to him what really happened all those years ago and whether in the telling he would finally rid himself of the haunting memories and remorse.

Days later Carrick fastened his seat belt and prepared for the long flight out to Australia and then on to New Zealand. He would be busy there with no room in his thoughts to dwell on the past and what might have been, and no time to speculate on the present and Julia Davis, whom he would shortly be leaving behind at nearly six hundred miles per hour.

As the plane taxied along the runway preparing to soar into the grey London sky, he closed his eyes and cleared his mind of all troubling thoughts.

26

JACK

It was Thursday, Jack's afternoon at the academy. He was almost trembling with a mixture of excitement and fear. Excitement that he'd finally finished composing the piece of music he wanted to present to Mr Devlin and fearful of what lay ahead if he shared what had been bothering him for months with the one person he felt would understand.

'Hey, Jack. How has your week been?'

'Fine, thank you. I've been working hard on a piece I've composed. I'd like to share that with you today, if that's okay?'

As Jack walked further into the music room, he saw Finn and his heart skipped a beat. He didn't know Mr Devlin had a dog, a dog like their old one, Judas. For a moment he couldn't speak, but his eyes conveyed a message that anyone could read.

'I didn't know you had a dog. An Irish terrier. We had one just like him. What's his name?' Jack couldn't hide his joy at what felt like seeing an old friend.

'He's called Finn. I don't normally bring him in when I have pupils. He can be a distraction.' Patrick raised his eyebrows at Jack with a quizzical look.

'I won't be distracted, promise, but can I just give him a pat?'

'Of course, but then we need to get down to work.'

SEVERAL HOURS later Jack had finished practising piano pieces and a more complex set of exercises on the drums. Mr Devlin had been impressed with the musical score he'd composed and promised to try it out with his band and see how it sounded.

Jack wondered if he still had the courage to talk to Mr Devlin. He might have had other plans or another student to teach after he left, so maybe the timing would be all wrong.

'You look like you've something on your mind, Jack?'

'Um...yes, I have. But you may need to get on or have another pupil coming in?'

'No. Free as a bird. All the time in the world. Shall we sit down in the comfy chairs? Do you want a drink—water, juice?'

'Just water will be fine, thank you.'

Finn had strolled across the room and was sitting beside Jack's chair, looking into his earnest face with the adoration only a dog's eyes can convey.

'So what's on your mind?'

Jack watched as Mr Devlin stretched out his long legs and settled himself back into the chair.

'You know my mum and dad are not together, don't you?'

'Yes. I gathered as much.'

'Well, you see, since that happened, well, my mum kind of...well, she's sort of made me the *man of the house*. I know she's trying to make me feel grown up, but I feel pressured and I don't know who to talk to who won't say something to her and make her feel bad. She's organising all my weekends, with boys coming over to stay and keeping me busy with things I don't want to do. She thinks it's what I want, and she isn't hearing me when I try to tell her that it isn't, and I don't know how to tell her that it's really annoying me.'

Jack was held in Mr Devlin's gaze. Silence hung between them for long seconds before Mr Devlin spoke.

'You don't. Not like that anyway. The thing is, Jack, your mum will only want the best for you, I'm sure of that, and maybe she thinks keeping you busy is a way of making up for you not having a dad around.'

Jack wanted to blurt out that he didn't care about not having a dad around. His dad had been disinterested in him and made him feel like he'd not been good enough to spend time with. Should he say that? Would that sound like he was whining? That was something his dad used to say.

'My dad isn't a nice person. He beat my mum up really bad.' There it was. He'd said it out loud, and now he couldn't take it back, nor could he stop the fat tears that suddenly escaped down his cheeks.

'I'm sorry, Jack. Truly sorry. That must have been awful for you to experience. Do you want to talk about that?'

'It made me sad, angry, afraid. But I'd been feeling like that for a long time before he hurt Mum.' He pulled his handkerchief from his pants pocket and blew his nose, realising that he couldn't go back now. There was only one way and that was forward. He would tell Mr Devlin everything.

Finn pushed his head into Jack's hand, and he found himself stroking the dog's head, which was very soothing, allowing time for him to gather his thoughts.

'My father has other children from his first marriage. I have two half-brothers.'

'I see. Do you keep in touch with either of them?'

'No. No, I don't. I will never have any contact with them ever again.' Jack took a deep breath before plunging in to tell the story of the trauma of his young life.

Mr Devlin phoned ahead to the school to let them know Jack would be late getting back and that he would see him safely to the school door. Jack had been relieved that Mr Devlin had been thoughtful enough to realise Jack would be in trouble if he didn't turn up for supper.

'There's a chippy around the corner. Fancy coming with me and we'll get something to eat and bring it back here?'

'That would be great, thank you, but I don't have any money on me.'

Mr Devlin laughed. 'No need to worry, I'm sure I can manage a slap-up supper for two at the chippy.'

They walked around the corner together, with Jack holding onto Finn's lead and feeling an enormous weight had been lifted from his shoulders. The bond between pupil and teacher had reached another level.

'WILL YOU BE OKAY TONIGHT? Back at the boarding house, I mean.' Mr Devlin glanced across at Jack before returning his eyes to the road ahead as they drove back to St Julian's.

'I'll be fine. Thank you for listening, for everything tonight. I feel a whole lot better.'

'That's good to hear. I'm always available to listen, Jack. I won't promise to have the answers, but sometimes just talking out loud helps.'

When they pulled up outside the school doors, Jack thanked Mr Devlin and gave Finn a final pat before heading inside. It had been a big night, and Jack felt exhausted and longed for the comfort of his bed and the company of his dormitory friends.

As the housemaster called for lights out and Jack snuggled down beneath the covers, Dan whispered across to him.

'Why were you late back? Did you have to have extra music time or something?'

'Yeah. Just music stuff. Something I've been working on. It took longer than I thought.' He didn't want to share with Dan what he'd told Mr Devlin. It was private and not something he wished to share, not even with his best friend.

'You're turning into a real music nerd. You know that, don't you?' Dan whispered back.

'Better than a maths nerd,' Jack responded. 'People come to listen

to a musician, but no one pays to watch a maths nerd doing sums.'
Smiling to himself, he closed his eyes and hoped sleep would envelop
him quickly.

An hour later, Jack remained awake despite feeling exhausted. He
was mulling over the conversation he'd had and the advice Mr Devlin
had given him.

He'd been amazing. He'd helped Jack look at everything in a
different way, and it had reminded him how, when he was younger,
his mother had been so determined he wouldn't be a victim.

Mr Devlin's words had been a timely reminder that you had
choices, and now he would be accompanying Mr Devlin on a
mission, a charitable mission before Christmas, and that excited Jack
in a way he'd not felt before.

27

JULIA

Julia had tried phoning Jack at the boarding house, but it seemed he was still at the academy and she wondered why there'd been a delay. He'd been working on something fervently over several weekends, and she'd guessed it was a piece he was composing, so maybe they'd spent extra time discussing his progress.

She was spending so much of her time working on various files and preparing complex documents for court she'd barely noticed whether Jack was in the music room or elsewhere. She knew she ought to be spending more time with him, but her work load was enormous, not only with the sheer volume of papers but also running the department and now as a member of the senior leadership team, there were even more meetings and more papers to read.

She wondered if Patrick had taken Finn with him to the studio. He'd promised he would when they'd talked at Louis's Café. She'd boldly asked him if he would take the dog in when it was Jack's lesson, explaining they'd had a dog just like him in New Zealand that they'd had to leave behind. Jack had pined for that dog for years.

. . .

Taking a break from reading, she made herself a pot of tea and sat back down at the table. Her thoughts drifted to Patrick. Meeting him in the café had been a surprise and sitting chatting with him had been easier than she could have imagined. He'd never mentioned his brother and she'd not heard from Carrick. Perhaps that was for the best she thought. She didn't have time for romance.

Her mobile beeped loudly, making her jump. She looked at the screen and saw it was Maria

'Hi Maria, what's up?

'Sorry to bother you after hours, are you free to talk?'

'Yes, of course. You're sounding mysterious.' There was silence for a second before Maria spoke

'I took some files home, ones that Marcus has been working on and which I've been concerned about.'

'Go on.' Julia thought she knew what was coming. Marcus, a young solicitor who she mentored together with several other young junior solicitors when she first joined Petries and took over running the department had been frequently late for work and seemed distracted. She should have taken him aside weeks ago but had let it go putting it down to girlfriend problems.

'There are three cases. One a domestic violence, the other a fairly straight-forward separation and the third a report from counsel for the child. I don't know what is going on with him, but I believe he's made some serious mistakes, I mean really serious.'

'Start with the domestic violence one. What's he done or not done?'

'The partner was badly beaten, Police called etc. He didn't apply for a non-molestation order or a restraining order despite the male being arrested. Fortunately this girl has family in Wales so she fled to them, but what if she hadn't?'

Jesus. Maria was right, this could have been a disaster and would still need a lot of careful handling and some quick action on the part of Petries to arrange for court orders to be in place to protect this girl Julia wagered.

'As far as the couple who are separating are concerned, it seems he's given advice to both parties and not advised the wife to seek independent legal advice. We acted for the husband before he married, so he's our client and I checked, we did Wills for them both and George's team acted on the conveyancing when they bought their first home. Now they've amicably parted ways, but all the same, she should have seen an independent lawyer, do you agree?'

'Absolutely. Even if she still retains Petries as her law firm for further conveyancing or a new Will, whatever. He should have advised her to seek independent legal advice so we can't be accused of having a conflict of interest. So what's the last one about?'

'You remember that client, William Bradbury?'

'Wasn't he the one with the difficult wife? Didn't she try to prevent access. As I recall, we went back to court several times and they appointed Counsel for the Child to sort it out.'

'That's the one. She was a right cow. Anyway, the report arrived a month ago and Marcus has done nothing with it. He's not arranged to see our client, nor sent him a copy of the report. The poor guy is still waiting on a decision from the court and hasn't seen his kids in ages. This should have been actioned immediately. It now looks to the other side like our client didn't care if he saw his kids or not.'

'You were right to phone me. Thanks Maria. I'm pleased you have been checking cases as we discussed. Is it only Marcus, or are some of the others making mistakes?'

'No. Just Marcus. I check files regularly to ensure we don't slip up. I don't know what's going on with him, but he's stuffed up big time. What makes my blood boil, he's hidden these files away, that's why I didn't find them earlier. I had to go looking when he was out of the office to find them. That would indicate to me he knows he's mismanaged all three.'

'Indeed. Leave it with me and I'll raise it with George in the morning. We have a meeting scheduled for 9:30 a.m. Thanks again Maria. Stop work now and enjoy the rest of your evening.'

'See you tomorrow, night Julia.'

This was not what Julia needed and it reflected badly on her department and the running of it which was her responsibility. They would have to act fast and fix this and Marcus had a lot of explaining to do.

28

PATRICK

After Patrick dropped Jack off at St Julian's, he drove slowly away and parked up in a lay-by down the road. His head dropped forward, forehead resting on his fists. He wept. He wept with an intensity that frightened him. Finn, who had been sitting in the back seat, squeezed his way forward, nudging his master's arm. Patrick let one hand drop from his forehead and stroked the dog's head the way he'd watched Jack do hours before. And like Jack, he gained comfort from the stroking and the dog's wet, warm tongue upon his hand.

PATRICK WEPT for the little boy, sexually abused and terrified, and for the young man emerging full of hope, full of love for music, for his mother, but tainted by the memories that remained with him. The anger, the bitterness, and sometimes the fear. How brave he was, thought Patrick. So much braver than I.

When he'd looked across at Jack and saw the teenage anguish radiating from him, he knew there was something big about to be disclosed, but he could never have imagined anything like this.

Finally, he regained his composure, started up the car, and drove slowly back to his apartment. To say he was shocked at Jack's revelations didn't do justice to how he felt.

He lay awake in bed unable to sleep, unable to stop Jack's words replaying in his mind. Patrick had heard some heartbreaking stories from the children he was involved with within his charity, kids who'd suffered from neglect, abuse, and disinterest. But all of them came from a place of poverty, born to parents who either hadn't wanted them or who had, but only as a means to claiming benefit from the government. They'd not been viewed as precious individuals who were owed love, a safe home environment, and a chance to better themselves.

But Jack's story was in complete contrast. He'd been wanted, loved, yet ultimately still harmed in a way which made Patrick's stomach knot.

He licked his lips and tasted the brine of teardrops and wondered whether this was God's way of washing out his eyes so he could see life with a clearer view again. He didn't think he believed in God. Not since Katie. But he couldn't blame God for that. The blame lay closer to home.

ALL EVENING he'd felt like a boat running before a storm, spinnaker straining in the gale, hull skipping across the wave crests, but knowing all the time that he couldn't outrun the maelstrom bearing down on him. It hadn't been only Jack's story that had overwhelmed him.

Learning that Julia had been severely beaten by a raging, violent husband had tipped the balance and forced Patrick to acknowledge he was falling in love with this woman.

He'd not asked nor wanted to fall in love again, but now, in the silent darkness of his room, he allowed himself to accept he loved her, and every fibre of his body longed to hold her, to love her to protect her from ever being harmed again and to give Jack the certainty that he would always be safe with Patrick in his life.

· · ·

He'd known, while vigorously trying to deny it to himself, since the morning she'd walked into Louis's Café that his feelings were no longer neutral.

When she'd laughed and he'd seen the glorious sparkling emerald green of her eyes brim with laughter tears, and the way her beaming smile showed she had two cute dimples on either side of her mouth, giving her a young, girlish look – that whatever happened next, he could no longer deny his feelings.

He'd never seen this more relaxed, fun side to her personality, and it had made him want to reach out across that little rustic table and hold her hand and never let it go. Instead, he'd looked away, unable and afraid to hold her gaze, fearful his eyes would reflect back that his frozen heart had begun to thaw.

When Jack had started by telling him how he felt about Julia's overprotective mothering, he'd stifled a smile. It was so typical of young men his age. Desperate to grab their independence in both hands, they overlooked the vulnerability and responsibility that came with it. How keen they were to shed the ties of parental constraints but still enjoy a warm home, food, and expensive privileges.

Ironically, they simultaneously embraced social and peer group constraints through doing almost anything to be liked, to be respected, to be an individual whilst desperately trying to fit in with their peers down to every branded item in their possession.

It would be funny if they weren't so terribly serious about exchanging one set of constraints for another in the pursuit of freedom of the self.

It brought back a sudden memory of how his parents had tried to shape Carrick's life into what they believed was best for him. He remembered the frustration, the sadness that Carrick wore like a shroud after one of his parents' many lectures about the need for an education, for a university degree.

It was only now, with the clarity of hindsight, that Patrick understood what it must have been like for Carrick living in the shadow of the talented older brother who would graduate with honours from university and go on to have a successful career in music. How that must have affected the way in which Carrick viewed himself.

He'd been the quieter of the two brothers, more reflective. Where Patrick had been bold and outspoken, Carrick had been reticent and shy. Carrick's choice to move to London in pursuit of his property development dream had exposed such a lack of faith from his parents that Patrick had sensed his brother's hurt although no words were spoken at the time.

Even now, with Carrick's evident success, his parents still didn't understand the shrewd business talent and dedication it had taken.

How clever he was with anticipating the property market and how many philanthropic activities he supported. Patrick had never known half of what Carrick had achieved. It only came to light when he'd met up with Liam and been told of his little brother's success.

This estrangement was silly, he thought. He should reach out to Carrick. This had gone on too long. He'd been jealous of the attention Carrick had paid to Julia the night of the charity event. She'd been responsive to him. He'd seen that from the stage, but maybe that was just her when she relaxed? He'd seen the same responsiveness at Louis's Café with him. She'd been relaxed and playful after she got over the shock of seeing him there.

He didn't need to believe she liked Carrick any more than he needed to believe Carrick had responded differently than he would have to any beautiful woman sitting at his table. This was all so juvenile. They were grown men. They were brothers who had at one time loved each other deeply. That must count for something. They would find each other again. Patrick would make sure of it.

He turned on his side, desperate to get comfortable both physically and emotionally. His thoughts drifted back to the conversation he'd had with Jack and his proposal that Jack should accompany him to his Christmas charity event at Evelina London Children's Hospital. Thankfully, Jack had responded enthusiastically and, Patrick believed, with comprehension that despite the bad things, Jack had so much to be grateful for and owed it to himself to give his life meaning and purpose each and every day.

Some of these children would never live to see what might have been, what could have been.

He hoped that by involving Jack, it would help him to understand his mother only wanted the best for him, and given time and a little more maturity, Jack would find the right words, the kind words to relieve his mother of the loving burden she unselfishly carried of filling Jack's life with love and good people so that he wouldn't have space for dark thoughts.

Sleep wouldn't come, so Patrick got up and put on his dressing gown, slipped feet into his slippers, and padded downstairs. He decided he'd make himself a cup of tea. He didn't need Baileys tonight.

Sitting nursing a steaming cup of camomile tea, he marvelled at Jack's strength of character. To have suffered as he clearly had and worked his way out the other side to become an extraordinary young musician was nothing short of a miracle in Patrick's eyes.

So many talented children came through his academy. Children of privilege whose parents could afford the fees and generally wanted the best for their child.

There were the occasional parents who enrolled their children for the wrong reasons, their lives lived vicariously through their child. Without the self-motivation and dedication it took to become outstanding, those children would struggle until Patrick could persuade the parents to support their child's fulfilment through an alternative artistic outlet more fitting to their talents.

Jack was the opposite. It was exciting to watch his progress, and Patrick already knew he had a musical prodigy on his hands. He imagined Jack being accepted for Juilliard if that's what he wanted.

Ultimately it would be down to Jack. His passion, his belief in himself, and the support he would gain from both his teacher and his mother meant he would get to choose.

Listening to Jack describe how he adapted the Grover Washington Junior piece of music made Patrick realise Jack was gaining an enormous sense of satisfaction from the creative process.

He'd said composing made him feel peaceful, and when he played an instrument, he could play out all his fears and anger. Music was a therapy for him. Patrick had little doubt that music held great power in the tool kit of emotional therapy. It was up to him to harness all that talent and give Jack the opportunity to soar like an eagle.

AS HE SHOWERED the following morning, Patrick wondered how he would broach the subject of Jack accompanying him to Evelina London Children's Hospital at Christmas with Julia.

School would have finished by then so Jack would have time to work on ideas for helping the children to enjoy playing an instrument. To enjoy the sound that instruments could make and to find comfort in both playing and listening.

He would make a point of calling her to discuss it this week rather than leave it until the last minute when she might have something else planned. It was the perfect excuse to call and then maybe, if he could pluck up the courage, ask her out for a coffee, or a wine, or dinner.

'God, for a man who has wined and dined as many women as you have, you're behaving like a teenager at his first disco where Julia is concerned,' he admonished himself out loud as he soaped away the sadness of his night's thoughts under the shower's steaming water.

He dressed quickly and went downstairs to make himself some breakfast before heading to the studio.

He let Finn out to the back garden, shutting the door quickly behind him as a cold rush of winter air invaded the indoor warmth.

Finn didn't mind the cold. He'd stay out in the garden sniffing and poking about without complaint long enough for Patrick to make himself a coffee and consume a bowl of muesli.

· · ·

REACHING the studio and letting Finn out of the car, Patrick sensed today wasn't going to be the creatively focussed day he had wanted it to be. He had no pupils scheduled and had intended working on some songs he'd written for the band. As he let himself in and climbed the stairs, he knew he'd rather be somewhere else.

The image of Jack sitting in the chair, racked with pain and anguish as he told his story, surfaced in Patrick's mind, and the enormity of what this child had suffered came crashing down around him.

But it wasn't just Jack; it was Julia as well. He'd not been able to fathom how she'd married someone who could harm her in such a way. He'd gleaned from Jack that his father was a lawyer, so an educated man, which made it all the worse as far as Patrick was concerned.

IIE MADE himself a coffee and sat down at his desk. He'd not thought about Katie's family in years, successfully making himself forget what had gone before and living in the present.

Now, remembering the rumours around the village of Katie's father's hot temper and readiness to use his fists, particularly where his family were concerned, and visualising what had caused the bruises on Katie's arms made him instinctively flinch as though receiving the blow himself.

But Katie came from a poor family, an uneducated family. A family he'd promised to take her away from, and he'd failed to do that. She'd loved her mother, but she'd been a beaten woman, too weak to stand up for herself or protect her daughter.

Julia didn't fit that profile. She was strong, resolute, in control. It was hard for Patrick to imagine something as ugly as this happening to someone like Julia.

Oh yes, he read in the papers all the time about domestic violence being the domain of all and the kingdom of none, but like many others, his mental image was always of families like Katie's.

Gazing out the window to the Thames, its sluggishly flowing cold grey waters reinforcing his melancholy mood, he wondered how Julia had coped afterward. After the assault. He'd not wanted to push Jack into talking further about it. It was obvious he'd been traumatised by seeing his mother injured. But Julia wasn't Katie.

Julia had pulled herself up and carried on for Jack's sake. She'd clearly been determined that Jack receive all the help he could get—occupational therapy, other therapies which Jack hadn't been able to explain fully and which Patrick knew little if anything about. Regardless, Julia had been the one person Jack could rely on.

He could see why Hamish had been so reticent to discuss them, and he felt ashamed that he'd been so quick to fire up the other night when Hamish had warned him to tread carefully around Julia.

It was not surprising he'd want to protect them both. He must have seen, as Jack's music teacher, how much music helped Jack to heal. How much music had become the therapy to replace most if not all others.

29

PATRICK

She'd agreed to meet him in a bar in Marlow. He'd passed the place many times but had never ventured in. The bar had a reputation as being quiet, sophisticated, great food; the type of bar he imagined she'd feel comfortable in.

He hadn't expected her to agree to meet up. When he'd summoned up the courage to call her, he'd feared that the conversation would be brief and to the point, but not in a good way. His expectation of rejection was such that her agreement to meet had taken him totally by surprise, even though that had been his greatest desire.

Truth be told, when she answered the phone sounding out of breath, he'd almost lost his nerve. Not like him at all. Now he was rushing back home from the studio to change and freshen up. Christ, when did he ever make so much effort, he thought to himself as he parked outside his apartment.

Finn followed him inside, and Patrick went through to the kitchen to prepare Finn's food and fill his bowl with fresh water.

As he showered, he felt an unaccustomed nervous energy roll over him. Out of the shower, he agonised over what to wear: tee or polo shirt, black jeans or denim?

'This is quite ridiculous,' he muttered to himself. 'It's a drink with a parent to discuss a child. Not *Blind Date*.' But his heart didn't agree with his head.

WHEN PATRICK WALKED through the door of the bar, the smell of food cooking made his stomach rumble and he realised he'd not eaten since the bowl of muesli at breakfast. He'd need to stick to one pint.

The space was very chic with a large horseshoe-shaped bar, soft leather chairs, and a separate area for dining. The sultry, smoky voice of Madeleine Peyroux could be heard coming from the large Bose speakers strategically placed high up in each corner of the bar, making it feel more like a French café than an English pub. Patrick settled himself on one of the leather chairs to wait. He wouldn't order drinks until Julia arrived.

He jumped up to wave as she strolled through the double doors. She was dressed in a navy tailored suit that hugged her body in a way that was both sophisticated and extremely attractive and a white shirt with cuffs that folded back on the sleeves of her suit jacket.

She was wearing her hair up with wavy tendrils trailing down the sides of her face, emphasising her high cheekbones and elegant swan neck.

She was arrestingly beautiful, and for a moment Patrick stood there, waving forgotten, just soaking up her beauty and elegance. She turned then, as though sensing his presence. The smile she gave him was almost his undoing.

'Hello, Patrick. Sorry if I kept you waiting. Just had to take a call in the car.'

'I've only just arrived myself. What will you be having? My treat.'

'Oh, that's nice. I'll have a red wine. Pinot Noir if they have it.'

'Why don't you sit down, and I'll bring our drinks over?' He looked at her close up and knew he could happily drown in the emerald pools of her beautiful eyes.

'So how has your day been?' Patrick asked minutes later as he took a sip of his pint.

'Excellent, as a matter of fact. But if you don't mind, can we avoid shop talk?' She smiled to reassure him it was not a rebuff, merely steering the conversation away from work and sensitive issues she couldn't discuss.

He laughed. 'Sorry, I should know better than to ask a lawyer how their day's been.'

'The reason I wanted to speak with you is about a music event I put on every Christmas in conjunction with the programme run by Evelina London Children's Hospital. It's for children with cancer.'

He took another sip of his pint before carrying on. She was giving him her full attention and, as before, he found her gaze quite unnerving.

'We get the children playing instruments and listening to music for a morning. They have music therapists who work with the children throughout the year, but this is just something extra we do at Christmas. It gives them the opportunity to play large or small instruments, make sounds, listen to proper musicians, that sort of thing. I'm making it sound a bit like organised activities, but really it's a sort of fun play-along, sing-along, do-something-different sort of thing for the children and the therapists.'

'That sounds wonderful, but I imagine it could be emotionally confronting for the musicians.'

'Yes. It can be. You look into some of those little faces and know they're not going to last too much longer. It's heartbreaking, and I don't know how their parents cope, but they're all so brave.' He hesitated, unsure how to move the conversation onto Jack without giving away what he knew.

'So how can I help?' She looked at him over the glass as she took a sip of her wine.

'I would like to take Jack with me this year. He's such a talented musician, and he displays an empathy for others, unusual for someone his age. Hamish told me Jack was always very caring of the younger kids at prep school. I thought it might be a great experience for both the children with cancer and for Jack.'

He stopped, waiting for her response before adding, 'I appreciate that you may have concerns, but I believe Jack has the emotional maturity to participate in such a meaningful act of giving to those less fortunate.'

'I think that would be a marvellous experience for Jack. Kids need to be involved in charitable acts as early as they can. It helps them understand that their experience of life is but one of many views, some better, some worse.'

'Absolutely. So you're happy for him to do this? She nodded her approval.

'That's wonderful. We'll need to leave for London about 9 a.m. and should be back late afternoon.'

'Okay, I can drop him off at the studio if that helps?'

'That's very kind of you but it'll be easier if I come pick him up when I've loaded the car, and I can return him home when we get back. The date is around the sixteenth of December, if that's a Saturday. It's always a Saturday. I'll text you as soon as I check the exact date. He'll be finished school by then anyway.'

'That'll be fine. Thank you for giving Jack this opportunity. I appreciate it.'

Patrick was beyond hungry but hesitant to ask if she wanted to join him for supper because it might sound pushy or too intimate or simply inappropriate. He needn't have worried. Julia took the lead.

'Do you have plans, I mean now?' She blushed slightly, and Patrick realised she was feeling as awkward as he was.

'I was going to ask if you'd like to join me for supper. Frankly, I'm famished.'

'Sure. Why not? I only snacked today, so, like you, I could eat my own arm about now. But on one condition: I pay. You've been so kind and generous with Jack, and he clearly idolises you. This will be my treat.' She smiled and her eyes twinkled with mischief.

Patrick found himself laughing out loud. She really was an enigma this woman. Full of contradictions. He found it difficult to get a measure of her. They ordered and spent the next hour chatting easily with each other.

. . .

SHE ASKED about his Irish heritage and how long he'd been living in London and why he had chosen Edinburgh University and not Dublin or London and what had prompted him to form the music academy.

At times he felt like he was being interviewed on a late-night TV show, but curiously none of her questions bothered him. In the past he would have been reluctant to discuss his decision to go to Edinburgh and not Dublin or London.

The link back to Katie had always been the exposed nerve in a tooth he never wanted his tongue to touch. But he believed Julia's questions came from a place of genuine interest, not just asking for the sake of conversation and then not listening to the answer.

Patrick quickly noticed she avoided any topic that might focus on her and her life. She was accomplished at steering the conversation in one direction and making that person feel they mattered.

He'd been out with so many women who'd asked a few questions about his life but before he could finish the answer - they'd be talking about themselves. This was completely different. She was completely different to anyone he'd known, and he wanted so much more of her.

When they spoke of Jack, her eyes would fill with love, the kind of love he'd seen in his own mother's eyes. He wondered again why he'd not made more of an effort to go home for Christmas. It was selfish of him.

'Would it be impertinent of me to ask about Jack's father?' The moment the words were out, he wanted to snatch them back, but it was too late, and he saw the closed look she gave him.

'It's not impertinent, just not important. We're divorced. He's moved on with his life and has his new partner, and I've moved on with mine. Jack has no contact with him. Kind of a mutual decision, if you like.' She sounded sour as though she'd just sucked on something bitter and wished to rid herself of the taste, of the memory.

'I'm sorry. That must be hard. Hard for you both. Boys need a positive male role model.' Jesus, why did he say that? It was what he believed, but it might have come across to Julia as though she couldn't possibly be both mother and father to her son.

'You're right, of course. They do.' She hesitated for a moment, looking down at her coffee that had just been delivered to their table.

'Jack's chosen not to have contact with his father. He was not the best father, plus Jack's had great male role models both at prep school and at St Julian's. And now, of course, he has you.'

She grinned at him, lightening the moment. Patrick felt relieved that she'd been able to talk about it without taking offence and turned the conversation around into something more light-hearted.

'I take a real interest in all my pupils. But I have to say, Jack is very different. There's something about him. The way he speaks, his passion, his dedication. He's mature for his age in a way, other boys aren't, but he's still a fourteen-year-old boy who wants and needs to be a fourteen-year-old boy and do all the stuff boys do at that age.'

There, he'd said it. He'd managed to slide into the conversation the summation of Jack's frustration with his mother. She was an intelligent woman and Patrick believed she'd think on what he'd just said. It wouldn't be lost on her.

'Yes. You're right. He is just a teenage boy. I sometimes feel like I've over compensated for his father not being there. But music is what drives him. I've never seen him so passionate about anything as much, particularly since he joined your academy. I've reorganised a room at home for him, made it into a music room, and he spends every minute he can in there or in his bedroom. I worry that he may isolate himself too much, you know, locked away in a room with instruments and composing for company. Should I be worried?'

'No. Not at all. He has all week to spend as much time as he wishes on other pastimes with his mates.'

Patrick smiled and reached his hand across the table to touch hers in reassurance, suddenly catching himself and pulling back as though he'd been burnt. Julia didn't react to his movement other than to smile back at him, but he felt acutely embarrassed that he'd almost crossed a line of familiarity with her.

'Jack is extraordinary. I would go as far as saying he's a musical prodigy. He has talent the like of which I've not seen in any other child I've taught. Locking himself away in his music room is necessary for him. For the way he is. For the way he feels about music. He lives and breathes it, and if he wants to have a really successful and enjoyable career in music, then he has to dedicate time and put in the effort to succeed.'

Patrick sat back in his chair, aware that he'd just given her a speech she probably was neither looking for nor wanting.

'I'm sorry. I hope I haven't taken a liberty when I shouldn't have in speaking so openly.' When he glanced at Julia, he saw tears in her eyes as she tried to compose herself.

'Please don't apologise.' She put a hand up to flick hair from her face, but Patrick recognised she was trying to wipe the tear that sat like a tiny crystal on her cheek.

'I think it's amazing you view Jack's talent with such enthusiasm and support. No parent could be prouder than me at hearing your words. Thank you. Thank you for being so frank and open with me.'

She dropped her head down, busying herself with folding her napkin.

'You know, when Jack was only, I'd say, about two, he pulled himself up on a friend's piano stool and sat there with his chubby little fingers stretched out like a proper pianist. He didn't just bang away at the keys the way most two-year old's would. He tinkled with the keys, his fingers going back and forth. So it was all there, even at that age, his passion for music.'

'It usually is in truly gifted children. They have an ear for music from the beginning.'

'Anyway, this has been lovely, but I probably should be off now.'

Patrick stood and waited while she picked up her bag and headed to the bar to pay. He felt awkward that she was paying. He wasn't used to that, but she'd insisted, and he knew that he would offend her if he did not respect her wishes.

He walked her to her car, holding the door open as she settled herself behind the wheel.

Patrick bent his tall frame forward, dipping his head inside the car door to say goodnight.

'Thank you again for supper. It's been a lovely night. Drive carefully.' He wanted to say so much more. He wanted to reach further into the car and kiss her fully on the mouth. But he wouldn't. He wouldn't risk spoiling what to him had been a beautiful evening by letting his desire for her take over.

He closed the door and stood to the side as she pulled out and drove off, lifting a hand to wave until he saw her turn the corner.

He stood there for some time after her car had disappeared from sight until the cold forced him to walk up the road to his own car. He'd been reflecting on their conversation and still couldn't imagine how horrendous it must have been for her, beaten and humiliated by a savage husband. He knew nothing of her husband other than him being a lawyer, but he couldn't view any man who beat a woman with anything less than contempt.

LATER, lying stretched out in his bed as Finn lay on the floor beside him, sleeping soundly, Patrick dissected their conversation in detail again. The evening couldn't have gone better. Well, yes, it could have, he wagered. He could have kissed her. But he knew he absolutely must not rush this or, more to the point, read too much into this tentative relationship.

He had no idea if she was viewing him with a lover's eyes or merely through the lens of a parent who admired the dedication of a teacher and his interest in her son. He was well aware this could be exactly how she viewed their relationship, and to assume otherwise would risk spoiling everything.

IT WAS 3 a.m. when Patrick woke from a dream—not a bad dream, an inexplicable dream. He reached his hand out to Finn, stroking the dog's head to reassure himself he was awake and it had been a dream.

'Let me go now, Paddy. I'm fine. Truly I am. You deserve to be happy. I'm okay with this. Please let me go.'

Katie was looking down at him, her black hair shimmering in a halo of light and her voice that of the young woman he'd left behind.

Her distinct broad Irish accent had been so clear. She was as real as if she were standing at the foot of his bed. In his sleep he'd reached out a hand to her, but she faded away, drifting out of sight like a smoky mirage.

He sat up in bed and looked about the room. She wasn't there. It was foolish of him to think she would be. He lay back down, pulled the covers up to his chin, and smiled. A smile of understanding, of moving on, of hope.

30

JULIA

Julia glanced again in her rear-vision mirror and could see Patrick standing at the side of the road still waving to her. It made her smile, but more importantly it made her feel cared about, and she'd forgotten what care from a man felt like.

As she drove, she mulled over the night's events and found herself welling up with tears. They coursed down her cheeks unchecked. She sniffed loudly and wondered where all this emotion was coming from. It was as though Patrick had lit the touchpaper to her tinder-dry heart.

Hearing him talk about Jack with such passion, such excitement, such dedication made her realise how right Hamish had been to recommend him and his music academy. She felt embarrassed at how harsh she'd been following their first meeting. It had been very judgmental of her to bitch to Hamish about Patrick being late, unshaven, hungover, and all the other adjectives she'd used to describe her disappointment.

How lovely she'd found the view was, standing on the moral high ground. Now she knew how wrong she'd been.

. . .

Since the night of the Irish music charity event, she'd felt a lightening of her mood, of her spirit. It was as though those melancholy Irish songs, mixed with the upbeat ones that the audience clapped and shouted too, had moved a mountain of grief within her and let it slide away. Not in an avalanche kind of way, but in a slow-moving, gentle gliding motion, making it less of a sudden awakening and more like a new dawn breaking.

She'd been able to manage that shift in her feelings without the need to analyse each and every particle of a past she dearly wished to leave behind.

She parked outside her cottage as it started to rain making her run for the door, struggling with her bag and keys. Finally inside, she was assaulted by Chino purring, meowing, and conducting figure of eights around her ankles to let her know he forgave her for staying out after work, provided she fussed and fed him this very minute.

'Oh, poor boy. I'm sorry to be late. But you do have biscuits. You're not exactly starving, are you?'

He rewarded her with a swivel around and between her stockinged legs.

She went to the fridge, took out his meat, and spooned a small amount into his bowl. Stroking his sleek coat as he purred and attacked his food with vigour, she smiled watching him, knowing he was that much older than when they'd first taken him in.

Although still in great health generally, she'd noticed the start of an arthritic limp. She'd bought some pet omega online and ensured he had some daily in the hope of slowing down the deterioration. He was a beautiful cat and such a great companion for Jack and herself ever since they'd moved out to Hambleden.

He was always there to greet her when she returned home, and on nights when she admitted to herself in the darkness of her room and her empty bed just how lonely she felt, he'd been the comforting presence, purring and padding to let her know he was right there next to her pillow.

Her landline rang, making her jump. No one ever rang the landline—well, not often anyway. She walked across to the table and answered.

'Hey, I was worried about you. Left text messages on your phone.'

It was Lizzie, and Julia suddenly remembered she'd put her phone on silent after she'd taken the call from a client before meeting with Patrick.

'Aaaah, sorry. I must have left it on silent. So what's up? Anything special or just a girly chat?'

'No, just wanted to say hi and how are you and you haven't been to see us in ages, that's all.' Lizzie laughed.

'I'm fine. Really busy with work, Jack, that sort of thing.'

'So that's it. That's all there is to report?'

'What do you want me to say, that I went for dinner with Jack's music tutor tonight and had a lovely evening?'

Julia could hear the intake of breath from Lizzie and imagined her pixie face breaking into a broad smile.

'And?'

'What?'

'Come on. Don't play hard to get. What's he like? I seem to recall you being pretty unimpressed with him, even though Jack thinks he's great. He phoned me last week for a chat.'

'Well, he is great—for Jack. I'm so glad he's attending this academy. It couldn't be better for him. Patrick is a truly gifted musician and teacher.'

'Awww, Patrick, eh? How sweet. And what exactly is Patrick like, pray tell?'

'He's tall, well built, slim hips, great arse, sexy Irish lilt to his voice. He's intense, intelligent, funny. Let me see, have I covered everything my schoolgirl friend would like me to say?'

'Wow. You fancy him, don't you? Did he kiss you tonight?'

'God. How old are you, Lizzie? You sound like we're back at school and dating for the first time.' Julia laughed. 'No, he most certainly did not. I'm not looking for romance.'

'Rubbish. You've just described your ideal man. You do fancy him?'

'No, I don't. He's lovely and not what I was expecting, but he's Jack's teacher, and that's where it begins and ends. Anyway, he's got a drop-dead gorgeous brother who I may have wished had asked for my number.'

'What? When did you meet his brother, or are you just teasing me?'

'Sorry. I haven't seen you for ages or talked to you for ages. My fault, not yours.'

'I did notice, you know. I assumed, rightly or wrongly, that you were a bit pissed with Michael pointing out to you months back that you were acting like a hermit.'

'Nah. It's all cool.' Julia wasn't telling a lie. It didn't bother her now in the least, but it would be disingenuous of her not to admit that his comments had infuriated her at the time, and she'd kept her distance from both Lizzie and Michael, not wishing to endure more pop psychology from Michael concerning his theories as to why she was avoiding meaningful relationships.

'Look, at the time I was really angry with Michael. But he was right to tweak my tail. I didn't want to hear it. Nobody does. The reality is my life is composed of Jack and work and work and Jack. I'm happy with that, truly I am.'

'Can't you see though, that it's not healthy to just have work and Jack as your only focus?' Lizzie sighed, and Julia could just imagine her frowning, probably doodling on a pad she always kept by the phone.

'Yep. I can see that, and that's why when Maria waved a ticket in front of me to go up to London to a charity event, I went—reluctantly at the time, I admit, but I went. Sorry you couldn't be there. She only had the two tickets at short notice. Anyway, trivial as it may seem, that appears to have been the catalyst I needed to shake myself out of my *hermit-like existence*, to quote Michael.'

'So what was it, this charity event?'

Julia had moved through the lounge and flicked the switch on the lamps as she balanced the phone under her chin. She kicked off her shoes and stretched out on the sofa.

'It's Patrick's charity to raise funds for the work he does teaching music to disadvantaged children at low-rated schools up in London.'

'Wow, he really is Saint Patrick, isn't he? Is he Catholic?'

'No idea. I didn't ask him what his religious beliefs were, nor how many women he's slept with, nor whether he's ever been married, although Hamish has referred to him as a single Irishman, so maybe not, and I've also not asked for his inside leg measurement.'

'You're losing your touch, girl. And you call yourself a lawyer?'

Lizzie was laughing loudly down the phone, and Julia realised it had been a long time since they'd both been so girlish and light-hearted with each other. That was down to her. She'd been the intense, serious one for such a long time it had become the norm.

'As I was saying, Maria and I went up to London for this event. It was all Irish music. You'll know some of the artists: Mary Black, Maura O'Connell—you know of them?'

'Yes, they're great. Wow, he must have quite a pull, this Patrick, to get those two on stage with him. I'm presuming he was playing?'

'Indeed he was, as was Hamish—you know, Jack's old music teacher from Heathstone?'

'Yeah, I remember. He's a lovely man. So what about the brother, then?'

'He was there in the crowd, supporting his brother. He's lovely, and I don't say that readily about any man these days.'

'What's his name? What's he do? Is he a musician, too?'

'His name is Carrick, and no, he's not a musician. He's a property developer.'

'Right. How successful a property developer? Is he loaded? Don't want to fall for a pauper, now do you?'

Julia laughed. 'You're awful, Lizzie. Strangely I didn't ask to see his bank balance, but I'm assuming he's done well. He's got property around London and overseas, and at this very moment is even looking at moving into the New Zealand market.'

'So, apart from money and success, what was so special about him, then? Come on, tell all.'

'Apart from being devilishly handsome, he's quite reticent, kind of shy but with a charming confidence as well, and I know that sounds like a contradiction, but he was so easy to talk to. Well, both brothers are, for that matter. It was—oh, I don't know, Lizzie. I'm sounding like some silly girl. He was just easy to be with, and I haven't known that in such a long time. It was a surprise—a delight, actually. When we left, I was sure he was going to ask for my number, but he didn't, and I've not heard from him since.'

'Why don't you contact him?'

'No. No, I couldn't do that. Honestly Lizzie, I'm not ready. I might have wanted him to ask for my number, but maybe that was more vanity and ego than actually wanting to become involved. I couldn't do that to Jack.'

'Maybe Jack would be happy if you found someone else. Have you ever asked him?'

'No, I haven't, and I'd find that rather awkward, and probably so would he. Anyway, enough of all that. How are you and Michael? Getting the house ready for Christmas?'

Julia could imagine Lizzie had already sorted out the Christmas decorations down to the very last bauble. Come the beginning of December, their home always resembled a Christmas film set from a New York movie. Julia loved it.

She didn't have Lizzie's creative flair for decoration. She could do home décor, but what Lizzie did was way above that.

'Almost. Just putting the finishing touches to a decorative piece I'm making for the table. I've not put anything up yet, of course. Hate these people who have decorations up from the day after Halloween and don't take them down until the Easter Bunny is hammering on the door.'

'Oh, Lizzie. Who do you know that does that? No one. You're exaggerating.'

'No, I'm not. There's a patient of Michael's who does exactly that. Drifts from one celebration to the next. She needs to get a life, that's what I say.'

'Speaking of a life, I need to keep mine intact for a big next few days at work, so I ought to get to bed.'

'Sure. It's been fab talking. I really miss you. Can you stretch to lunch, maybe next week? I'll meet you in Maidenhead.'

'It's a date. I'll book us a table and text you. Night, Lizzie. See you next week.'

JULIA RANG OFF, smiling to herself, glad they'd had a chat. She'd been a bit precious to have avoided contact. What was wrong with her that she could be so judgemental and unforgiving over any perceived slight? The Julia of old would have laughed it off.

Michael had only meant well, nothing more. His comments had come from a place of care and love, not criticism as she'd chosen to view it.

Rummaging through her bag, she pulled out her mobile and checked the messages. Several from Lizzie as expected, and one from Jack saying he was fine and had had a good day at school. He'd talk with her tomorrow. The last one was from Patrick.

PATRICK: Thank you for a delightful evening. I trust you arrived home before the rain? Patrick

That was sweet of him, she thought. He really was very thoughtful and kind.

She toyed with the idea of responding. Well, he had asked a question, hadn't he? One that ought to require an answer, or did it? Was it a rhetorical question? She read it again. No, it had a question mark. He only wanted to know she'd arrived home safely. She'd text, brief and to the point. That would be polite.

JULIA: Home safe and sound, just as the rain started. J.

There, not too gushy nor too dismissive. Satisfied, she turned out the lights, scooped Chino into her arms, and retreated upstairs to bed. She'd sleep peacefully knowing tonight had been another step in her moving forward.

She felt she'd turned a corner, and not a corner that ended with a brick wall immediately in front of her that was beyond navigation. She'd turned a corner to light and hope.

31

PATRICK

Patrick spent the rest of the evening dissecting every moment of his time with Julia. The more time he spent in her company, the deeper his infatuation. He kept telling himself not to read too much into anything, but his heart was pushing him on, allowing him to hope, and he wasn't sure how to contain these emotions or even if he wanted to.

He remembered that he was going to call Liam and see how life was treating him in Dublin. He made the call and they chatted. After discussions about London and Ireland the conversation moved on to Carrick.

'You know Carrick is out in New Zealand chasing down some property deals. He's not coming back for several months. Decided to spend the summer out there. Can't blame him. It's bleedin' cold and miserable over here, and I can't imagine London isn't any better.'

'Oh. I hadn't realised he was going so soon and for so long.'

'Nor did I, but I think he wants to check on his properties in Australia as well. It's a long way to go for a few weeks, I guess, or he's running away from a possible love interest.'

'What love interest would that be then?' Patrick asked realising his voice sounded accusatory.

'I think your little brother was a bit smitten with that Julia woman we met at the charity. You know, the lawyer.'

'I know who you mean. I hadn't realised they had an interest in one another.' Patrick was fishing for information at the same time his heart was racing with the expectation he may find out something he'd rather not know.

'Oh, I'm not sure she was interested, but Carrick certainly was. Anyway, he's gone, so it must have been a fleeting moment for him. You teach her child, don't you? Did I hear that right?'

'Yes. Jack, her son is a pupil of mine. Particularly gifted young man.' Patrick found it easier to steer the conversation away from Julia and settle more comfortably on Jack.

'He's lucky to have you as his teacher then Paddy. Lucky boy indeed. I must be off now my friend, I have a call to make to the States, they should just about be up. Thanks for the call.'

Patrick rang off. His emotions were churning from Liam's comments about Carrick and Julia, and he was curious as to why his brother would be spending so much time out in New Zealand and Australia.

He didn't buy the explanation Liam provided that it was a long way to go. Carrick would give no more thought to jumping on a long-haul flight than other people would give to hailing a taxi.

H E W ENT UPSTAIRS, picked up his Alhambra Spanish guitar, and began to play. As his fingers adjusted from the feel of his normal Gibson guitar to the wider neck and nylon strings, his thoughts moved to his parents.

If Carrick wasn't going back to Ireland for Christmas, then he really ought to. He needed to stop making excuses and just go. It wasn't the other side of the world. He could be out there and back in time for the gig at New Year.

He'd book flights in the morning and then call his mother. He picked out the melody to Sting's "Fragile" and played it through to the end. He'd not played this particular piece in years, but his memory had served him well, picking out every note without fault.

Why wait until morning? Patrick decided it was better if he booked the flights to Dublin straight away. Before he had time to dream up another excuse not to go.

An hour later, he'd booked a flight out in the early evening of Christmas Eve to Dublin, returning on December 29, which gave him ample time to rehearse with the band ahead of the gig on New Year's Eve.

He'd made a note to phone his mother in the morning. It hadn't occurred to Patrick that his parents might have made their own plans for Christmas. They were always home at Christmas. Always. The farthest he'd known them to move from the glowing fireplace would be his father venturing outdoors to the woodpile in the backyard.

He retired to bed, content he'd done the right thing. The only thing a son should do at Christmas. He'd let the past and Katie dictate his whole adult life.

What a waste. In the grieving and anger, bitterness and guilt, he'd stolen from himself the opportunity for marriage, for children, for a different life. He was too old now to start a family. The thought of nappies and bottles and sleepless nights held no appeal.

However, having a teenage boy in your life, one that was a musical prodigy, well, that was an entirely different matter.

THE FOLLOWING EVENING, Patrick was rehearsing with his band and regaling them with how excited his mammy had been when he phoned to say he'd be home for Christmas. He'd been right not to concern himself that other plans had already been arranged by his parents.

They were set in their Irish ways and Christmas was at home, should always be at home. She'd been thrilled that at least one of her sons would celebrate Christmas with them.

'Now, I want you all to have a look at the sheet music I've put out.' He beamed at them all as he watched their astonished looks.

'Grover Washington Junior? Haven't heard that name in years,' Phil said.

'Nor had I, but I just want us all to have a go at playing from the sheet music and see how it sounds.'

They spent time going through the musical score until finally everyone felt comfortable enough to play.

Phil started the intro on keyboards, and Patrick picked out the guitar section. Johnny came in on drums, and then Jules performed the saxophone solo.

It was a bit ragged, Patrick thought of the first attempt. He reminded them all to go with the music as written and not be tempted to improvise.

After a couple of hours, it had come together nicely and Patrick called, 'let's take it from the top one last time and I'll add in the lyrics this time.'

The band really let themselves go, especially Jules on the saxophone. Patrick looked across and saw how they were all totally in the groove. He was bursting with pride when they finished and announced this was the work of his pupil, the one he'd been telling them about.

'He composed this for his mum because he'd heard her playing it a few times on the hi-fi. Quite remarkable.'

'Shall we add it to our repertoire for New Year's Eve?' Johnny asked.

'We could, if everyone is happy too?'

'Well, it's kind of funky in its own way, different from our usual covers. I'd be happy to add it,' Phil said. The rest of the band nodded in agreement.

PATRICK SAT at his kitchen table, an old scrubbed pitch pine table he'd picked up in a second-hand shop. A light sanding and several lovingly applied coats of wax had restored the natural glow to the beautiful grain.

He heard Finn give a low growl, signalling the postman was about to push something through the letterbox flap in the front door.

'It's all right, boy. Just the postman. Nothing for you to be bothering about.'

Finn lay back down on the sandstone-tiled floor, heaving a sigh and stretching himself out, head on paws. Patrick finished his bowl of muesli and, picking up his cup, he headed for the door to retrieve the mail.

Flicking through a mix of Christmas cards and bills, he recognised his brother's handwriting on one envelope.

He returned to the kitchen and spread the post out across the table. He opened the envelope from Carrick, which contained a card.

On the front was a caricature of Santa and Rudolph standing beside a sleigh, with the caption from Rudolph saying, *"What can I say? Weather's crap, sledge is buggered, Fatty's in a strop – Just another Christmas Replay."*

CARRICK'S NOTE READ:

Merry Christmas, big brother. Just letting you know I'm out in New Zealand and Australia. Couldn't get excited about another cold Northern Hemisphere Christmas, so I'm enjoying some sun and sea Down Under. Lots of exciting opportunities here so might stay a while and return for Easter and some spring sunshine.

I hope you have a peaceful Christmas and know I'll be thinking of you and hoping that you find the courage to ask Julia Davis out.

I could see the night of the charity event that you have a special connection, even if you were pig-headedly trying to pretend that you didn't.

I'm your brother so don't go denying it now! I think she's lovely and she'd be good for you, if she doesn't find your bachelor behaviour too annoying, that is!

I'll look forward to catching up with you for supper and a pint, my treat when I'm back. I went home to see Ma and Pa before I left, but I'm only a phone call or email away if you need me.

Carrick

PATRICK REREAD the card several times. This was so un-Carrick-like. He normally did short, staccato emails or a very brief text. To take time to buy a card, one Patrick would find amusing, and then write a proper message was out of the ordinary.

Patrick couldn't help laughing at the caption on the front of the card and then reread Carrick's words once more. So his brother had picked up on Patrick's infatuation with Julia. Not surprising really, Patrick mused. Carrick had always known when his brother liked or didn't like someone, ever since they were young boys playing together.

He'd nudge Patrick and whisper to him, 'You don't like him, do you?' or 'You're sweet on her, aren't you, big brother?'

TIME WOULD TELL, Patrick thought as he drove to his studio. He didn't know how Julia felt about him and it was far too soon to start trying to push things.

He could see from the way she spoke when they'd had supper together that the mention of her ex-husband still affected her. Not surprising, given what she'd been through, or at least what he knew from his conversation with Jack.

He would take things slowly and see where they led. He had to be prepared for it going nowhere. She might not view him with romantic eyes, and, should that be the way it was, he would have to accept her feelings and move on.

· · ·

At the studio, he had to push thoughts of Julia out of his mind. A busy day lay ahead teaching, with one older pupil who was practising for an important audition and needed additional time to go over the pieces he would be performing.

As he switched on lights and filled the kettle to make himself some coffee, his phone beeped a message. Glancing down, he saw it was from Julia.

Julia: Morning. You'll need my address when you pick up Jack, and also, if you need anyone to look after Finn while you're up in London, I'm happy to take him for the day as long as he doesn't hunt down cats??

Cheers, J.

Oops, almost forgot, address is - "The Forge" Pheasant's Hill, Frieth, Hambleden.

Patrick reread the message, savouring every letter. Smiling to himself, he tapped out a message in response.

Patrick: Thank you for the offer, I accept 😊. Finn will love having a day with a lady. And, he's afraid of cats, gives them a wide berth. I'll text when I'm on my way, but assume I'll be there by 9 a.m. Saturday 18th. Patrick.

He hummed a tune to himself as he returned to making a plunger full of strong coffee. The day was just getting better and better.

He'd felt warmed by Carrick's card and his words. It seemed they were getting back on track with their relationship, and now it was up to him to mend the broken bridges of the past.

He'd waited far too long for Carrick to come to him and admit his stupid schoolboy crush had caused so much heartache for Katie and that he, Carrick, had been responsible for the trauma that followed, ending in Katie's death.

Carrick had never acknowledged what he'd done. Never apologised directly to Patrick, and that had been at the centre of all Patrick's bitterness and anger.

It seemed futile to continue holding on to all those old emotions. It had been easy to become anchored in righteous condemnation allowing himself to remain stuck in the darkness of bad memories.

Memories that were emotional quicksand, exerting a strong downward pull on his psyche. The past had trapped him in unexamined clutter, bitterness and emotional garbage filling the rooms of his heart, leaving no room for new and better relationships to find a home; letting him believe that there was no space for anything but music and empty short-term relationships.

Since Patrick's strange dream about Katie, he'd felt more centred. Like driving a car with one badly unbalanced wheel. Sure, you could still drive it slowly without having an accident but trying to drive to the car's potential would swiftly expose the fact that it couldn't perform as it should.

Patrick had been like that unbalanced car for too long, unable to embrace his potential in all aspects of his life.

The refrain of an old Burt Bacharach song popped into his head: "Three wheels on my wagon, But I'm singing a happy song."

But it wasn't so. Patrick's wagon had had three wheels for many years, and yes, he'd accomplished much but he'd missed out on the true happiness of sharing his life with someone special.

It didn't need to stay that way, and now he'd acknowledged to himself how he felt about Julia, it was up to him to put that fourth wheel back on his wagon.

32

———

JACK

It was Saturday, school had finished, and he wouldn't be returning to the boarding house until the New Year.

Today Jack would be travelling with Mr Devlin to London. He was both excited and nervous. He'd Googled the Evelina London Children's Hospital and been saddened by the large number of children with cancer and whether anything he was going to do today would make a difference.

He'd never been face to face with a child who was dying. Well, he hadn't met anyone who was dying, so he had no idea what to say. How do you start a conversation with someone who's dying? Anyway, he reassured himself, they weren't all dying, only some.

When his mother told him she'd be having Finn for the day, he'd immediately asked if that meant Mr Devlin would stay for supper.

'I hadn't thought about that. He's probably playing somewhere or out with friends, Jack.'

She'd not even considered the possibility of Patrick staying for supper after he dropped Jack off. If it had been anyone else, she would automatically have invited them, but she'd been so caught up with having the dog, she'd not considered the owner.

'Can you ask him, please? It would be the right thing to do when he's taken me up to London for the day.'

'Like I said, Jack, he's probably got something on. But yes.' She sighed. 'I will, out of courtesy, I'll ask him.'

JACK HAD BEEN LOCKED in his music room since he finished school, practising and composing in equal measure. His progress with the saxophone as well as the keyboard was exciting.

His mother had surprised him with a second-hand keyboard, and Mr Devlin had lent him a saxophone from his studio, so he was always practising either keyboard, saxophone, or drums. His mother had remarked at breakfast how thrilled she was at hearing some of the music coming out of his room.

'Is that you or a CD?' she'd teased.

'No, it's me, of course. Do you think I'm getting better?' He knew the answer but was fishing for a compliment and reassurance that he wasn't hitting too many bum notes.

'You sound amazing, truly you do. I wouldn't say that, Jack, if I thought you sounded like nails on a blackboard. You do need to get out a bit, though, get some fresh air and exercise.' She'd looked across the table at him, raising an eyebrow.

'I will. I do stretches in between instruments, and I've even started doing some yoga positions when I get stiff from sitting. I need one of those mats you use for yoga. But I know I need to get outside as well. If we had a dog, I'd be able to take it for walks and get all the fresh air I need.' He looked at her pointedly.

'Yes, well, we don't have a dog and will not be getting a dog. So you'll need to think of something else, my boy. And what's with yoga? When did you start doing yoga?'

'We do it at school sometimes, one of the new exercise programmes they introduced. I love it, so I'm doing a few yoga positions after each session.'

'Impressive. You'll be able to teach me a thing or two, then?'

'Hardly. Do you think Chino will be okay with Finn here?'

'Patr—Mr Devlin said he's frightened of cats, so I don't think that will be a problem. Anyway, Chino visits that cottage across the field and they have a dog. So I can only assume he's not too fussed about canines.'

'I can't wait to see him. He's really gorgeous, just like our Judas.' Jack beamed as he munched through his fourth piece of toast.

JACK HAD BEEN WATCHING from his mother's bedroom and saw Mr Devlin pull into the driveway. He raced down the stairs and grabbed his sticks and a bag with food his mother had made up for him. Enough for himself and Mr Devlin, Jack thought when he'd peeked inside.

There was homemade bacon and egg pie, ham and tomato sandwiches, yoghurt, fruit, and nuts. A real feast, plus two bottles of fizzy water.

Jack opened the door as Mr Devlin was about to knock.

'Morning, Mr Devlin. Hello, Finn. Come in. Mum's in the kitchen. I'm all sorted and ready.'

'Good for you,' Mr Devlin responded, patting Jack on the shoulder and calling Finn to follow him indoors.

'Morning, Patrick,' his Mum said, wiping her hands on her apron. Her hair was pulled back in a ponytail and she was wearing a long jumper over tight jeans.

Jack was so intent on fussing with Finn he didn't see the smile exchanged between his mother and Mr Devlin and the slight flush to his mother's cheeks when she asked Mr Devlin if he would like to stay for supper when he dropped Jack back.

'That would be grand. I'd love to, if it's no bother.'

'No bother at all. It's the least I can offer after you've had Jack for the day. Maybe text me when you are on your way back?'

'Sure, we can manage that, can't we, Jack?'

'Yep. I'll remember, Mum.' He stood up from stroking Finn and kissed his mother goodbye.

She walked them to the door and stood waving as Mr Devlin reversed out of the driveway and they headed off to London.

'What's in the bag, Jack, besides your drumsticks?'

'Lunch. Mum made enough for both of us. I'm always starving after I've played.'

'I'm a bit the same. That was nice of her. Does she like to cook?'

'Yes. I don't think she does during the week when I'm at school; she doesn't like eating alone. But she sure goes all out at the weekend, especially if I have friends back.'

'So she's a good cook, then?'

'No. She's a great cook.' Jack grinned across at him.

Mr Devlin laughed, and Jack felt he couldn't be happier with the way the day had started. He hoped when they got to the hospital he'd know what to say to the children and how to make them feel special.

Jack had seldom visited London without his mother. Michael had taken him to Lord's for the cricket, and when he was at prep school Lizzie had taken him several times to the Tate Gallery and the Natural History Museum, but apart from that and the odd school trip, he'd only ever been up in the company of his mother. This was a real boys' day out, making Jack feel quite the adult.

'Today will probably be a little confronting for you, Jack, to start with at least, but I'll be there by your side. We'll be working as a team, so don't feel nervous, okay?'

'I am feeling nervous, actually. I'm frightened I won't know what to say, how to make the kids feel special.'

'You'll be fine. They'll love having someone more their own age to interact with. Some of the really young children will especially love having a big boy there.' He smiled across at Jack before returning his gaze to the road.

Jack thought Mr Devlin was a good driver, fast but attentive and courteous. There really was nothing not to like about Mr Devlin, and he was thrilled he was going to stay for supper. It might give Jack the opportunity to take him into his music room and play the new piece he'd been working on and see what he thought, see if he was on the right track.

It was going to be such a cool day, and his nerves from earlier had vanished, leaving him feeling settled and eager to help these children experience playing an instrument or listening to him play.

IT WAS hard for Jack to see children his age completely bald, some wearing masks, some too weak and sick to leave their wheelchairs, but what struck Jack most forcibly was their smiling faces and positive attitudes.

He had a lot to be thankful for, and he could understand why Mr Devlin had wanted him to come, to appreciate, despite their trauma, that these children were so excited to be given the opportunity to play an instrument or just to sit in their wheelchairs and listen to music.

It made Jack realise that, despite his own trauma in early life, he would go on to fulfil his dreams. He would grow up and probably marry and have children. Many of these children would not see out the next year.

ONE PARTICULAR LITTLE girl had touched Jack in a way he could never have imagined. She was six years old with the biggest blue eyes he'd ever seen. She wore a pretty turquoise scarf around, what Jack presumed, was a completely bald head and was dressed in a simple cotton dress that matched her head scarf.

She'd wanted to try the drums but was too weak to sit on the stool by herself. Jack had looked to Mr Devlin for advice.

'Can she be lifted up to sit on my knee? Would that be okay?'

'I'll check with her mum, but I'm sure it'll be fine. Just talk with her while I ask.'

'So what's your name?' Jack crouched down so he was making eye contact. She was so small, way smaller than a normal six-year-old, Jack thought.

'Tilly,' said the little girl.

'That's a lovely name, and you want to play the drums? Mr Paddy'- that's what the children all called Mr Devlin – 'is asking your mummy.'

'All good, Jack. You sit on the drum stool and I'll lift her up,' Mr Devlin said when he returned.

Jack settled little Tilly on his knee. She was as light as the choux pastry his mother made and probably just as fragile, making him feel nervous that she might slide off his knee and fall to the floor.

But he needn't have worried. Tilly fastened her little legs around his, hooking her ankles together to help her balance.

She placed her hands on Jack's as he started to play a soft and gentle rhythm. She giggled loudly when they reached out and hit the cymbals.

Her back pressed into Jack's chest, he could feel the thinness of her tiny frame through her cotton dress. She had a strange smell about her, a smell foreign to him but all too familiar to the children she shared a ward with. After five minutes they stopped for a break, and Jack could see despite her elation she was tiring.

'Do you want to get down now, Tilly, and we can play the piano together?'

'I'd like to, but I think I need a little rest now. Thank you, drummer boy.' She looked up into his face with her beautiful big blue eyes and a cheeky grin, making Jack laugh as he handed her across to her mother.

'Thank you.' Tilly's mother led her across the room to a nurse who walked Tilly through the double doors away from the music therapy room and back to the ward.

'It's Jack, isn't it?' Tilly's mother was back standing beside the drum kit.

'Yes. I'm Jack. She's very cute, your little girl.'

'Yes, she's quite the character at times.' Tilly's mother smiled.

'She's got acute lymphoblastic leukemia, diagnosed at three years of age. But we're about to try a new drug and we're hopeful.'

She blurted out this news like she couldn't wait to hear her own voice announce those words of hope - that by saying them aloud to a stranger maybe this time they'd be lucky. That's how it sounded to Jack. He'd been startled by the conversation, and he could see how difficult it was for a mother to talk about her little girl and continue to hope for a cure.

'It's wonderful that Paddy has brought you here today. The kids enjoy seeing someone young. It takes their mind off things, for a while at least. Anyway, I best get on and let you play.' She placed her hand on Jack's arm as she left. 'Thank you again for being so patient with my little girl.'

Jack nodded in response, too choked with emotion to respond. He'd known it would be difficult, but nothing had prepared him for how it would make him feel inside. Seeing the sorrow in parents' eyes, the heartache that they must feel. He realised he was so lucky he was healthy, loved, and alive with an exciting future ahead of him.

NEXT, a ten-year old boy wearing a mask asked if he could play piano. Jack took him across the other side of the room where the piano sat, but before Jack could sit down at the stool, the boy had opened up the lid, sat himself down, and started to play. He could play well, and when Jack asked if he wanted to play a duet, the boy launched immediately into the famous "Chopsticks" waltz.

Such was their playing that the other kids gathered around the piano to watch and listen. One older boy, who looked to Jack to be about fifteen and was wheelchair-bound, clapped and called out, making all the kids laugh.

As the afternoon drew to a close and Jack helped tidy up the music therapy room, Mr Devlin asked if he'd enjoyed the opportunity.

'Yes. Very much. You were right to bring me here. To help me to see how tough some kids have it. It's reminded me that I'm a survivor, and some of these kids won't survive, will they?' He looked across at Mr Devlin, who was packing away his guitars.

'No. No, they won't, Jack, and I can't imagine what that must be like for their parents. But we've given them hours of fun today, right before Christmas. It all helps ease the burden of sorrow.'

Jack didn't respond. He was deep in thought and struggling to control his emotions. He'd loved playing with the kids, especially the little ones who banged on the little solid drums, screaming with delight at the sounds they made.

They'd plucked at ukulele strings and beat out uneven rhythms on the xylophones. They'd tired easily, and it was hard to hear the cries of protest from the younger children as they were taken back to the ward to rest when clearly all they wanted was just one more go.

JACK CHATTED COMFORTABLY with Mr Devlin on the way back home in the car. He was so easy to talk to, and it highlighted for Jack once more just how difficult it had been with his father.

He'd never been able to chat in a relaxed way with him. He'd never understood who Jack was, and now he never would.

He'd never get to see Jack perform or share in his excitement about the music academy. Jack had no intention of ever letting him back into his life. The man sitting beside him, looking across and smiling at him as they joked about music genres, this was the man that would fill the void.

'I'LL TEXT Mum and tell her we are on our way,' Jack said, pulling his mobile out of his bag and switching it on. It had been turned off while they were at the hospital.

'Oh, there's a message from Mum. It says Lizzie and Michael have asked us over to theirs and would you like to meet her there. She'll bring Finn with her.' He looked across at Mr Devlin, hoping he would say yes and not back out.

'Who are Lizzie and Michael?'

'They're my godparents. Lizzie is Mum's best friend from school. They've been besties forever. They're great. You'll like them.'

Jack hoped he didn't sound too desperate. He just didn't want the day to end with Mr Devlin dropping him off at Lizzie and Michael's, collecting Finn, and driving away. It wouldn't be right.

'Where do they live?'

'In Henley, so handy for you,' Jack replied hopefully.

'Well, that's easy enough, isn't it? Let's do that. Shall we stop for some wine? Can't go empty-handed. You can help me choose. You'll know their tastes.' He grinned across at Jack.

Immediately, Jack felt like he'd morphed into an eighteen-year-old. Mr Devlin needed his help to choose wine. Well, yes, of course he would. Jack did know everyone's tastes.

33

JULIA

Julia was busying herself making a rolled pavlova to take to Lizzie's for dessert.

She'd had a wonderful walk up through the woods at the back of the cottage and across the fields with Finn. She'd forgotten just how wonderful it was walking with a dog by your side. He was so well behaved.

She made a mental note to compliment Patrick on how thoroughly he'd trained him. It took time and patience to end up with a dog who was so attentive and willing to please as Finn was.

JULIA HAD TAKEN the call from Lizzie late in the morning, and when she'd mentioned where Jack was and with whom, Lizzie had squealed with delight, insisting she contact Patrick immediately and invite him. Julia wouldn't do that at all. She'd text Jack and let him be the bearer of good or bad news, whichever way Patrick wished to view it.

When she'd not received a response, she began to fret that Jack had left his phone behind. She searched his bedroom and the music room, but there was no phone. Then it dawned on her that he would have it switched off if he was in a hospital. She'd have to be patient and wait.

Eventually Jack texted to say they were on their way back and, yes, Patrick would love to join them. *Love to join them.* Those would have been Jack's words. She couldn't imagine Patrick being animated at the thought of entering a stranger's house with three people who were close friends, two of whom he'd never met.

Still, she thought, he could have found some excuse, but clearly he hadn't. She couldn't help but be a little excited at the prospect of Lizzie and Michael meeting him. It had all the makings of an interesting night.

Julia fed Chino, topped up his biscuits and water bowl, and bent to stroke him as he purred loudly, attacking his meat like he'd not been fed in a week.

'You'll have to content yourself with your own company tonight, Chino. I'll leave the lamp on and the radio, so you'll be fine.'

She wasn't sure why she was having this out-loud conversation as though the cat could understand and respond if she talked loudly and slowly enough. She'd gotten into the habit of talking to him all the time. The perils of living alone—well, mainly alone, she thought.

SHE ARRIVED at Lizzie's before Jack and Patrick returned. She had the pavlova to deliver safely into Lizzie's fridge and wine to chill, even though she knew Lizzie would chastise her for bringing wine. *We have plenty, Julia,* she'd say. *Michael buys it by the crate!* Regardless, Julia wouldn't arrive empty-handed.

'So what time do you expect them to be here?' Lizzie asked, pouring two glasses of bubbly. 'And you two are staying the night?'

'What?' Julia had just finished slipping the pavlova onto the top shelf of Lizzie's fridge, pushing it to the back far away from the possibility of careless hands grabbing at something and tipping it out on the floor. She looked startled at Lizzie's statement.

'You and Jack, I mean.' Lizzie grinned. 'You thought I meant you and Mr Irish, didn't you? Dirty dog.'

'Don't be daft. Just caught me by surprise and stop calling him *Mr Irish*. You'll slip up and call him that by mistake. I know what you're like.' Julia sighed.

'In answer to your question, Jack and I will stay. I've actually packed a few things, which reminds me I must go and get them from the car. I really didn't fancy driving back late tonight.' She headed for the front door to rescue her overnight bag.

Just as she was locking her car door, she saw Patrick's car pull into the driveway. She stopped and waited, bag in hand.

'Hello, you two.' She greeted Patrick and Jack.

'Hi, Mum,' Jack said. 'We've got wine. I helped choose, so hope I got it right, otherwise blame Mr Devlin.'

His face creased into a smile, and Julia found herself smiling back, thrilled to see her son so upbeat. He'd obviously had a great day.

'Hi, Julia. How was your day?' Patrick had walked up alongside her car and was staring at her in that intense way he had.

'Great, thank you. Finn and I went for a long walk this morning, and he's spent the rest of the afternoon spark out in front of the fire with Chino.' Holding up her phone to show the picture she'd taken as Jack and Patrick leaned in to view the photo.

'Wow. Never thought I'd see the day when he'd be so relaxed with a cat. He normally slopes off out of sight.'

'He's so well-trained, Patrick. You've done a great job. It's not always easy with terriers.'

'Practice, I guess. We had dogs as kids. So where is the big boy, then?'

'Oh, in the kitchen with Lizzie, hoping to receive a tit-bit. Don't worry, she won't feed him anything naughty. You'll be lucky if you get him back. She'd love to keep him the way she's fussing.'

Julia laughed, putting her arm around Jack's shoulder and inviting them both inside to meet their hosts.

'Lizzie, this is Patrick Devlin. Patrick, this is Lizzie Grace. You'll get to meet her other half shortly.'

'Hi, Patrick. I've heard so much about you. From Jack,' she added quickly. 'He's so thrilled to be at the academy, aren't you, Jacko?'

Jack crossed the room and hugged Lizzie. 'Sure am. It's the best, and today was really great.'

'It's nice to meet you, too, Lizzie, and thank you for the offer to stay for supper. Appreciated.'

'Our pleasure. Michael will be back soon. Just had to nip down to the surgery for an hour. So, Jack, tell us about Evelina,' Lizzie said.

'It was amazing, and sad and rewarding and confronting, all of those things.' Jack turned to Patrick for support.

'He did a grand job, so he did. Jack's got the magic touch with little kids. And I think it's taught him something about how tough life can be for some children through no fault of their own. Makes you realise how lucky you are.'

'I'm grateful that you offered Jack the opportunity, Patrick. It was generous of you. Now, what would you like to drink? Lizzie, what's on offer?'

'You name your poison, Patrick. We're bound to have it. Michael loves his beer and wine.'

Patrick settled on a Guinness and sat down on the leather sofas in the vast kitchen/dining room. Finn, seeking out his master, nudged his hand looking for a pat before settling down at Patrick's feet.

'If you ever want a dog-sitter, I'm your girl,' Lizzie chirped. 'He's so delightful.'

'No way, we'll take him anytime, Patrick,' Julia chimed in. 'Jack would be mightily upset if you didn't ask us first.'

'Wow, he really must have made a good impression, then. I'll bear that in mind.'

Jack was sitting on the sofa watching and listening to the conversation. Julia glanced across at him and noticed how tired he looked.

'Mum, I'll take the bag upstairs if you like?'

'Sure, that would be great. Thanks, Jack.'

'Lizzie, I take it from the extent of the Christmas decorations, that you like to celebrate the event?'

Patrick took a sip of his Guinness and looked across at Julia with laughter in his eyes.

'I do. I absolutely adore Christmas, so, yes, I go all out and make no apologies for it.'

'It's wonderful. Can't say I've ever seen a house so beautifully decorated.'

'What are you doing for Christmas, Patrick? You're welcome to join us. The more the merrier.'

God! Julia inwardly groaned at Lizzie's boldness. *Next she'd be suggesting they could have the wedding on the lawn in early summer!*

'Thank you for the offer, Lizzie, but I'm afraid I'm flying out to Dublin on Christmas Eve. I'm going home to my parents. Just a fleeting trip. I have to be back in London for a gig on New Year's Eve.'

'Oh, that's a shame. Still, I'm sure your mum and dad will be thrilled to have you home. Is your brother joining you?'

Julia thought he'd wonder how Lizzie knew he had a brother, but of course Jack could have told her, so she needn't worry that Patrick might think she'd been gossiping about him and Carrick to her friend.

'No. Not this time. He's out in New Zealand. Won't be back until the spring.'

Julia was surprised to hear Carrick intended staying in New Zealand for so long, but it confirmed her thoughts, that he hadn't been interested in her in any serious way. There had never been any intention on his part to ask her out.

Julia realised Jack had not come back downstairs, and she excused herself to go and check on him. When she climbed the stairs and walked along the landing to his room, the door was ajar and she could see he was spreadeagled on the bed, fast asleep.

It must have been a pretty harrowing day. She'd leave him be, and maybe when Michael arrived home he could go up and wake him.

As Julia reached the bottom of the stairs she hesitated, watching Patrick through the open doors to the kitchen.

He was chatting animatedly to Lizzie, his long legs stretched out in front, one foot crossed over the other, one arm stretched around the back of the sofa. He looked relaxed and comfortable.

She stood watching, unable to move. With his free hand she saw him reach out and stroke Finn's head. His long musician's fingers massaged the dog's head before he lifted his glass from the table and took another sip of his Guinness.

He was handsome in a rakish kind of way, and she realised that she was finding herself very attracted to him.

He was so easy, so relaxed, so completely different from Nick. Patrick looked up as though sensing someone staring at him. His eyes locked on hers, and it was she this time who was forced to look away, a slow blush creeping up her neck to her face, highlighting her cheekbones.

'Is he okay?' Patrick asked, standing as Julia walked into the room.

'He's fine. Sound asleep. Must have been quite a day?'

'It was. He was brilliant, kind, intuitive. He had one little girl, Tilly. She's been in and out of Evelina's since she was, I don't know, probably about three. She wanted to play the drums, and Jack was so gentle and patient with her. Despite her circumstances, she's got the biggest heart and wildest spirit of any of the children in there.'

'What type of cancer has she got?' Julia asked.

'Very aggressive lymphoblastic leukemia. She has had times of remission, but it always comes back and every time it's worse. Her mother said today they're going to try a new drug, so she's hopeful. But, frankly, I was shocked when I saw Tilly. She's wafer thin and so pale she looks translucent. Completely bald, not one hair on her head. I would love to think some new drug would save her, but I've my doubts.'

'I can't imagine what that would be like. Don't want to imagine what it would be like.' Julia shuddered.

'It's a wonderful thing you do, Patrick, to give the children a special day right before Christmas.'

'It's little enough in the scheme of things, and it brings them so much joy. Especially today, with Jack there. Someone more their age seemed to lift their spirits.'

· · ·

THE DOOR BANGED, and Michael called out. Finn jumped up at the sound of the door and a male voice, and Julia watched as Patrick laid his hand on the dog's head, reassuring him all was well.

He really did have a way with children and animals. If that had been her Judas, he would have bounded to the door, barking his head off.

Introductions were made, and she could see Patrick warmed to Michael immediately. It would be difficult not to. Michael was very easy to get along with. No airs and no arrogance, unlike other doctors she'd met or represented in divorce cases.

It was only her ex-husband who hadn't managed to get along with Michael. *There's a surprise*, she thought to herself as she watched the two men pouring themselves another Guinness and going off to the family room, presumably so Michael could show off his jazz collection to Patrick. Michael was a jazz nut, and there wasn't much he didn't know about that genre.

'Well, now they are out of earshot, he's delicious, Julia. I approve wholeheartedly.'

'Lizzie, he's here for supper, not to ask for my hand in marriage. You're shocking, playing cupid like you are, even if you're rather good at it.' Julia smirked, holding out her empty glass for Lizzie to refill.

'There's chemistry between the two of you. I can feel it, so don't bullshit me.'

'Yes, all right, I admit I do like him, quite a lot, actually. He's wonderful with Jack. I've never seen Jack so…I can't think of the word, but he's touched Jack in a way no other man has. And that's not to say that Michael hasn't been wonderful and had a positive influence on Jack…it's just, I don't know, the X factor that Patrick has.'

'X factor or not, I can see how infatuated Jack is with him. Well, that's not the right word either. He's very at ease with him, like they've known each other for years. Does that make sense?'

'Makes perfect sense. I'm glad you see it and it's not just my imagination.'

Lizzie groaned out loud. 'Oh God. Michael's punishing the poor man with jazz tracks.'

They could hear Count Basie giving it something on the piano. 'If we see Patrick running out the door, we'll know who to blame!' She laughed.

'Don't be daft. He's a musician. He plays a bit of jazz himself. He's probably loving it.'

'Right, good luck with that thought, girlfriend. Shall we start supper now Michael's home? Do you want to wake Jack?'

'I was going to send Michael up when he came in, but I'll go. Be back in a minute to give you a hand.'

THEY ENJOYED a beautiful meal Lizzie had prepared, followed by Julia's rolled pavlova, which had been a big hit with Patrick.

'Is this a New Zealand speciality or is it an Australian one?' He winked at Julia across the table.

'You aiming to start the next war, Patrick?' said Michael, helping himself to another slice.

'Just counting down the seconds to the explosion, actually,' Patrick replied while a beaming smile lit his face.

'We Kiwis know we are the founders of pavlova. Nothing more to say, really. But this is my very own particular speciality.'

Julia looked across the table to Patrick, half expecting a witty retort, but he held her gaze as he spooned the light and fluffy raspberry-infused delight into his mouth. The sensuous gesture was not lost on Julia. She felt herself blush before turning her gaze to Lizzie.

'That was, as usual, a delightful meal. Thank you, Lizzie.'

'It's wonderful to have you here and to finally meet Patrick,' Lizzie said.

'You could catch a cab home, couldn't you, Patrick? Leave your car here and pick it up in the morning. I thought we might move into the family room and enjoy a liqueur or brandy by the fire. Everyone up for that?'

'If you're sure, Lizzie. I could probably walk to my place from here, but it's pretty cold out there so I'll order a cab a bit later. A brandy sounds like the perfect end to a lovely evening.'

'No. What would be perfect, Patrick, is if you would play something for us. We'd love to hear you play.' Lizzie gave Patrick her best pretty-please look, making him laugh.

'As it happens, I do have two guitars in the car—'

Before he could finish the sentence, Jack interrupted.

'I can get them for you, if you like?'

Patrick flicked his car keys across to Jack, who caught them in one hand.

'Still got a good catch on you, Jack,' said Michael. 'You playing cricket next summer?'

'No. Actually, I'm not going to be playing sport at all once the new term starts. I have to dedicate the time to music.'

'Shame. You're a talented sportsman.'

Michael frowned, and Julia hoped he wouldn't launch into the merits of balancing physical exercise with music or study. He was very passionate about sport, all sport, and he enjoyed sharing in Jack's successes on the sports field.

THE WARMTH of the fire and the thick rich Amarula Cream liqueur Julia was drinking made her feel relaxed to the point of soporific.

Jack sat on the end of the sofa as close to Patrick's chair as he could manage as he watched him tune his acoustic guitar.

He started by playing an acoustic piece by Bert Jansch called "Angie," which Julia thought was very catchy, and she could see out of the corner of her eye Lizzie tapping her foot in time with the rhythm.

Next, he played "Cavatina" with its soulful notes, followed by "Blackbird" an old Beatles song.

Lizzie had dimmed the lights, and as Patrick began to play and sing Sting's "Fragile" within the glow from the open fire, there resonated a deep longing in Julia. A longing to be loved, truly loved.

She listened to the sound of his husky voice, and the words called out a reminder to her that she was fragile. However much she wanted to believe she had healed, there were still wounds that needed the healing balm of love before they could truly mend.

When Patrick ended the song, a round of applause from Jack, Michael, Lizzie, and Julia made him blush. Julia smiled remembering back to the night of Irish music in London when he'd had the same bashful look.

After they said their farewells at the door, Lizzie, Michael, and Jack walked back inside, leaving Julia to wait with Patrick for his cab to arrive.

'You play and sing beautifully. That was a wonderful end to the evening. Thank you again.'

'My pleasure. I don't often get to play my acoustic. I only had it with me for the kids at the hospital.' He stomped his feet, swinging his arms around himself to keep warm.

Despite being wrapped up, it was extremely cold, and Julia thought they should have stayed inside until the cab arrived.

'I've had a lovely evening. Thank you for inviting me.' Standing on the bottom step looking back at Julia, Patrick's face was caught by the soft outdoor lighting. It made Julia feel she ought to skip down the last two steps and kiss him full on the mouth.

As this thought hung in the air between them, the bright lights of the cab fell on their two figures, banishing the magic of those fleeting ideas.

Julia waved goodbye from her place on the step before retreating indoors. She could hear Jack talking to Lizzie in the kitchen as they cleared away the supper dishes.

'He's great, isn't he, Lizzie?'

'Absolutely, Jack. You're very lucky to have someone as talented as Patrick to teach you.'

'Yes, but it's not just the music; it's him, as a man, I mean. He's so cool. Why do you think he's still single?'

'I don't know. Maybe he just hasn't found the right person. Being married to a musician can't be easy with all those late nights.'

'I guess. Do you think he likes Mum?'

'Well, of course he does. She's the parent of his pupil; why wouldn't he like her?'

'No, I mean like her in, like…fancy her?'

'I don't know, Jack. Would it worry you if he did?'

'I don't know. I'd love Mum to meet someone else. Someone special who would look after her.'

'That's sweet of you. We would love her to meet someone, too, but she worries about you and I don't think she has room for anything else.'

'She doesn't have to worry about me. I'm fine.'

Julia coughed to alert them to her presence before walking into the kitchen.

'Patrick get off all right?' Lizzie asked, turning to place a large platter in the cupboard.

'Yes. Fine, but, God, it's cold outside. Almost feels like snow.'

'We might get a white Christmas this year. Wouldn't that be fun, Jack?' Lizzie said, putting the last of the dishes away. Jack smiled at her in response.

'Come on, Jack, you need to get to bed and so do I.' Julia put her arm around his shoulder, giving him a hug. 'I'm proud of what you did today.'

'I had a great day. Too tired now to talk about it, though. I'll tell you more in the morning,' he said, stifling a yawn.

'Okay, off you go upstairs. I'll see you in the morning,' Julia said, yawning herself, aware how weary she felt and how much she longed to rest her head on the pillow and fall asleep.

'Did you hear any of that?' Lizzie asked after Jack had gone.

'I did. It's so unselfish of him, you know, to want me to have someone in my life.'

'It is. But what do you want, Julia?'

'I do want someone. Of course I do. I'm just not ready.'

'When will you be ready, do you think?' Lizzie looked at her, raising a quizzical eyebrow.

'I don't know, Lizzie. It's going to take time.'

'It's been five years, Julia, and, yes, I know your priority has been

Jack, but you can see he's growing up. He's fine. You've done a wonderful job.'

Julia's phoned beeped, startling them both. She glanced at the screen and saw it was a text from Patrick.

PATRICK: Sorry, the cold must have frozen my brain, I forgot my dog! How could anyone forget their dog? Are you okay to keep him at Lizzie's overnight?

'Jesus.'

'What?' asked Lizzie. 'What is it?'

'Have you seen Finn?'

'He's right here with me,' Michael announced, looking bemused at the two women staring at him in the doorway.

'I took him out the back for a run when Patrick left. He wanted the toilet. What's the problem?'

'Patrick has just texted to ask if we can keep him until the morning.'

'Well, of course we can. That's what I thought, anyway. How was he going to take him home in a cab?' Michael shrugged in exasperation.

'Where do you want him to sleep, Lizzie?'

'He can sleep with you or Jack. I don't mind.' She turned to Julia. 'There's an old picnic rug in the cupboard under the stairs. I'll fetch it and he can sleep on that.'

WHEN JULIA RETIRED upstairs to bed with Finn padding alongside her, she checked on Jack. If he was still awake, she would let Finn sleep on the floor by Jack's bed.

She pushed his door open gently with her foot but could see by the landing lighting that he was fast asleep. She quietly pulled his door to and went along to her own room.

An hour later, Finn was breathing contentedly by her bedside, but she was still wide awake despite feeling desperately tired.

Jack's conversation with Lizzie had taken her by surprise. He'd hinted at her getting a boyfriend before, but she'd laughed it off as a joke and not taken him seriously at all.

He was growing up, and she knew she needed to give him more space and not keep organising his life. It had become a habit after Nick left to keep Jack busy and not allow him time to wallow in the past.

Her mind drifted to Patrick's guitar playing this evening and how mesmerised she'd been watching his hands, his fingers, the deftness of his movements from one end of the guitar to the other.

He had beautiful hands and long slender fingers, and lying in her bed alone she allowed herself to wonder what those hands would feel like on her skin, tracing the contours of her face, fondling her breasts, caressing between her legs.

The thoughts were arousing, but she quickly slammed them back in their box. She wasn't ready for a relationship, too afraid to be intimate with a man again.

It wouldn't be forever, she kept telling herself, just not now. Holding onto that reassurance, she drifted off to sleep.

34

PATRICK

Across town, Patrick lay awake in bed. He couldn't believe he'd forgotten Finn until the cab was at the end of the driveway.

He couldn't blame the drink as he'd not had that much. He'd blame it on the women and song instead, smiling to himself as he reached to turn the bedside lamp off. He didn't feel in the least bit sleepy, his mind teeming with thoughts and memories of the day's events.

He'd driven out to Julia's cottage in the little village of Hambleden, one of his favourite places.

He'd enjoyed a pint or two at the Stag and Huntsman many years ago and thought it was likely to have been the last time he'd been out that way.

He could appreciate why she loved living out there. The cottage was beautiful, set back from the road with woods and fields behind it. Must have been wonderful for Jack as a young boy with all this space, he'd thought, as he'd driven through the gates and parked outside.

When Jack had shown him through to the kitchen and he'd seen Julia standing there, wiping her hands on her apron, her face flushed and her hair pulled back into a ponytail, she'd had the look of a young girl about her. In that moment, he'd wanted nothing more than to sweep her up into his arms and hold onto her, never letting go.

JACK'S instant response to the children at Evelina's had been heartwarming, and he'd make a note to talk about it further with him at their next lesson. It had been a lot to absorb on the day, so many experiences that were new to Jack, some quite confronting, but he hoped that the reason behind why he'd asked Jack along had not been overtaken. He'd wanted Jack to see how, when faced with adversity, your attitude mattered.

The night had been full of surprises, including meeting Julia's best friends and sharing a meal together. They were nice people, and he was glad Julia had friends like Lizzie and Michael. He had no doubt she'd relied heavily on them when coming to terms with past events.

It had been clear that Lizzie was intent on matchmaking at every opportunity, and he loved her for that. He'd imagined Michael might be starchy and formal, but he couldn't have been more mistaken. He was down to earth and interesting to talk too. So passionate about his jazz music.

He recalled the vision of Julia standing on the steps above him when, for a moment, he'd thought she was going to bridge the gap between them and he would hold her in his arms. But the cab arriving had been the worst timing and the moment had passed, snatched away and lost to the dark night.

MORNING CAME ALL TOO QUICKLY, Patrick thought, as he glanced at his watch and realised he needed to be up and out to fetch Finn. He had band rehearsal in the afternoon and final lessons he needed to look over before his students would finish for the year.

He sent a text message to Julia to say he was on his way to fetch

Finn, but he'd walk, so probably get there in half an hour or so. A message beeped back almost instantly.

JULIA: 'Hi, I'm texting for Mum. She's driving. I'll let Lizzie know you're coming. We're on our way home. Thank you again for an awesome day yesterday, Jack😊

Patrick couldn't deny the disappointment he felt. He'd been looking forward to seeing them both this morning. He sighed. That would teach him to sleep too late.

Dressing quickly, he jogged downstairs and grabbed his jacket and scarf from the hall stand.

THIRTY MINUTES later he walked up the drive to Croft Cottage and was once more in awe at the beauty of the property and its setting.

He'd been a little star-struck last night when he and Jack had arrived back from London. Such an imposing frontage with its slate-tiled roof, cedar and rendered walls nestled against a backdrop of magnificent rural views.

He'd been blown away by the sheer size of the space inside. Whoever had redesigned it had done a magnificent job. It might once have been a cosy cottage, but now it was a magnificent contemporary country residence.

He pressed the buzzer and could hear the doorbell ringing out its chime through the house. Lizzie appeared at the door with Finn by her side.

'Good morning. Come in out of the cold.' She ushered Patrick inside.

'Thanks for taking care of Finn.' He reached down to scratch his dog's head as Finn wagged his tail at seeing his master.

'It was no hardship, believe me. He's gorgeous. Do you want a coffee, something to eat?'

'Thank you, but no. I need to be on my way. I've got rehearsals later and music to prepare for the final lessons for my students for the year. Otherwise, I'd have been glad to sit and enjoy your hospitality again. It was a lovely evening.'

'Glad you could come. Michael and I have been looking forward to meeting you. Jack, as you can imagine, has talked about you a lot.'

'He's a grand young man. Incredibly talented. I'm lucky to have the opportunity to work with him.'

'Awww, listen to you. Such a lovely thing to say. Sure you won't stay for a coffee? Michael's just out in the garage. He'll be in in a minute. He'll be sorry if he's missed you.'

'You are persuasive. Yes, thank you. I can't stay long, but a coffee will be great.'

'Did you say last night you're off to Dublin on Christmas Eve?' Lizzie asked as she busied herself making coffee and getting down mugs from the cupboard.

'Flying into Dublin, then I'll drive down to Baltimore in County Cork where my parents are. I haven't been back in a while, so it's timely.'

'Are they retired, then?'

'Yes. My father was principal at our local school and my mum was a teacher there also. Now they've escaped the schoolhouse and bought a property on the outskirts of Baltimore. It's worked out well for them.'

'Morning, Patrick,' Michael called as he walked into the kitchen.

'Staying for a coffee? You'd have been lucky to escape without having a coffee with Lizzie. Have we got any of those pastries, Lizzie? I'm a bit peckish.'

'Sure, they're in the pantry in that blue container. You get them out and I'll grab a plate. I'm sure Patrick won't say no to one of my pastries.' She looked across at Patrick.

'Sounds good to me. Thank you.' He glanced around the kitchen, marvelling at the modern architecture and spaciousness. The whole downstairs was painted white, with some of the rooms having floor to ceiling windows, inviting in the rural scene across the garden.

'Much on today, Patrick?' Michael asked as he tucked into a pastry and took a sip of his coffee.

'Band rehearsal and need to organise final lessons with students before Christmas. How about you?'

'Oh, I've got a day off, which is delightful. Too cold to play golf so I'm hanging about, annoying my wife.' He winked at Lizzie.

'He's on call on Christmas Eve, but at least he's got Christmas Day off this year.'

'Where's your surgery, Michael?'

'In Marlow, so not far from here. Been there a long time now, before I met Lizzie.'

'Marlow has expanded a lot in the past ten years. You must be busier now?' Patrick asked, taking a sip from his coffee and sinking his teeth into one of Lizzie's pastries, which he found were delicious.

'You're absolutely right. We've expanded from three doctors to twelve. It allows all of us to get a break and recharge. By the way, I hope I didn't cause offence last evening mentioning Jack and his sport?'

'No. Of course not. It was Jack's decision and his alone to ask to be excused from school sport. He's totally committed, and to be honest, if he wants to enjoy a successful career in music, he has to be single-minded. Julia was quite agreeable to the change, as I understand.'

'Oh, I'm sure she was. I was just voicing my disappointment, that's all, not a criticism. He's a great little sportsman, good across all codes, but I hear what you're saying. He'll spread himself too thin if he tries to keep up with sport at the level he's playing.'

'More coffee, Patrick?' Lizzie asked.

'No, thank you, and those pastries were gorgeous, so they were, but I must be on my way and let you two get on with your day. Thanks again for looking after Finn.'

'Anytime,' Michael said.

Patrick climbed into his car with Finn sitting on the passenger seat beside him, waved goodbye, and pulled out of the driveway heading to the studio to work before he met up with the band for rehearsal.

· · ·

On Monday afternoon, Patrick was scheduled for a lesson with Jack, his last for the year. It crossed his mind that Julia might still be working and he wondered who would bring Jack across from Hambleden. He decided to text Julia and offer to pick Jack up.

Patrick: Just thought, how is Jack getting to his lesson this afternoon? I can pick him up if you like?

Julia: Morning, Patrick. All good. Jack's at Lizzie's and she'll drop him off and pick him up, but thanks for the offer, really kind ☺

When Jack arrived in the afternoon, Patrick was surprised to see no Lizzie.

'Lizzie not coming in?'

'No. She said it was my paid lesson and therefore she shouldn't take up your time or mine,' Jack replied.

'Before we start, I wanted to ask you how you felt about Saturday at Evelina's.'

'It was an amazing experience. It's made me think a lot, a lot about the children, what will happen to them, and I know some won't make it.'

'It's sad, I know. But they are filled with hope, and that's something I find quite remarkable.'

'It's hope, it's joy, it's staying in the moment. It reminded me of what Mum used to say to me, that you can choose to be a victim or you can choose to move on. She had this expression. I hope I can remember the exact words.' He hesitated before carrying on. '

She said "moving on is not condoning." Does that make sense to you?'

'Indeed, it does. She's very wise, your mum. You saw those children on Saturday, how music lifts their spirits, keeps hope alive. It's a wonderful therapy.'

'I know. I couldn't believe how much they enjoyed it and how much they all wanted to be involved.'

'Exactly. You use music as your therapy too, Jack. It's like your external heartbeat. I see that in the way you play.'

'I know that composing makes me feel really peaceful and playing gives me the release I sometimes need. Especially if I've had a day when dark thoughts visit me.'

'I'm glad you recognise how healing music can be, in more ways than most people can imagine. Anyway, we need to get started. There's a lot to cover. I'm going to give you quite a lot of homework to work on and think about during the break.'

'Great, bring it on.' Jack grinned.

35

JACK

Jack had been staying at Lizzie and Michael's for the past few days while his mother finished up at the office. They'd bought Chino across with them. He'd stayed there a long time ago, but the cat hadn't forgotten all the special places in the house where he could stretch out and follow the sun around from room to room, which was how he spent his lazy days.

Michael had set up one of the spare rooms for Jack to practise music. He'd brought with him his keyboard and the saxophone, leaving his drum kit behind. He'd not wanted to waste a day where he couldn't practise or compose so Lizzie and Michael had hardly seen him.

He came downstairs looking for something to eat and drink.

'Hey, Jack, you've finally emerged into the light,' Lizzie said, rubbing the top of his head.

'Are you looking for food and water? I was about to make a snack for you.'

'Thanks, Lizzie. I'm starving.' He went to the fridge door and poured himself a chilled water from the ice and water dispenser.

'I just thought, Mr Devlin will be flying out in a day or so and he didn't say what he was doing with Finn. Do you think I should text him and offer to have him? Would you mind?'

'No, of course not. That's a great idea. I imagine he's probably got him booked in with someone, but text him and see.'

JACK: Hi, Mr Devlin. Lizzie and I wondered what you were doing with Finn when you go back to Ireland. Do you want us to look after him? Jack 😊.

LIZZIE PUT a plate of chicken and tomato sandwiches in front of Jack. He'd not realised just how hungry he was. A while later, Jack's phone rang.

'Hello, Mr Devlin.'

'Hi there, Jack. Thanks for the text. Your timing couldn't have been better. I had organised one of my bandmates to take him, but he's just called to say his mum is poorly and he's travelling up to Leeds. So, I was just about to call when I got your text. Are you sure this will be okay with Lizzie and your mum?'

'Sure. It'll be wicked, but Lizzie's right here—do you want to speak with her?'

'Okay, put her on.'

'Hi, Patrick, I've just switched to speaker phone of course it's absolutely fine. We'd love to have him. Do you want to drop him off tomorrow morning?'

'That'd be grand. Thank you so much. You've bailed me out of a hole. I'll bring all his food and bedding with me. See you tomorrow morning.' He rang off, leaving Jack grinning from ear to ear.

'It's going to be so cool having a dog at Christmas. I keep nagging Mum, but she won't let me have one. I know why, but it's annoying.'

'If the weather isn't too perishing cold, you'll be able to take Finn across the fields with Michael for long walks. It'll be great.'

'Do you know what time you expect Mum back tonight?'

'No, sorry, she didn't say. I know she's got quite a lot of work on.

Christmas is a funny old time for lawyers and for doctors as well. Everyone always seems to get sick at this time of the year or chop off a finger while they're making Christmas lunch.' She pulled a face at Jack, making him laugh.

He finished his plate of sandwiches and poured himself another water, which he carried back upstairs.

He needed to practise the saxophone. He'd spent most of the day on keyboards, mastering Beethoven's "Für Elise" and Mozart's Symphony no. 40 in G Minor and Piano Sonata no. 11 in A major. He loved playing Mozart. It was clean and precise with a playfulness about it, in contrast to Beethoven's more fiery pieces, which Jack imagined using for dramatic movie musical scores.

He warmed up with "Melody in F" before moving onto the pieces he really enjoyed. He'd mastered Dave Brubeck's "Take Five" and it was this he was playing when his mother tapped on the bedroom door.

She opened the door and stood watching him. He turned and nodded, finishing "Take Five" before moving onto "The Girl from Ipanema."

He'd been so immersed in playing he hadn't noticed Michael and Lizzie had joined his mother. As he finished the final note, they clapped and shouted loudly.

'You are unbelievable, Jack. I would never have imagined you could take to another instrument like this, so different from the drums,' Lizzie screeched. 'You're phenomenal.'

'Thank you,' Jack said, suddenly feeling embarrassed at all the attention but inwardly thrilled that they'd enjoying his playing.

He knew he had a long way to go, and some of the notes were slightly off, but it was only a matter of practice. That's what Mr Devlin kept reinforcing. *Practise, practise, and practise some more, Jack.*

When Jack had finished his final lesson for the year, Mr Devlin had handed him a folder with music he wanted him to practise and piano pieces he wanted him to transpose.

They were not simple pieces, and at first Jack panicked when he read through Mr Devlin's note to him. Now, having given himself time to digest what was being asked of him, he felt empowered by the task ahead.

DOWNSTAIRS, Lizzie was making supper and his mother was pouring drinks.

'Would you like a very tiny glass of red wine, Jack, since it's almost Christmas?'

'Yes, please.' He watched as his mother carefully poured a small amount of red wine into the glass.

'Your playing was wonderful. You've suddenly gone from knowing how to use all those little levers and keys to make the notes to being able to play a whole piece smoothly with a really nice tone,' his mother said, handing him the glass of wine.

'Especially when you weren't supposed to be learning saxophone until next term.'

'It's not without fault, Mum, but I think I'm getting my own tone, which is all about how you balance how hard you blow with how much pressure your mouth puts on the reed.'

'Well, that seems very complicated, but it certainly sounded great to me,' she said with a smile.

'I've got a long way to go, but I'm really loving the saxophone. It's a wonderful instrument. I made great progress with keyboards, so Mr Devlin agreed to let me try out the Sax to see how I'd go. Glad he did.'

His mother raised her glass to him. 'Here's to you and the music academy.'

Jack clinked glasses, feeling proud of his progression in a short space of time.

THE NEXT MORNING, Mr Devlin arrived to drop Finn off. Jack was excited to see the dog, but also because he wanted to give Mr Devlin a Christmas present, something his mum and he had chosen. They'd spent hours deciding what to get him and eventually agreed on what they both thought he would appreciate.

'There you go, Jack. You can take him, and I'll bring his bedding and food.'

'Come on, Finn, let's go.' The dog followed obediently at Jack's side as he led him through to the kitchen where Lizzie was making coffee.

'Got time for a coffee, Patrick, before you head off?' she asked.

'Sure. I wanted to have a word with Jack anyway, so a coffee would be grand.' Patrick sat down at the dinning room table.

'So, Jack, the folder of work I gave you, how are you finding it?'

'It was a bit scary at first, but I'm getting into it now and seeing it as a challenge.'

'That's the spirit. It wasn't meant to be easy. I set it to challenge you while I'm away.'

Lizzie poured their coffee and handed a cup to Patrick.

'I think Jack has something for you. It's a shame Julia can't be here; she had to go into the office for something urgent. Always the same on Christmas Eve.'

'Oh, I didn't realise she wasn't here. That's a shame. I'd like to have wished her a Merry Christmas. Guess a text will have to do.'

He looked down into his cup and Jack noted the sudden change in mood. Perhaps he was right and Mr Devlin did fancy his mum?

'Merry Christmas. This is from Mum and I.' Jack handed across a beautifully wrapped small box.

'Can I open it now?'

'Sure, you can,' Jack said, smiling and inwardly hoping they'd made the right choice of gift.

'A Waterman Carène pen! How beautiful, and with its own leather case. Gosh, I've never been given a high-quality pen before. And Jack, as you are well aware, I use a pen all the time. This is beautiful. Thank you so much.'

Jack beamed as he saw how genuinely thrilled Mr Devlin was. They'd been right to choose this one.

'I have something for you also, Jack. When I've finished my coffee, I'll go out to the car and fetch it.'

Jack soaked up the smile from Mr Devlin. He would miss him

over the break but having him in Lizzie's kitchen on the day before Christmas was better than he could have hoped for.

When he left to go out to the car, Jack said to Lizzie, 'Do you think he was really pleased with the gift we got him?'

'One hundred percent. It's a beautiful pen, and they're not cheap. That was generous of your mum and you. I presume you put something towards it and didn't leave your mum footing the whole bill?'

'No,' Jack said indignantly. 'I put money towards it. He's been great to me. I wanted to get him something really nice. Something that would remind him of Mum and me.'

'I don't think he'll have any problem remembering either of you.' Lizzie laughed.

'Here you go, Jack.'

He took the large box from Mr Devlin's hands, wondering what it might be. He couldn't imagine, but he'd soon find out as he ripped the paper away.

Sitting in front of him was the most beautiful and ornately carved and painted long box. The lid was carved in the shape of a Celtic knot inlaid with something Jack didn't recognise.

He'd learn later it was mother-of-pearl. Jack had never seen anything quite like it. He felt a sudden wave of emotion and, terrified he might cry, made a fuss of trying to fold the Christmas paper that he'd unceremoniously ripped off minutes before.

'Open it up. There's more inside.' Mr Devlin looked at him expectantly.

'Wow. Oh, my goodness. This is amazing.' He lifted the lid to find the inside lined with red velvet. Nestled in the red softness lay a number of drumsticks.

'This was mine when I first started playing the drums. My mum gave this to me with one set of sticks. The others were ones I played with when I was in my first band, Platonic. They're yours now, Jack. I wanted someone with exceptional musical talent to have this, and I've waited a long time for such a person to walk through the doors of my academy.'

Jack looked up, hearing a slight catch in Mr Devlin's voice. He went across and hugged him. They stood together, caught in the moment of emotion and pleasure.

'I don't know what to say, well, except a thousand thank-you's.' Jack was finding it difficult not to cry. The importance of such a gift was overwhelming, and he was relieved when Lizzie came to his rescue.

'That's an extraordinary gift, Patrick. I'm so sorry Julia couldn't be here to thank you in person, but I'll do it for her.'

Jack watched as Lizzie embraced Mr Devlin, and he could see she had tears in her eyes. It was such a wonderful gift to pass on to another musician, and Jack felt honoured that he was the one Mr Devlin had chosen.

'I'll be ever so careful and take good care of this,' Jack said, nervous that he had something so precious, a bit like when his mum had given him his granddad's pocket watch, which still sat on his dressing table nestled in its box.

'Well, don't be too careful. I want you to play with those sticks. They brought me a lot of luck and they might do the same for you. We Irish believe in luck, so we do.' He laughed, pulling Jack into a fierce hug.

'You see you look after your mum over Christmas, and I'll look forward to seeing you when I get back.'

'Are you going now?'

'Yes. Reluctantly, I have to. I've got a million and one things to do before my flight tonight. Thank you for the coffee, Lizzie, and thank you again, Jack, for the beautiful pen.'

AFTER THEY'D SAID their goodbyes and he waved until Mr Devlin drove out the gates, Jack wondered if he'd ever felt happier in his life than he did right then.

36

JULIA

Jack was upstairs in his room and Michael had been called out to a patient, so Julia poured Lizzie and herself a glass of wine while they stood side by side in Lizzie's kitchen preparing supper.

'So, now with Jack upstairs, what happened today that had you racing into the office?'

'Something that needed my urgent attention.'

'Which was?'

'We have a problem with one of our young solicitors. He's dropped the ball on several Family Court hearings. I thought it was his love life, but it's much more serious.'

'Serious in what way?

'Drugs. He's developed an appetite for cocaine. George and I have been working on a strategy for the past few weeks. We had a meeting today with all of the partners and the senior leadership team. You can imagine how well that went down on the last day before Christmas.'

'Oh, shit. Not happy bunnies then. What will you do, sack him?'

'Yes. That's where I think it's heading. He's lied to me, lied to Maria. He's lying to himself, like all addicts do. I should have seen the signs earlier, but I missed them or at least didn't think his mistakes were drug related.'

'He's the one with the problem Julia, not you. Don't go blaming yourself. How bad are his mistakes, with the clients, I mean?'

'Bad enough, but we've worked out how to minimise the damage to Petries and ensure the clients are given the legal representation they should have had in the first place.'

'I was reading the paper this morning, and there was an article about the spike in criminal acts and domestic violence. It's always the same at Christmas. Instead of drinking eggnog, they fill themselves up with pints or bottles of bourbon and run amok,' Lizzie said, shaking her head.

'Tell me. I've worked in family law long enough to know this is our busiest time of the year through until about March.'

'Well, some head of the church was ranting on in this article about the need for tolerance and understanding, blah-blah. That's all very well but tell that to the woman who's been beaten up by her husband or partner and her kids have had to witness it.' Lizzie raged.

'There's so much violence, particularly towards women at this time of the year. It's weakness and lack of self-control.'

'And what about women who are raped and won't get an abortion, or their church makes them feel so guilty they don't feel they've got a choice. The hospital should give them the morning-after pill, just in case. Not even tell them. That's what I'd do.'

'Yes, I'm sure you would and be arrested later.' Julie raised an eyebrow at Lizzie.

'Changing the subject, if I may?'

'Please do,' Julia said.

'What did you think of Patrick's gift to Jack?'

'Amazing, which reminds me I ought to phone him and say thank you, but he's probably on his flight by now.' She looked at her watch. 'I'll call tomorrow.'

'I wish you'd been here. He was quite emotional.'

'Who was? Jack or Patrick?'

'Both, actually. But I was referring to Patrick. He got quite choked up. He really does have a special relationship with Jack, don't you think?'

'Hmm. Yes, they both have something special going on. It's lovely. Wonderful for Jack.'

'It's probably pretty wonderful for Patrick as well,' Lizzie commented. 'Single man, never married, maybe would have loved to have had kids, who knows?'

'Exactly, who knows? I certainly don't. What I do know...well, I don't know, but I'm sensing there is something between him and his brother. I saw it that night at the charity event.'

'What sort of something?'

'I don't know. I just sensed there was some history, something sad, maybe even unresolved.'

'Really? What made you think that? And don't say *just a sense or a feeling.*'

'They didn't talk much, I mean, in the breaks. Maybe it was different after, when they had the backstage party, but we'd gone by then so I don't know what may or may not have happened. I remember during a particularly powerful song they exchanged glances, you know, in the way people do when the song reminds them of something. Or maybe I just imagined the whole thing.' She sighed, taking another sip of her wine.

'Well, some siblings just aren't that close. You can't compare everyone else to you and William. You two had a special brother-and-sister bond.'

'Yes, I know. I miss him a lot, especially at Christmas. He always made such a fuss making sure I felt special on Christmas Day, probably to make up for Mum doing nothing.'

'Let's not dwell on those times.' Lizzie changed the subject, and Julia knew her friend did not like to remember her childhood Christmases with her father arriving home drunk on Christmas Eve and spoiling the next day with his antics.

Julia had a sudden image of an aunt, who spoiled her and William at Christmas. The memories of this much favoured aunt had faded with time, but she recalled being given a beautiful brides doll with real hair, at least she thought it was real and William had been given a Hornsby train set.

Something happened soon after that Christmas and they never saw or heard from the aunt again.

'He seems quite well-off.'

Julia was shaken from her moment of reminiscence.

'Who is well off?

'Patrick. I'm talking about Patrick.'

'How do you know that?' Julia asked.

'Well, he's got that nice studio in Henley—well, I say nice; I only dropped Jack off and didn't go in. But it can't be cheap rent, unless he owns it? There's a thought. Perhaps he's stinking rich and looking for a wife. Someone who's about five foot eight tall, slim, gorgeous long dark wavy hair, beautiful eyes, and preferably named Julia.'

'Lizzie, really.' Julie raised her eyebrows and tutted.

'He doesn't own the building; he leases it, but for an unusually low amount.'

'And how, Miss Marple, do you know this? Been snooping again, have we?'

'An unkind, uncaring kind of person may think that. But someone who's meant to be your best friend and who is kind and caring would never dream of painting me in that unflattering light.' Julia put on a mock-hurt look and then relented with a smile.

'All right, then. I did some searches on the studio address and his home address. He owns his apartment, no mortgage, paid cash, but the studio he leases at way below the current commercial rates.'

'You really have been busy, haven't you? May I ask why the interest?'

'Because, Little Miss Cupid, I like him, and I wanted to find out a little more without grilling him like he was being interrogated at the local police station.'

'Finally. You've admitted it. You fancy him.' Lizzie beamed.

'No, I didn't say *fancy*, I said *like*. That's all I'm prepared to admit to at this stage. Case closed.'

.   .   .

Julia tried unsuccessfully to make contact with Patrick on Christmas Day, but the network message was the same time and time again: *All the lines are busy at the moment. Please try again later.*

Eventually she gave up and decided to phone him on Boxing Day when hopefully the rest of the Irish nation had tired of talking on the phone to distant friends and loved ones.

37

———

PATRICK

Patrick was surprised at the level of emotion he'd felt handing over his box and drumsticks. He'd cherished them for years, all through university and now, middle aged, it was time he passed them on.

He'd have no children of his own—too late for that—and Jack was the most deserving person he knew and the one who was most likely to treasure the box and the sticks the way Patrick had.

He'd never really been a drummer, he acknowledged to himself, as he drove back to his studio. He'd enjoyed playing when he was much younger, but a year into his university studies he found his real passion was guitar. Even though he could play almost any instrument and usually quite well, it was the guitar that was his real love.

The card had been tucked inside with the pen when he'd unwrapped it. He'd not dwelled on reading it at the time, wanting the opportunity to be alone so he could appreciate the words.

As he sat waiting for his flight to taxi down the runway, his seat belt fastened, he took the card out from inside the pocket of his laptop bag. It was an Irish Christmas card with a message on the front reading: *Blessed be your holidays, Cosy be your hearth, Merry be your Family, Peaceful be your Hearts.* On the inside of the card Julia had written a note.

MERRY CHRISTMAS, Patrick. I hope you have a wonderful time with your mum and dad. Thank you for your patience and generosity with Jack. He's loving the opportunity, and under your tutorship I'm sure he'll go on to have a wonderful career in music.

Look forward to catching up when you get back.

Best wishes

Julia and Jack

HE REREAD THE CARD, pleased that she'd written a note to him herself and not left Jack to write something, but disappointed it had not been signed *with love.* Best wishes were not the same as love and kisses.

After placing the card back in its envelope and tucking it inside the side pocket of his laptop bag, he sat back in his seat, closed his eyes, and let the exhaustion of the last few weeks catch up with him.

Sleep came quickly and he didn't wake until they were about to land at Dublin airport. He had a four-hour drive ahead of him to reach his parents' house before eleven, so he was glad of the sleep as he made his way through the airport to the rental car pickup desk.

HIS MOTHER WAS STILL up when he parked in the driveway outside the front door. She hugged him fiercely before Patrick held her away from him so he could take a good look at her.

'You look tired, Mammy. I'm sorry I've kept you up.'

She was still a beautiful woman, but Patrick had been surprised at the change since his last visit. She appeared thinner, more fragile.

'Nonsense. I'm fine. I wouldn't have settled until I knew you were safely here. Come on, let's take your bag through to your room. Your father's had a big day stacking wood, so he went to bed an hour ago, but he'll be pleased to be seeing you in the morning. Night, Paddy. Sleep well.' She kissed him goodnight and pulled the door shut.

Patrick lifted his bag onto the bed, clicked the numbers for the combination, and opened up his suitcase. He'd not packed much, but he'd still needed a suitcase rather than an overnight bag given the bulk of the jumpers, thick socks, a scarf, hat, hiking boots, and shoes.

Once he'd transferred his clothing to the chest of drawers and retrieved his toilet bag and dressing gown, he zipped his suitcase and placed it up on top of the wardrobe.

Looking about the room, he noticed it had been decorated since last he was there. Gone was the old-fashioned floral wallpaper for which the previous owners had a penchant. Now the walls and woodwork were freshly painted in soft grey tones.

The curtains, which had matched the floral wallpaper, had been replaced with Roman blinds in a charcoal grey, making the whole room look clean and crisp.

The large Georgian dresser, furniture left over from his grandparents' home, sat proudly against the far wall. On top of the dresser his mother had placed a vase of wild Irish flowers and herbs bold enough to brazen out the harsh winter winds of the Irish coast. She loved flowers, and even in the dead of winter she would be out on the hillsides foraging for something to put in a vase.

He snuggled under the goose-down duvet, which his mother insisted on having on all the beds all year round, regardless of the temperature, but tonight he was glad of its insulating warmth.

HE WOKE to the sound of Irish Christmas carols playing somewhere in the house and the smell of a cooked breakfast. It was traditional in the Devlin household not to have their Christmas meal until the evening, leaving time for outdoor pursuits. Sailing, if the weather would permit. However cold it might be, as long as the sea was calm enough, they'd take the boat out.

If that wasn't possible, then a long hike over the hills was another Christmas Day family tradition that Patrick and Carrick had enjoyed as young boys and loathed as they grew into their teenage years when all they wanted to do was open presents, eat a big breakfast, and return to the comfort of their beds to listen to music until they'd be forced to help peel tatties, prepare sprouts, carving with care the cross in the top of the stalk.

Patrick lay warm and comfortable in his bed, reminiscing about Christmas' past and wondering what Carrick was doing today. It was already Christmas evening in New Zealand. He thought it might be nice to surprise his parents and make a call to him to wish him Merry Christmas. It would be the start of the journey to rebuild their friendship, their love for one another. Carrick had sent the card. Patrick would make the call.

His mother would be both delighted and appalled that he'd be phoning long distance on Christmas Day, the most expensive day of the year. She had no idea about mobile phone plans—it was a step too far for either of his parents. Their mobile phones had been bought out of necessity in case of emergencies.

PATRICK PUSHED his chair back from the table, feeling satiated with the large breakfast his mother had served up. His father, he could see, was equally full of bacon, sausage, eggs, mushroom, tomatoes, and homemade hash browns.

Patrick pulled his phone from his pocket and dialled Carrick's number. It rang several times before finally he answered.

Patrick pressed the button for the loudspeaker and greeted his brother. His father sat up, astonished that suddenly he could hear the voice of his youngest son, and his mother turned from the sink, towel in hand, beaming from ear to ear.

'Hello, everyone. Merry Christmas. I've just spent the day at the beach. What's the weather like there?'

'Balmy, Carrick. We've been stretched out on the deckchairs. This global warming is really having an effect here in Baltimore.'

Patrick's father roared with laughter, and his mother called out as though she were speaking to the hard of hearing.

'He's so full of Irish blarney, Carrick. Some things never change. Whereabouts in New Zealand are you, Carrick?' she asked.

'I'm in the Bay of Islands on Ninety Mile Beach. I've been in Auckland, and after New Year I'll be heading to Wellington and then the South Island for business. It's beautiful here. You'd love it.'

'I don't think I would, Carrick, you know how I am with the heat, but I'm glad you're having a lovely time.'

'So what's news in Baltimore? Anything I should know about?'

'Oh, well, I don't want to spoil your Christmas, but Colleen Fitzpatrick passed away a few days ago. A blessing really, poor woman, suffering like she did. And your father's bought himself a new kayak, a Christmas present, he said it was, but I think that's an excuse.'

'It's a beauty, Carrick. A two-person. You'll have to come out with me when you get back. It'll be spring by then. Good weather for a paddle.'

'Sounds great, Pa. When did you get there, Paddy?'

PATRICK WAS STILL RECOVERING from the shock of his mother's news about Katie's mother. Why hadn't she told him last night? But then why would she? Why would she think it would be of any interest to him?

'I flew into Dublin last night and drove down. Got here before eleven. It's cold but a fine day. Might even get out with Pa in his new kayak.'

'I'm sorry to hear about Colleen, Mammy, but as you say a blessing. When's the funeral?' Carrick asked.

'Oh, I think the day after Boxing Day. Can't do it before that.'

'How's business in New Zealand, Carrick, and have you been to Australia or are you doing that on your way back?' Patrick quickly changed the subject. He did not wish to dwell on the death of Katie's mother, not today.

'No. I stopped off on my way over. It's all good there, and business in New Zealand is interesting. Some great opportunities. I'll tell you all about it when I get back and we have that pint I promised.'

'I'll keep you to that. Anyway, we'll say our goodbyes and wish you a Merry Christmas and Happy New Year.'

'Bye, my boy. We love you and miss you. Take care of yourself out there,' his mother said.

'Merry Christmas, son. We'll see you in the spring.'

'Bye, everyone. Thanks for the call.'

Patrick had made his mother's day and probably his father's, if the look on their faces was anything to go by.

'It sounds like he's having a grand old time out there,' said Patrick's mother. 'Thank you for phoning him, Paddy. That was a lovely gesture.'

LOUGH HYNE LAY silver in the bright light of a winter's afternoon sun as Patrick helped his father launch the kayak.

Despite the cold, it was a calm and sunny day. Patrick enjoyed the feeling of being back on the water, not the same as a sailboat, but there was a calming peace to kayaking that he'd never appreciated before.

As they paddled out, he was glad his father wasn't one of those men who felt that silence needed to be filled with words. The only sound was the cry of sea birds and the sound of their paddles as they sliced through the water.

Patrick's father took the front seat, and after a shaky start they quickly settled into a rhythm. It was surprisingly fast, and soon they'd reached Castle Island before turning back and slowing their pace.

'She sits well in the water, don't you think, Paddy?'

'I don't know much about kayaks, Pa, but this is one of the most relaxing water sports one could do. I'm loving it.'

WHEN THEY GOT BACK to the house, stored the kayak, and opened the back door, the mouth-watering smell of cooked turkey greeted them.

Patrick had no doubt his mother would have prepared and cooked enough food to feed the village, but he wouldn't complain.

Being out on the water had made him hungry in the way he used to feel as a boy after a day's sailing.

'He's a natural with the kayak, Rosie. I told you he'd enjoy it.' His father turned to Patrick.

'Your mother convinced herself that neither you nor Carrick would take to kayaking, not after sailing.'

'It's completely different to sailing, obviously, but I really loved it. If the weather holds, I'll go out again before I leave. You've still got a sailboat, haven't you, Pa? I thought I saw it in the back of the shed?'

'Oh yes, indeed we have. That won't be going anywhere.' His faced creased into a cheeky smile, and for a moment Patrick glimpsed the young boy in him still, yearning to be out on the sea with the mainsail cracking above his head.

'I don't get out on her now.' His faced saddened as he looked at Patrick. 'I'm becoming an old man now, Paddy, swimming in the tide water of my seventh decade.'

'Rubbish, Pa. You're as fit as a fiddle.' Whilst Patrick knew his father was still very fit, he had aged a lot in the past couple of years.

'When Carrick comes out in the spring, I'll come with him. We'll all go out sailing. How about that?'

'I'll put it in the calendar so I don't forget to remind you.' He chuckled, obviously thrilled at the prospect of sailing with his two boys.

LATER IN THE EVENING, seated around a roaring open fire and feeling stuffed full of food and wine, Patrick wanted nothing more than to drift off to sleep, but his mother and father wanted to know all about the academy.

'I'm teaching a young man who I would consider to be a musical prodigy.'

'Really?' his mother exclaimed. 'And how did that come about?'

'Hamish. You remember, from university.'

'Oh, yes. I seem to recall you brought him home once. Nice lad, gifted musician as I recall.'

'That's right, Mish is a gifted musician. He teaches at a prep school in Berkshire. You remember he married Susan? They've got nine-year-old twin girls.'

His mother nodded in acknowledgement.

'Mish was Jack's music teacher at prep school. By the time he auditioned for the academy he was already an accomplished drummer, and I mean outstanding.'

'You used to love the drums once,' his mother reminded him.

'Long time ago now, but yes, I did. Anyway, Jack wants to compose. It's quite unusual in a lad of fourteen, but that's what he wants to do, compose musical scores for movies, TV, that sort of thing.'

'He's come to the right person, then, hasn't he?' Patrick's father remarked. 'You wrote some wonderful musical scores as I recall at university?'

'I did, and I still write when I have the time.'

'Avril O'Brien said you were playing a charity event in London a while back. Mary Black and Maura O'Connell performed, no less. Was that true?'

'Yes, they did. It was to raise money for my charity with the disadvantaged school kids. How did Avril O'Brien know?'

'She's some distant relation—and I mean distant—to Mary Black. She reminds us on a regular basis. Avril, that is, not Mary. She probably hasn't a clue who Avril is. Avril was always one for bragging, was she not, Brendon?'

'She was, Rosie. A pain in the arse, if you don't mind my saying?'

'Oh, but I do, Brendon Devlin. There'll be no swearing on the day our Lord was born.'

'Consider yourself reprimanded, Pa.'

Patrick laughed as he watched his father pull a face. He was reminded of how small Ireland was, and he felt shabby that he hadn't thought to invite his parents out to London to share in the event or even tell them it was happening. It hadn't occurred to him that they'd want to travel across to London.

· · ·

With the soft glow from the fire and only the side lamps lighting the room, Patrick studied his parents.

They were aging, of course they would be, but it was more than that. They appeared to be crumbling like some of the old ruins that adorned the winding road from Cork to Baltimore.

His mother was still beautiful, but her hands were arthritic, the skin stretched across them like thin sheets of tissue paper barely containing all the bones and veins. He hair once thick and dark was now completely silver.

He looked across to his father, more stooped than Patrick could remember him being. He used to be over six foot, but now he seemed hunched, somehow drawn into his body.

He'd retained his fitness, but the big-framed man he remembered from childhood was much thinner, a gauntness about his features weathered from years of sailing and braving the harsh Atlantic winds.

Patrick woke from sleep feeling chilly and needing the comfort of his bed. It was after midnight and his parents had retired upstairs, leaving him sleeping peacefully as the last of the embers glowed in the fireplace.

It had been years since he'd last felt so relaxed, but he also realised he was extremely tired. It had been a big year and he wondered what the new one would bring.

Images of Julia swam before his eyes, and he wondered where she was and what she was doing. She'd be asleep at Lizzie's, of course. They were staying there until Boxing Day and then she'd go back to her cottage with Jack and Finn.

That's where he'd head to as soon as he got out of the airport in London. He'd drive straight to her. He had the perfect excuse, after all: fetching his dog.

He'd felt excited telling his parents about Jack. Seldom did he ever speak of his pupils, even though many had gone on to have successful careers in music, and he'd been genuinely delighted that they had, but no one had touched him in the way Jack did. He'd never taught anyone as gifted as Jack.

His mind flicked back to the conversation about the death of Katie's mother. It had been a shock, as though someone had burnt his skin with a match.

He couldn't avoid thinking about Katie, about her family, not now he was out here where it had all happened and here where it all ended, but he hadn't expected the past to visit on Christmas Day.

KATIE'S MOTHER had been a kind and gentle woman, Patrick remembered. Once quite beautiful, but the ravages of time spent outdoors in the harsh Irish weather helping her fisherman husband had stripped the youthfulness from her skin.

Being used as a punchbag during the rages of her drunken husband had robbed her of her inner beauty and spirit, leaving her broken, unable to defend either herself or her daughter. He wondered if the piece of shite husband was still around. He'd ask his mother in the morning.

ON BOXING DAY, Patrick took himself off to climb Mount Knockoumah. He pulled on his hiking boots as his mother handed him the thermos of hot coffee and pack of food she'd prepared for him, which he stowed in his backpack. He'd been desperate to strike out on his own for a hike and find some quiet time to reflect.

The view from the top down into Lough Hyne and out to the Atlantic Ocean was far more stunning and dramatic than he'd remembered as a boy. Back then it would have been more about beating Carrick to the top than admiring the raw beauty of the place.

After taking off his backpack, he sat down on a large flat rock, poured the thick black coffee from the thermos, and took a bite from the bacon and egg pie his mother had made.

She'd been reminding him this morning as she'd rolled out the homemade pastry how she'd made the very same pie when he and Carrick had headed off one sunny summer's day to do the climb.

He remembered that morning well. As they'd walked off, Carrick had been badgering him about Katie Fitzpatrick. Was he seeing her? Did Mammy and Pappy know? Did her parents know?

He'd wanted to grab Carrick by the shirt and punch him. Not something that Patrick had ever done to his little brother, but in the heat of the moment and with a cocktail of fear and raw emotions, Patrick had made a fist with his hands and punched Carrick's backpack instead.

'Shut up. You don't know what you're talking about. I don't know Katie Fitzpatrick.'

'You're lying. I know you are. You fancy her, and why not? She's beautiful. The most beautiful girl in Baltimore. That's what I think.' He'd laughed, almost skipping ahead of Patrick as they started their climb.

'Who cares what you think? You're a child. You've never even had a girlfriend.'

It had been a cruel and bitter conversation, leaving Patrick feeling angry and guilty in equal measure. He'd never lied to his parents or his brother, but now he had, and he couldn't undo the lie nor could he admit to it. To do so would be to acknowledge he was seeing a Catholic girl from the wrong side of the tracks.

His parents would be disappointed and would insist he stop seeing her, and Carrick would be smug in the way that only a younger brother could be, that he knew all along, that Patrick would never be able to keep a secret from him. They were brothers and told each other everything. Except that hadn't been true. Up until he met Katie, there was nothing he hadn't shared with Carrick.

The crushes he had on girls in school, the fear of not making the first fifteen team in rugby, the frustration he felt having both parents teaching at their school.

His frustration that the music teacher was less than average, and Patrick wishing he could go off to a big high school in Dublin where they had a real music department. All these wishes and grievances he'd shared with his little brother, until Katie.

HE'D BEEN PLAYING a rugby game against the school Katie attended. It was the first time her school's team had made the final and the first time Patrick's team had played them.

On the sidelines the girls cheered as they always did every weekend, only this time Patrick had seen someone different as he jogged back up the field. At the end of the game he'd gone across to the beautiful girl standing alone looking awkward and slightly fearful.

IT TOOK ONLY one conversation for Patrick to know he wanted this girl more than any other. At that stage in his life he'd only ever kissed girls, nothing else. It seemed every girl he met knew his parents or her parents were friends with his.

There was no way he could avoid his parents knowing who he was seeing, who he might wish to ask out, who he would be taking to the school formal. He had no privacy, and so he'd taken to avoiding girls and concentrated on rugby and music instead, until Katie.

As he looked out to the Atlantic and poured himself another coffee, Patrick remembered the thrill of the forbidden. He could feel it still in every fibre of his body.

The way his nerves tingled with the excitement of their illicit tryst. The ways they devised to see each other without anyone knowing.

The secret meetings in his parent's boat shed that he had the key too, hiding the spare key in his bottom drawer so there would be no chance of his father or Carrick disturbing them. He'd not realised until he met Katie how devious he could be, how easily he could lie to his parents about where he'd been and who he'd been with.

· · ·

THEIR RELATIONSHIP HAD GROWN from a tentative getting to know one another to a growing passion that neither felt they could deny for much longer.

Katie was unintentionally the forbidden fruit in the Garden, she was the siren singing from the storm-lashed rocks, and like the moth drawn to a fiery end in a candle flame, there was nothing Patrick could do or wanted to do to step back from their dangerous love.

CARRICK HAD KNOWN. Patrick knew he'd always known, and however much he wished to believe otherwise, he'd had to admit six months into his relationship with Katie that Carrick was a potential problem. As the saying goes, keep your friends close and your enemies closer. Not that Carrick was the enemy; it was just easier to have him on your side than not.

So it began that Carrick would accompany them when they went out sailing. Their parents never realised there were three on board and not just two.

It had been a dangerous game, and as months went by, Patrick could see Carrick was also falling head over heels in love with Katie. In the beginning he'd been amused at his younger brother's attempts to gain Katie's affection, then it began to trouble him, the same as it troubled her.

PATRICK SIGHED. He should have been making his way back, but he felt anchored to the spot, mesmerised by the stunning views and trapped within the memories of the past.

He'd promised he'd take her away to London as soon as he finished university. That had been the plan. She would save as much money as she could and maybe get to London ahead of him and find a place for them both.

They'd planned and schemed and dreamed and it had all been just that, for deep down Patrick knew she'd find it impossible to leave her mother behind to face the drunken, violent husband alone.

He also knew her father would never let her leave Baltimore and go off to London. He needed her on the fishing boat. He'd pay her a meagre wage, and he'd make it impossible for her to leave.

THE NIGHT before Patrick was to leave Baltimore for Edinburgh, he'd met Katie one last time in the boat shed. It was late, his parents were in bed, and he believed Carrick was over at a friend's house. They had time, time alone and time to say their final goodbyes.

They'd been seeing each other in secret for almost a year, during which time Patrick learned of a woman's body, of the pleasure to be had and the pleasure he could give.

The sexy magazines which lay at the bottom of his drawer, along with the spare key to the boat shed, were a poor second in comparison to the real experience. The ecstasy and the agony. The fire and ice.

On that last night, when he'd lain with Katie on the rug in the boathouse and made love to her one final time, he'd shed tears of joy and sorrow. Joy that she was his and his alone, and sorrow that in a few hours he'd be leaving her.

As they lay naked in each other's arms, Patrick had reached a hand up to her cheek and felt his fingertips touch the hot tears. He'd pulled himself up on one elbow and looked into her sad blue eyes.

'Don't go, Paddy. Stay with me. You can go to university in London. Why Edinburgh?'

He could still remember how her words were like a dagger to his heart, for hadn't she over all these past months talked only of his music and how important it was and how gifted he was and how he must take this opportunity?

'Fly like an eagle, Paddy, but come back to me when you graduate.'

Now she was saying the opposite. He'd stood up and begun to dress himself, angry, fearful, and hurt.

'I'm sorry. I shouldn't have said that, but it's how I feel.'

'You've known all along I was going to Edinburgh. That was a fact from the beginning, from when we first met. I can't change universities now even if I wanted to, which I don't, by the way.' His words had been delivered with a savagery he'd not known he possessed.

He held her clothes out to her, shaking them in her face, insistent she get up and dress, and had turned away from the sadness in her eyes, too hard to witness, raging within himself at the unfairness of her plea tonight, their last night.

Why hadn't she said how she felt before? But before when? Before they'd even started seeing each other? Before he'd taught her to sail, when he'd take her out sailing after midnight when it was forbidden and dangerous?

Before they'd made love and lost their virginity to each other? As his thoughts whirled around him, Patrick had heard a noise outside. He froze and Katie raced to dress herself.

Patrick looked across to check she was fully clothed before he carefully opened the door of the boat shed.

The moon was full, suspended like a giant orb from an invisible line in the ink sky. Illuminating the water, the moon's beams caressing the sails of the yachts moored in the tiny marina like shadow puppets as the sails moved gently with the night's breeze.

Patrick looked from left to right but saw nothing other than an upturned fishing pot, which he assumed a cat had jumped into, perhaps hoping there was a little leftover catch in the bottom of the pot.

Katie was crying as she wrapped her coat around her shoulders. Shrugging off Patrick's attempt to comfort her, she had run ahead of him, away from the boat shed and up onto the road before disappearing from sight.

There was nothing Patrick could do to stop her going, and he'd turned back to the boat shed, retrieved the blanket from the floor, and restowed it on the boat before locking up and walking slowly home. It was not how his last night was meant to be, and he'd never felt so wretched.

· · ·

IN THE MORNING as his parents had driven out of town heading for Dublin and the airport, his eyes had searched the streets for her, hoping to catch one last glimpse.

His heart had been filled with such sorrow and anguish he'd hardly been able to utter words to his parents. They'd put it down to nerves at leaving, starting a new life in Edinburgh. He'd not even thought of Edinburgh, had hardly been able to pack his bag.

Carrick had cried off coming with them to Dublin, saying he was unwell and didn't want to be carsick. Patrick knew he was lying but didn't understand why, and when he'd gone to Carrick's room to say goodbye, he'd been asleep or pretending to be, so he'd tiptoed out of his room and silently closed the door.

PATRICK SCREWED the top back down on the thermos flask, packed it tightly in his backpack, and started his descent.

He thought he might take the kayak out when he got back if it wasn't too late. Just the single one his father stored in the shed. He'd enjoyed the peaceful calm out on the lough with his father and revisiting the memories of the past had made him feel unsettled. The water would soothe him as it always had done.

As he made his way down, his phone rang, and he stopped to retrieve it from his jacket pocket. A wintery sun's rays shone on the face of his phone so he couldn't see who was calling.

'Patrick Devlin.'

'Hello, Patrick. It's Julia.'

His heart churned like milk to butter at the sound of her voice.

'How lovely to hear from you. Everything okay—Jack, Finn...you?'

'We're all fine. I didn't get the chance to text or phone—well, actually, I tried on Christmas Day but couldn't get through. Bloody British Telecom.'

She laughed, and he could picture her standing in her kitchen with her apron on, as she had been that day he'd collected Jack, her hair pulled back in a ponytail, looking young and fresh. He wanted to reach down the phone and grab hold of her and kiss her with all the passion he'd been storing up for months every time he thought of her.

'Well, you've got me now. How was your Christmas?'

'You sound puffed. Where are you?'

'I'm walking down Mount Knockoumah. It's a bit steep in places.'

'Walking down, so presumably you walked up. Was that to walk off Christmas lunch?'

'Something like that. Tell me about your Christmas. Oh, and thank you, by the way, for the beautiful pen. It was the perfect gift for me.'

'You're welcome. My Christmas was lovely, low-key, peaceful, just what I needed. Jack has been locked away practising every day. He's played for us a couple of times. Can't believe how well he's handling the keyboard and the saxophone. Amazing.'

'That's music to my ears, if you'll excuse the pun. He's remarkable, and I'm looking forward to getting back and seeing how he's handled all the homework I gave him.'

'I think he's managing just fine—well, so he says—but you'll be the best judge of that. Anyway, I'll let you enjoy the rest of your steep decline. Just wanted to say hi and Merry Christmas. And to thank you for that beautiful box and drumsticks you gave Jack. I can't tell you how much it means to him. That was a truly lovely and generous thing to do, Patrick.'

'It was my pleasure. They couldn't have gone to anyone more deserving.'

'Oh, and also I wanted to say Finn isn't missing you at all. He's having daily walks across the fields, playing ball in the garden with Jack—when he can drag himself way from his music—so you needn't worry. I'll send you a picture of the two of them.'

'Thanks. I'd like that. Lovely of you to call. I'll come straight out to yours when I get back to pick Finn up, that is if I can pry him away from the two of you.'

'What time does your flight get in?'

'Can't remember the exact time, but I imagine I'll be out at your cottage by eight o'clock, something like that. Is that okay?'

'Sure. Do you want to stay for supper, or will you have eaten on the plane?'

'Supper with you and Jack is far preferable to an airline meal. That would be lovely, thank you.'

'Okay, see you then. Enjoy the rest of your time. Bye, Patrick.'

He smiled as he put his phone back in his jacket pocket. His memories of the past faded into the background, replaced by a rush of hope for the future.

WHEN PATRICK ARRIVED BACK from his hike, the day was closing in and his aching body told him to rest up for kayaking tomorrow.

'How was it, then, Paddy?' his mother asked as he walked into the kitchen.

'Grand, just grand. I'd forgotten how magnificent the view is from up there. Where's Pa?'

'Gone into town to have a pint with one of his old friends. I'll put supper aside for him, so you and I can dine together.'

'I'll have a shower first and then pour you a drink.'

His mother lent across from stirring the pot on the stove and kissed him on the cheek.

'It's lovely to have you home for Christmas, Paddy, it truly is.'

He reached out and hugged his mother to him. She always had a smell of lavender about her and it was no different now as he kissed the top of her head.

'I love you, Mammy. I'm sorry I'm not back as often as I should be. I'll make more of an effort in future.'

'Don't be daft, my boy. I know you're busy with the academy and the band and, of course, your charity work. I just...' She left the sentence unsaid, but he knew what she was going to say. *I would love you to settle down with a special woman in your life, Paddy...*

He'd disappointed his parents by not marrying, by not providing grandchildren. He knew they'd longed for at least one of their sons to produce grandchildren and both had failed.

After his shower and a change of clothes, Patrick poured his mother a red wine and they sat down by the fire to chat.

'I mentioned to Carrick, you know, when he visited, about the Fitzpatricks.'

Patrick could feel himself stiffen, but his interest was piqued, and he wanted to hear what his mother had to say.

'What about them?'

'Well, as I was saying to Carrick, Kevin Fitzpatrick died a while back, leaving poor Colleen to cope alone in a hospice. She never recovered, you know, from Katie, from Katie's death.'

Patrick wanted to leave the room. He didn't want to hear, didn't want to think of Katie's death.

'Kevin Fitzpatrick was a poor excuse for a human being.'

'Why do you and Carrick have such hatred for a dead man? Carrick was very bitter about him.'

'He used his wife as a punchbag, and when that wasn't enough, he started in on his daughter. He was a lazy, violent drunk. Probably Carrick feels just as strongly as I do.'

'How do you know all this? How do you even know Katie Fitzpatrick? You didn't go to the same schools or mix with the same crowd.'

Patrick realised immediately that this was something that had been gnawing away at his mother. She was circling the subject like a fox surveying a henhouse.

'What you really mean is she was from the wrong side of the tracks so how could we possibly be mixing with her?'

'That's not it at all. Doesn't matter to me where she came from,' she said indignantly. 'I'm just puzzled, that's all.'

'Kids all know each other, Mammy, whether we went to the same school, ran with the same crowd, it's all much the same in the end. Anyway, everyone in the village knew he beat his wife and daughter. You didn't have to be best friends to know about that.'

'Yes, you're right, of course. There was a lot of gossip about them, including some silly stuff about Carrick being sweet on Katie. I thought that was utter rubbish and said so to Carrick when he was here.'

'And what did he say?'

'I can't remember his exact words, but along the lines that people talk and make things up all the time about who's sweet on whom. He's right, of course. That is the character and sometimes the curse of a small village.'

'Indeed it is.' Patrick wanted to change to subject to something less fraught, but it seemed his mother was intent on talking about the Fitzpatricks.

'I can't imagine how that poor woman coped losing her only child. The spark went out of her. She didn't even have a body to bury. They never recovered anything other than the boat, a necklace, and her shoes. There were so many rumours at the time, nasty rumours, but the coroner ruled death by misadventure. I don't know why they refer to suicide as misadventure. It's a foolish way to describe someone feeling so miserable that life isn't worth living.'

She took a sip from her glass and gazed into the fireplace.

'She rowed out to sea in that creaky old boat of her father's. Some said she was heading for his fishing boat, but that can't have been right because it was on dry dock at the time getting repaired.'

PATRICK KNEW she would not have rowed out. The dinghy had an outboard. His mother was repeating a rumour.

'It was a long time ago Mammy. We'll not be finding any new truths now, will we, so let's talk about something else.'

Patrick felt sick. Images of Katie flashed before his eyes, her thin sinewy arms pulling hard on the oars of her father's old rowboat the way he'd watched her do countless times.

Her strength for a girl so slight had surprised him. Then they'd bought the outboard motor and rowing became something from the past. Where had she been going to that night? He was never sure she'd intentionally wanted to die, but something had made her go out on the water that night and never come back.

His father arrived home, and he sat up talking to him long after his mother had gone to bed. They reminisced about sailing together and driving Patrick to Dublin for music events he performed in. They were always by his side, always encouraging.

As a teenager he'd thought they were too strict. Like most teenagers, he'd wanted far more freedom than would have been good for him. They were right to hold onto the reins and not let him veer off course. His childhood had been a happy one, and for that he had his parents to thank.

PATRICK WENT to bed with a heavy heart. All this talk of Katie's death had been sad and unsettling, and he hoped his mother would not raise the subject again.

There were more rumours than what his mother had disclosed. Stories that had filtered back to him across the water to Edinburgh. Rumours that told of Carrick seeing Katie. That she was in the family way, that his little brother was in way over his head.

When confronted with these accusations, Carrick had vehemently denied them.

'We were friends, that's all. She needed a friend after you left,' Carrick had fired back, but Patrick knew he was keeping something from him.

He believed Katie had found comfort in his brother's arms and Carrick had welcomed her wholeheartedly. Patrick had found music to be his therapy. The most dedicated of all therapists, music was the balm to anoint his heart. It remained the one constant in his life.

IN THE MORNING, he rose early and went down to the shed to take out the single kayak. It was freezing cold but calm, and he thought the cold air and time on the water would settle the turmoil boiling away inside him.

He paddled around the lough, marvelling at the birds and the beauty of the place so peaceful at this time of day.

After breakfast he'd drive into the village and pick up the Newspapers for his father and then help his mother clean out the loft space.

She'd been nagging his father for months, apparently, without success. He'd help her; it was little enough given how much his mother had fussed and run around after him since he'd arrived. She'd enjoy sorting through the paraphernalia in the loft with her son by her side.

As he continued to paddle, his mother's words kept surfacing, looking for answers and forcing him to think back to the time of Katie's death.

After that awful last night, he'd not contacted Katie and he'd not returned home at the end of the first university term.

It wasn't a punishment, as Carrick had once accused him of it being. He really hadn't had the time to come back. He had music he needed to compose, instruments he needed to practise, theory he had to learn, plus he had landed a part-time job in a pub to help pay his university fees. There just wasn't the time.

He knew in his heart, whilst all of it had been true to a degree, it was a glaringly transparent excuse, not a punishment. He'd been hurt and disappointed with Katie for asking something of him that she must have known in her head he couldn't fulfil.

Sadly, it had been her heart, not her head, that had called out to him not to leave but he had silenced his heart with his reply.

He understood Carrick's hurt and anger. He'd been in love with her, just like Patrick had. Loving Katie had caused them both to miss out on so much in life. Marriage, children.

For Carrick a home in which to settle. At least Patrick had his apartment and was happy there, whereas Carrick seemed to wander the world as though he were still searching for her.

Patrick paddled back to shore for the warmth of his mother's kitchen and another of her hearty breakfasts. No good could come of thinking about what might have been.

. . .

A WHILE later he drove into the village and collected several papers for his father, which he placed on the passenger seat before locking the car and striding down the road, hands in pockets, shoulders hunched in his jacket, his breath trailing him in the cold air.

He walked past the old schoolhouse where he and Carrick had been raised. Little had changed—a new roof, perhaps, and probably double glazing, otherwise it remained much the same as he remembered. He strode on down towards the boat shed.

When he reached the place where he'd spent so much of his young life, it wasn't the image he'd remembered. It was bigger, grander somehow. Each time he returned home, he'd avoided this part of town, never wishing to fall down that rabbit hole of memories entwined with both happiness and tragedy.

His father's boat shed had been long sold, and the new owners had repainted it royal blue and white. It had always been black and white for as long as he could remember, but he was glad someone had updated it, moved on from the traditional, and given it a new lease of life.

He stood staring out at the water, remembering the nights when he and Katie would set sail late in the evening. The water dark and moody had made it all the more daring and exciting.

As he turned to leave, he glanced back at the boat shed once more and acknowledged it would never have worked between him and Katie.

When she'd asked him to stay, to attend a London university instead of Edinburgh, he'd subconsciously known that her avowed support for his musical ambitions was not deliberately insincere but lacked true depth of understanding as to what it meant to him.

Even at that supposedly carefree age he'd had his life all mapped out before him. If he worked hard at university, a career in music lay waiting for him, and he'd wanted that more than anything else.

Now, in the cold light of a winter's day in Baltimore, he admitted he'd wanted a life in music more than he'd wanted a life with Katie.

She would have been far happier with Carrick. He was the one brave enough to strike out on his own in London, and Katie would have been by his side because Carrick would have found a way to combine his dreams and his love for her.

What a terrible waste of three lives, Patrick thought as he made his way back to the car.

38

JULIA

As Julia drove back to the cottage with Jack and Finn, she felt relaxed and content. This had been a lovely Christmas, and she couldn't remember the last time she'd allowed herself the freedom to just *chill*.

She wouldn't go into the office, but there was some work she would need to do before the new year began.

Jack would be happy locked in his music room, taking breaks to walk Finn, and that would give her the freedom to work without feeling guilty.

She'd asked Jack before they left Lizzie's if he wanted to ask any of his friends over, but he'd firmly refused.

'No, Mum, I've got too much homework to complete for Mr Devlin and I'd far rather do that. I've got Finn, anyway. He's my friend for the holidays.' He'd smiled at her and run outside to give Finn a walk before they packed the car.

For once Chino wasn't howling in his cat cage. He seemed to draw comfort from having Finn sitting on the back seat with him. There were so many bonuses to having this dog around. Julia smiled to herself.

The call to Patrick on Boxing Day had been special, she admitted. When finally she did get hold of him, they'd had a lovely conversation, leaving her feeling pleased that she'd be seeing him before New Year's Eve.

Perhaps *pleased* was a little self-deceptive on her part, she thought as she pulled up outside the cottage. *Excited* might be more honest.

JULIA RECEIVED a text from Patrick to say he was leaving Heathrow and would probably be at the cottage within forty minutes, traffic permitting. Perfect timing, she thought. She'd made a traditional Irish stew, even going to the trouble of making her own soda bread to soak up the juices from the meat and vegetables, to be followed by a crème brûlée for dessert.

Beer and wine were chilling in the fridge, the fire was burning brightly in the lounge, and she'd lit some perfumed candles, making the whole cottage smell exotic.

SHE RETREATED upstairs to change into something more suitable. Her flour-dusted jeans and top looked somewhere between shabby chic and peasant housewife. Checking her watch, she thought there'd be just enough time for a quick shower.

As she soaped herself down, she realised she hadn't prepared a meal for a man since Nick left. *It is well overdue.* She smiled as she let the water wash off the soap before stepping out and towelling herself dry.

In her bedroom she pressed play on the CD player and the room filled with the sultry tones of Aretha Franklin singing "You Send Me." She loved this song and found herself singing her heart out and swaying her hips to the sensuous beat. Pulling her knickers on, she picked up her bra and swung it round her head as she sang the lyrics. *"I want you to marry me, please take me home, yeah, yeah, yeah."*

She fastened the hooks on her bra, still singing and swaying whilst pulling a lacy camisole over her head. The music was so loud she didn't hear the tap on her bedroom door and nearly jumped out of her skin when Jack put his head around the door, a huge grin spreading across his face.

'Wow, you're really getting into it, Mum. I did knock, by the way.' He was still grinning at her.

Julia began doing up the zip on her trousers before reaching for the silky shirt she'd chosen to wear.

'You gave me a fright. Just getting into the groove. Your old ma still enjoys a boogie, you know. I used to dance a lot back in the day'. She pulled the shirt over her camisole and slipped bare feet into suede loafers. As she stood in front of the mirror to put her earrings in, she could see Jack still standing in the doorway, his face a picture of amusement.

'What's so funny?'

'Nothing. I'm happy to see you so chilled. Wouldn't be anything to do with a guest coming to supper, would it?'

She looked at him through the mirror without turning around. 'I'm happy, that's all, but yes. It will be nice to see Mr Devlin, and I'm sure Finn will be thrilled to see him.'

'Well, I won't be thrilled to see Finn go back home. He's such a cool dog. I don't want to be disloyal, but he's much better behaved than I remember our Judas being.'

'Reluctantly, I have to agree. We never succeeded in training him out of some of his annoying habits. But we loved him all the same.'

Before they could speak further, they heard the sound of a car in the driveway. Jack turned and took the stairs two at a time. Julia laughed. He was as pleased to see Patrick as she was.

She checked herself once more in the mirror, sprayed some of the Angel perfume Lizzie and Michael had given her for Christmas across her chest and the back of her neck, and started downstairs.

She stopped halfway down as she saw Patrick standing in the kitchen looking up at her, a bottle of champagne in one hand and a package in the other.

He was wearing a beautifully cut sports jacket with a snug-fitting black tee shirt underneath, his long legs clad in tight jeans, emphasising his slim hips.

His eyes locked on her caused her to worry she wouldn't be able to make it further down the stairs. Her legs had turned to jelly and her heart was beating so fast she was sure it was visibly pulsating like in the cartoon film when Roger caught sight of Jessica Rabbit.

'Hello. You look beautiful.' He hadn't moved his gaze from her eyes, and they might have stayed caught in the moment if it hadn't been for Jack making a discreet cough as he held up three champagne glasses.

Julia moved her gaze to her son, his face a picture of elation, and she saw the approval in his eyes. She gathered herself and continued down the stairs.

'You look relaxed and refreshed,' Julia told Patrick. 'Ireland agrees with you.'

'I'll pour, if you like,' Jack said. 'May I have one as well, Mum?'

'Yes, you may, and thank you, Patrick, for bringing champagne. My favourite.' She smiled cheekily at him.

'I'll leave these on the benchtop for later.' He placed the wrapped box on the far corner of the bench before turning to Jack. 'Well, where's my dog, then?'

'He's sparked out in front of the fire with Chino. They're inseparable, so Finn will have to stay otherwise Chino will fret and probably die.'

Jack rolled his eyes at Patrick as he expertly pulled the cork from the bottle the way Michael had taught him.

'Oh, I see. Well, that's a dilemma, then, isn't it? Patrick said, a playful frown on his face.

Jack handed his mother a glass then gave one to Patrick before lifting his own glass holding it up towards his mother and his teacher.

'Here's to wonderful opportunities ahead in the new year for all of us.'

'Wow, that's a toast and a half.' Julia smiled. They sipped the champagne, savouring its creamy smoothness, each caught in their own private thoughts.

'I hope you're hungry?' Julia smiled at Patrick.

'I'm starving, actually. I haven't eaten since breakfast. Didn't want to spoil what I knew would be a great supper. So, Jack, tell me, how are you going with the homework I set you?'

'It's been challenging, but I've enjoyed it. I'd like to play something for you, maybe before supper if that's okay with you, Mum?'

'Sure. Shall we go through to your music room?' Julia had no idea what Jack was going to play for Patrick, but assumed it was one of the pieces he played over Christmas to Michael and Lizzie.

'Mum loves this song. It's been covered by a few people, but Mum's favourite is the Diana Krall version.'

Julia was lost for words. She had no idea Jack knew much about Diana Krall. Intrigued, she watched as he settled himself in front of the keyboard.

'I've arranged this myself using the synthesiser. See what you think.'

JULIA RECOGNISED THE PIECE IMMEDIATELY: "Just the Way You Are." It was her all-time favourite of Diana Krall's.

By the conclusion, she was fighting back the tears. The way he'd interpreted the piece, he'd brought in the drums and saxophone at exactly the right times. His playing was smooth and without fault.

She glanced across at Patrick. His expression was one of joy, of pride, of love as he moved across to Jack, still seated at the keyboard, and put his hand on his shoulder.

Jack leaned his head back into Patrick's body. Julia had never seen her son so relaxed with another male, other than Michael. She'd never once witnessed this closeness between Jack and his father. The contrast between the two men could not have been greater in that moment.

She continued to watch as Patrick bent his head down. She heard him say, 'That was sensational, Jack. I'm so immensely proud of you. This is just the beginning, my boy.' Jack stood and the two hugged.

Jack moved across to his mother and hugged her, holding her with a new strength she didn't know he had.

'You were amazing. I feel privileged that you've chosen a song I love so much and played it so beautifully.' She kissed the top of Jack's head.

'Will you keep Mr Devlin company while I get supper sorted?'

'Of course. We have lots to catch up on.' Jack smiled and danced through the doorway back out to the lounge.

WHEN JACK and Patrick went through to the lounge, Finn's head flicked up, his sleepy eyes adjusting to the image of his master standing in front of him. He whimpered with excitement, licking and whining as Patrick crouched down to talk to him and run his hands all over Finn's body.

'He's certainly pleased to see you,' Jack remarked.

'We've loved having him here. I shall miss him a lot.'

'I'm sure it won't be the last time you get to look after him. It's great for me knowing I can leave him with someone who cares for him in the way I do.'

With supper was over, they retired to the lounge for a coffee and opened Patrick's box of Belgian chocolates. Jack excused himself and went up to his bedroom to make a call to Dan.

'That was a beautiful meal. You're a good cook.' Patrick was sitting on the sofa opposite Julia, looking straight at her with his intense gaze.

'I enjoy it, when I've got someone to cook for. I'm afraid during the week when I'm on my own without Jack, I don't bother.'

She took a tentative sip of her hot coffee and put the cup down on the blanket chest that sat between the two sofas.

'He's sensational. You know that, don't you?'

'I'm blown away by his progress. To be honest, he locks himself away in that music room and I don't like to disturb him, so I have no idea what he's working on. That song, I can't believe he picked that out for me. It was beautiful.'

Julia felt her voice catch. She looked down, not wishing Patrick to see the tears that had sprung from nowhere and were welling in her eyes.

'What plans have you for New Year's Eve?'

'None. Well, apart from being at Lizzie and Michael's. We always go to theirs for Christmas and New Year. Lizzie loves entertaining—guess you probably figured that out?' She smiled, relieved he'd led the conversation away from the emotional subject of Jack.

'I'm gigging in London. Same thing every year. When do you start back at work?'

'Already have, in a way. Not in the office, but I've been working on some files while Jack has been locked away with his music.

I'll be back in the office the day after New Year's Day. I've got a lot on and some of our solicitors are away until mid-January.'

'When does the academy start up again? Do you have the same term time as school?'

'No. It doesn't work like that. I have adult students who attend university, so I make myself available from the third of January. That way, if they need additional tuition, I can accommodate it easily.

If Jack wants to come in outside term time, he's welcome too, of course.'

'Thank you. I'm sure he'd love that, although school isn't out for long at this time of the year.'

'You may have noticed there's a door at the back of the studio?'

She'd noticed it the first day she met Patrick and assumed it was some sort of entertaining area. She wondered where this conversation was going.

'Yes, I had noticed.'

'It's a recording studio, not very big, but it works well for the needs of the academy. Jack will have his turn in there before too long. His progress is astonishing.'

· · ·

Julia was watching him sitting on her sofa, relaxed and at ease. He made her feel the same, something she'd never felt with Nick, not even in the beginning. There'd always been an edge, a friction between the two of them. Patrick had a way of making her feel safe, secure, and he looked devilishly handsome tonight.

'I should be going. I've got rehearsals in the morning. It's been a delightful evening. Thank you again for taking care of Finn and for the lovely meal. I feel very spoilt, and here's me thinkin' I'd had plenty of spoilin' from me mammy.' He deliberately accentuated his Irish accent, making Julia laugh out loud.

'It's been my pleasure on all counts. I'll call Jack down. He'll want to say goodbye.'

They stood outside the cottage, waving as Patrick drove out of the driveway, and Julia wondered if Jack was feeling the same as she was, like someone had just removed a brightly burning candle from the room, the richness of life's colour bled away in the subdued light, the way their life had been before they met Patrick Devlin.

JACK

Jack was going across to Lizzie and Michael's for the day as his mother had to go into the office. He'd pleaded to stay at home and practise music, but she'd insisted he go to Lizzie's.

As a compromise, she'd sent a text message to Patrick asking if there was time available for an over enthusiastic pupil.

Just as they were about to leave, a reply had come back from Patrick saying he'd love to see Jack around 1 p.m. if that worked. Jack was delighted.

'Will Lizzie be able to drop me off and pick me up, do you think?'

'I'm sure she will, and then I'll be back as soon as I've finished work to get you, okay?'

'Fine. I've got plenty to keep me busy.'

When they pulled up at Lizzie's, Jack reached across the seat and kissed his mother before grabbing up his music papers and jumping from the car. He ran up the steps to the front door.

'So how are you, my gorgeous boy?' Lizzie asked him.

'I'm great, thank you. I've got a music lesson with Mr Devlin at 1 p.m. and Mum wondered if you would be able to drop me off and pick me up?'

'Sure, no problem. I didn't think you started back at the academy until term time?'

'Normally that would be the case, but I'm keen for another lesson and Mr Devlin was available.'

Lizzie made Jack a hot chocolate and they sat chatting in her kitchen.

'You know the night Mr Devlin came to supper, when he came back from Ireland?'

'Yes, I do.'

'Well, I went upstairs to see Mum; I could hear music playing and guess what?'

'I don't know. What?'

'I knocked on the door, but the music was so loud she didn't hear.' He took a sip of his hot chocolate.

'Is that it? She was playing loud music? Stone the crows!' Lizzie slapped her thigh.

Jack laughed at her antics. 'No, when I put my head round the door, she was boogieing away to the music and dancing around the room and singing really loud.'

Lizzie put her hands to her cheeks in mock horror. 'How outrageous! And a woman her age, having a good time! Whatever next?'

'You're nuts. It was just great to see her so chilled out. Since Dad left, it's like she got lost somewhere. She's so happy these days. I love this new, happier Mum.'

'I'm sure you do. I think it's difficult for you—or for any of us, come to think of it—to appreciate how tough it's been for her. Worrying about you and dealing with what your father did to her. It's a lot to deal with, and to come out the other side without bruises, it's a big ask, if you get what I mean?'

'Sure. I understand all of that. She doesn't have to worry about me anymore. I'm fine, I truly am.'

.   .   .

JACK WASN'T EXAGGERATING when he said this. When he started at the academy, he was still experiencing moments of often uncontrollable rage towards his father.

As the months had gone by and he was spending more and more time composing or playing, the anger and the bitterness and the bouts of rage had dissipated. He knew they could come back, but at that moment he was enjoying not carrying around every day the burden of all those negative emotions.

Music was like a bright light that left nowhere for dark thoughts in the shadows, and the more he immersed himself in music, the better he felt. It was the therapy that Mr Devlin had spoken of months before. Music, both the playing and the composing had healed Jack in ways that a fourteen-year-old boy could not describe.

'And do you know what else, Lizzie?'

'You're sounding like a right old gossip, like someone from *Coronation Street* telling the neighbours all the news. Well, go on then. I can't wait to hear more.'

'Well, Mr Devlin told Mum she looked beautiful.' He sat back in his chair, eyes sparkling like he'd made the revelation of the century.

'She is beautiful, though. He'd have to be the silliest person alive to not think that. So is that it? Is that all you've got?' she asked mischievously.

'Oh, you're not taking this seriously. I think he loves her, don't you?'

'I don't know, Jack. I don't know him well enough, nor have I seen him with your mum enough to be able to confirm that. How would you feel if he did—love her I mean?'

'I've thought about it a lot, actually. Well before that night. I suspected he fancied her, but now I think it's moved to love,' Jack said stoically, but noticed Lizzie having to look away. He was sure she was about to laugh, and he wondered if he could make her understand this was a serious conversation.

'You haven't answered my question. How would you feel about that?'

'I think it would be wonderful for Mum, if she wants him to love her, that is.'

'Yes, but how do you feel?'

'It feels okay; fine, in fact. I think he's the coolest man I know. Not saying Michael isn't cool, it's just different.'

Lizzie laughed. 'You don't have to apologise. Your relationship with Michael is special, but that doesn't mean you can't have other special relationships.'

'I guess what I'm trying to say is, if I had to choose someone for my mum to be happy with, well, to be in love with, Mr Devlin would be my first choice.'

'That's lovely, Jack. You are such an unselfish young man and so mature. I'm very proud of you.' She reached across the table and squeezed Jack's hand.

'Is there another hot chocolate on offer?' He grinned at her.

40

————

PATRICK

Patrick was looking forward to seeing Jack this afternoon. He had something he wanted to run by him, and he was keen to see how far he'd progressed with the homework he'd prepared for him prior to Christmas.

Despite Jack's confident response when he'd asked him that night at the cottage, he wanted to see for himself just how well he'd managed what had been set.

He'd been busy with rehearsals and playing on New Year's Eve and hadn't allowed himself the luxury of thinking about Julia and that lovely evening they'd shared.

He found if he had a lot on, he had to discipline himself not to think of her. She could so easily become a huge distraction. He was in love with her. But he would take it slowly. There was no rush and she was worth the wait, and he was still unsure how she felt about him. He'd read messages in her eyes, but then found himself questioning whether he'd imagined it or not.

.   .   .

As HE SAT GAZING out his studio window at the Thames, he realised he did not fear the feelings that welled up inside him whenever he thought of her, whenever he saw her. He would follow his heart this time, and whether they found each other or not, he was not going to run away from the opportunity to love and be loved again.

WHEN ONE WAS YOUNG, every feeling was intense, painted in 3D technicolour, volume control set at ten, and impossible to ignore.

Love was deep, hate was strong, anxiety could cripple, sadness overwhelmed. With age came a mellowing.

The feelings were all there, but the pictures were in pastel colours, the volume was set at a sensible four, and maturity had equipped you with the wisdom to tame the impulsive ways of love.

Patrick thought he had mastered good fun by enjoying selfish arms-length relationships, yet there he was, unable to deny that his emotions were fizzing, the colours were getting brighter, and his hand was itching to turn up that volume knob so that he could be uncontrollably young at heart and in love.

WHEN JACK ARRIVED, the two sat down and went through all the work Patrick had set him.

'You've done well. There are just one or two things which you need to progress further, but they're only minor and I'll go through those with you when term starts. No need to bother with it now. On a different matter, I wanted to run something by you.'

'Sure, what is it?' Jack looked expectantly at him.

'The piece you composed for your mum, the Grover Washington Junior one.'

'Yes. Did the band not like it?' Jack looked crestfallen.

'On the contrary. They enjoyed playing it. Your composition was very sophisticated, and I insisted they get it right and not improvise.'

'That's such a relief. Thank you.'

'Anyway, what I wanted to run past you: how would you feel if I got the band in here to the studio to play that piece for your mum?'

'Awesome. Really, you would do that?'

'I think it's important for you to hear something you have arranged yourself. To understand how that fits with all the musicians. How they have interpreted your arrangement.'

'Wow. That would be so cool. Mum would love that.'

'Do you think so?'

'Of course. Could Lizzie and Michael come as well?'

Patrick laughed. 'Of course, they can. I haven't sorted a date yet. I wanted to check with you first.'

'Thank you. I'm thrilled you and the band think it's good enough to play.'

'But one thing, Jack?'

'Yes?'

'This should be a surprise. Do you think you can manage that?'

'Sure. I won't say anything.'

JACK SAID his goodbyes and went downstairs to the street to wait for Lizzie. Patrick had several pupils to see and his teaching wouldn't be complete until early evening. Then he'd have to look at the calendar and work out when all the band members could fit in coming out to the studio to perform.

School term had started, and Patrick had only managed to find one night when all the band's members could make it out to his studio in Henley. He just hoped Julia would be free.

It wasn't so important if Lizzie and Michael couldn't make it, although he knew Jack would be disappointed, but Julia had to be here. He wanted her to see how much Jack had advanced.

Arranging Diana Krall's song had been clever, and Jack had played the piece so well, but this was a far bigger piece of musical arrangement where he'd had to write the score for all the instruments. It was an outstanding achievement for someone so young.

· · ·

As it eventuated, Julia had taken that day to work from home, and when Patrick had sent her a text to ask if she could drop by the studio to discuss Jack's term work, she'd responded immediately.

Jack had spoken with Lizzie and Michael and sworn them to secrecy so they would turn up at the studio just after Julia. The band would already be there, set up and ready to go.

When Julia arrived, she'd been taken aback at seeing a bunch of musicians tuning up on the small stage at the back of the studio and Hamish standing talking to Patrick.

'Sorry, did I get the time wrong?' She looked flustered, and Patrick took the opportunity to explain there would be a performance first, if she didn't mind.

'No, that's fine, of course. Hi, Hamish. How are you?' She went across and gave him a hug.

'I'm fine, Julia. Just catching up briefly with Paddy.'

The buzzer sounded and Patrick pressed the button to let Lizzie and Michael enter downstairs. He watched as Julia looked with astonishment and then dawning suspicion as they walked through the door, followed moments later by Jack emerging from the back room.

'So what is this? A coincidence, possibly, or have I been duped and we're all here for what, a performance of some sought?' Julia looked theatrically from Jack to Patrick.

Jack sat down beside his mother. 'We got you here under false pretences, I'm afraid. You'll just have to be patient, Mum.' He squeezed her hand and smiled.

Lizzie and Michael took their seats beside Julia and Jack, and Patrick left them to walk to the stage and pick up his guitar.

He leaned into the microphone.

'Thank you for coming, and I apologise, Julia, for leading you astray. It was a surprise Jack and I thought you would enjoy. This is my band, *Soft Rock and Blues*, and they've all made the time to come out to Henley tonight to play a piece which I am led to believe Jack's mother plays quite often.' Patrick beamed at Julia.

'Jack came to me a while back having rearranged this piece. He wrote all the score for every instrument, and we decided he should hear how his work sounds.'

THEY BEGAN TO PLAY, and Patrick sang. His eyes closed, immersing himself in the words.

When he opened his eyes, he looked straight at Julia. Beside her Jack was tapping out the rhythm, and Patrick could see he was listening to every beat, every sound the band was making. Leaning forward in his seat when the saxophonist played the solo part to the song, Jack's face, eyes closed, was a picture of ecstasy, lost in the moment.

WHEN THEY FINISHED to a standing ovation from the small group, Jack walked up to thank the band members individually, shaking their hands.

'What else can you do?' Lizzie called. 'Or have we given up our evening for just one song, albeit beautifully played?'

Patrick threw his head back and laughed. 'I'm sure we can pull a few tunes out of the hat for you, Lizzie. Why waste the opportunity? Might encourage you to come and watch us play.'

'Well, before you do, why don't I open a bottle of champagne to toast the composer here?' Hamish looked across at Jack.

'It's all chilled, Hamish, ready and waiting, and I'm sure our young musical arranger will help you serve. He's a dab hand at popping a cork.'

Patrick was in his element. This was the best the band had played this song. They'd realised how important this was for Patrick and his young pupil so were determined not to let either of them down. Now they'd have the opportunity to play some of their own stuff and perhaps win over some more fans.

41

———

JULIA

Julia made final edits to her report and emailed it to George. Marcus' employment with Petries was at an end. If he didn't get to a rehab clinic, then his legal career would also be at an end.

AT LUNCHTIME, Julia took a break from the tedium of spreadsheets and went downstairs to the kitchen to make herself a coffee and retrieve her homemade sandwich from the staff fridge.

As she passed reception on her way back to her office, hands full of coffee and sandwich, the receptionist held up a package that had just been delivered for her. Tucking it under her arm, she proceeded back to her office.

After placing her coffee and sandwich on the desk, she looked more closely at the package. She saw it was an international satchel from a law firm in New Zealand. *How odd* she thought.

Sitting down behind her desk, she took a sip of her coffee and bit into her sandwich, slowly turning the package round with her spare hand. She was still doing that when Maria walked into her office.

'What's that?' she asked as she came through the door with a file in her hand.

'Something from a legal firm in New Zealand.'

'You're treating it like it contains anthrax,' Maria said.

'Here's a novel idea: why not open it and find out what it is?'

'Why the sarcasm?' Julia gave Maria one of her withering stares.

'Sorry. I'm feeling a bit down about Marcus. I still can't believe he's got himself tied up with drugs. Not what I would have predicted. He could be arrogant, but I always believed his heart was in the right place when it came to clients, doing the best job he could for them and for Petries. Shows how wrong you can be.'

She slumped down in the chair looking dejected. Julia looked across at her as Maria twirled a strand of red hair around her index finger.

'You know, I thought it must have been an upset with that "Miss Perfect Jodie" that he was dating. He seemed quite serious about her. Don't you think?' Maria looked at Julia expectantly.

'Yes. That's how I missed the real issue. I put his sudden behaviour changes down to his love life. Big mistake on my part.'

'Don't go blaming yourself Julia. How could you possibly know he was snorting cocaine? How could any of us know? I hope George isn't giving you a hard time about it?'

'No. He's been really good. Worried of course, but glad we've been able to sort everything out with the minimum of fuss.'

'Well that's good then. I guess I should leave you in peace and get back to my desk, I've a few things to sort out before I take a lunch break. She moved away closing Julia's office door behind her.

Alone again, Julia took the last sip of her coffee and opened the satchel. On the top was a letter addressed to her.

Dear Ms Davis,

We are writing on behalf of our client, the late Grace Elizabeth Seddon, your aunt, who passed away peacefully on 26th December 2004.

As executors of her estate, we wish to inform you that as the only surviving relative, you are the sole beneficiary for the bulk of your aunt's estate.

We have enclosed a copy of your aunt's last Will and Testament and a list of items including personal effects which we will need your written authority to either sell in conjunction with the sale of her property in Oriental Bay, Wellington, New Zealand or that you arrange for the uplifting of same prior to the property being placed on the market for sale.

At your aunt's request, we have also enclosed documents of a personal nature which your aunt wished you to have at the time of her death or as soon thereafter as practicable.

You may, of course, wish to seek your own legal counsel to peruse our client's last Will and Testament and to advise on the list of items and personal effects. Your aunt was particular and precise in the handling of her estate and all items have been valued prior to her death, so we believe the figures are an accurate assessment as at the date of this letter.

We look forward to hearing from you at your earliest convenience. If you wish to discuss any of the above matters by phone, please contact Malcolm Braithwaite on the number listed above.

Yours faithfully

Malcolm Braithwaite

Braithwaite Stone & Lucas

JULIA WAS STUNNED. She had not seen or heard from her aunt Grace since she was a little girl, and how the hell had she tracked her down to England? She would phone this Malcolm Braithwaite and speak with him. In the meantime, she opened the long white envelope containing her aunt's Will.

Apart from the sum of $2,000 to the Cats Protection League, $2,000 to a Dog Sanctuary and Rescue Centre, $2,000 to the Wellington Arts Society, and $2000 to Hospice New Zealand, the remainder of her estate was gifted to *"my niece, Julia Anne Davis (nee Drummond)"*.

At the bottom of the second page, Julia read of her aunt's wishes once she had passed over.

I do not wish there to be any funeral in celebration of my life. I am to be cremated immediately following my death and my ashes retained and to be given to my niece, Julia Anne Davis (nee Drummond), to be scattered in England at a place of my niece's choice.

'Oh my God! How bizarre,' Julia exclaimed aloud.

She reread the Will several times before turning her attention to the list of items.

She gasped at the expected sale price for the auction of her aunt's apartment and was stunned at the figure estimated for a Tom Esplin original painting, *Chateau Vitre Brittany*.

In total there were four original paintings, two antique Georgian dressers, a French armoire, an antique clock of French design, two rings, four sets of earrings, and two necklaces, plus a large collection of vinyl LPs and a vintage Linn turntable. The remainder of items were basic household effects of little value.

She couldn't believe what she'd just read, so read it again to be sure she wasn't hallucinating.

It was the wrong time of the day to phone New Zealand, so she'd have to wait until this evening and phone Malcolm Braithwaite from home.

In the meantime, she had a lot of work to press on with. She folded the Will and returned it to its envelope along with the list of personal effects and put the satchel in her briefcase to read again once she was home.

Throughout the afternoon as Julia worked on budget predictions for her department for the remainder of the year, her mind kept wandering back to her aunt.

It was a shock not only to learn she had passed away, but that Julia had been the surviving relative to benefit. The amount she was to inherit was not trivial.

She had only faded memories of her aunt visiting when she was a little girl.

The very glamorous aunt sitting in their kitchen, taking tea with her mother and father, her dark hair piled high in what Julia now knew to be a chignon.

She dressed in wild, colourful clothing that had intrigued Julia as a little girl, and she'd been instantly drawn to this larger than life figure who plied herself and William with sweet treats and beautiful Christmas presents.

She had a vague recollection of visiting her aunt at her own home. It had been a large house with an equally large garden, which Julia remembered running around in with William and hiding behind big hedges and trees. That was the last she could recall of her encounters with her aunt.

As a little girl, Julia believed the mysterious aunt had vanished in a puff of smoke, never to be seen again like someone in a fairy tale.

She never knew why her aunt had stopped visiting and they in turn had stopped visiting her, but as a young child her curiosity was soon occupied by other matters and the aunt promptly forgotten about, as children do.

42

CARRICK

Carrick had flown into Heathrow the evening before and driven to his house in Lymington.

This morning he would phone Patrick and suggest they meet up for that pint he'd promised him. He only had a day to spare before flying out to Dublin to meet up with Liam who had phoned asking if he could return from New Zealand earlier than planned. He needed his help in Dublin.

'Morning big brother, hope I haven't caught you at a bad time?'

'No. I'm up and about. Where are you, still in New Zealand.'

'No. I'm home. Got in last night. I thought we might meet up for a pint later today. I promised you I would.'

Carrick was trying to sound casual and upbeat, but his heart was beating faster than usual.

The meeting with Patrick was not just about a pint and a chat. He had decided to take Liam's advice and tell his brother what really happened with Katie.

It was time, way overdue in fact, but the nervous tension inside him made him question once more if this was the right thing to do. Should he let sleeping dogs lie? The truth wasn't always helpful nor healing.

'That's a great idea. I've got lessons up until about 3 p.m. then I'm all yours. Where are you - in London?'

'No'. Carrick hesitated. Patrick had no idea that he owned a property in Lymington their estrangement for so many years meant Patrick new little if anything about Carrick's life.

'I'm in Lymington, but I'm coming up to London. I'm flying out to Dublin tomorrow evening.'

'Lymington. What's in Lymington. Have you got a woman stashed away there?'

'Chance would be a fine thing, so it would. No - I have a home here.'

Carrick heard the sharp intake of breath. Patrick would be surprised and probably confused as to why Carrick had never mentioned this before.

'Wow. Okay, maybe tell me about that when I see you. If you're coming up to London, why don't you get up here later today and stay the night. We can go to the pub or stay in and I can cook.'

'That's a great idea, but how about I cook. I seem to recall cooking was not your forte, unless you've been receiving lessons from Delia Smith.'

Patrick laughed loudly, making Carrick hold the phone away from his ear.

'You're right of course. You cook, I'll get the wine in.'

'Great see you around 4 p.m. then.'

Carrick disconnected the call and sat down at the kitchen table. He gazed out the kitchen window across the fields to the woods beyond content to sit for a moment and mull over the conversation.

Patrick sounded happy, warm and genuinely pleased his brother was coming to visit. This was a positive start to what Carrick sensed would be a difficult evening.

43

JULIA

Julia had a long conversation with Malcolm Braithwaite, the solicitor handling her aunt's estate, and felt she had a clearer understanding of the next steps.

She decided she would ask George to handle the matter on her behalf. It would allow her to keep a professional distance from the executors, and she preferred that.

When she opened the envelope in the satchel addressed to her, she found several pages of typewritten notes.

Dearest Julia,

I dare say you may not remember who I am, so for the benefit of clarity, I'm Grace Seddon, your mother's sister. I knew you and your brother William when you were very young. Due to circumstances which I will explain around your mother's decline, I was no longer allowed to see either of you, a circumstance which I found deeply saddening as you were both such delightful children.

.   .   .

I DIGRESS and should start at the beginning and write to you of your mother.

She was a gifted artist, attending art college with the intention of one day becoming recognised and earning a living from her paintings.

Unfortunately, your mother as a young woman was easily led. I blame this on our parents. They were will-o'-the-wisp people, too much money that they inherited making them irresponsible and reckless. One of Gandhi's seven deadly sins *"wealth without work"* This applied to our parents.

We were well loved but lacked boundaries and any sort of discipline. This impacted your mother more than I. Nevertheless, she worked hard to attain a place at art college and did well the first year.

By the second year she'd fallen in love with her art teacher, a married man. He knew what he was doing, so she was not the first young student to be seduced and certainly not the last.

Unfortunately, they were discovered, and those were times when women were frequently held responsible as the perpetrators of inappropriate relationships.

She was stood down from art college whilst the teacher remained with his job intact and reputation untarnished. She never picked up a paint brush again, which was a great tragedy.

I FOUND her a job at the law firm I was working at, Cullen, Jacob & Son, a typically chauvinistic example of the profession. I should have known better. I knew she was vulnerable, needy some might say, and too susceptible a girl to be working amongst such men.

Six months later I left the firm. I was off to London for adventure, and nothing and no one was going to stop me. Selfish now, when I think back. Age bestows one the wisdom to appreciate how different life may have been if only the impatience of youth hadn't dominated one's every thought and action.

It's about the only thing age has got going for it, wisdom…of sorts.

· · ·

Soon after starting at Cullen's, your mother met your father. I was never quite sure how that meeting came about. Your father said he met her when he delivered a piece of furniture to their offices that had been commissioned by Old Man Cullen, a letch whose eyes would settle on my bosom rather than my face every time I entered his office.

Your mother told everyone that she met your dad at a local dance. Your father was inherently shy by nature and had the misfortune to be born with two left feet, so I never believed that to be the manner of their meeting, merely assuming that she thought this story more glamorous than confessing to a chance encounter with a delivery boy.

Truth be told, your father was already making a name for himself with his beautiful creations, and while he liked to hand deliver to his clients, he was certainly no delivery boy.

Regardless, your father believed he was punching above his weight where your mother was concerned, and I suspect she encouraged such thoughts. Her own fragile self-esteem had not fully recovered after the art college debacle.

They loved each other of that I was sure. She wrote to me in England to tell me they were to marry and that, no, she wasn't pregnant; they just couldn't wait to set up house and become husband and wife.

I couldn't afford to return for the wedding, which took place in the local registry office. Nor did our parents attend, being uncontactable overseas somewhere at the time. It was sad for her, and for your father. Nevertheless, she wrote many letters to me expressing her joy at married life and then to tell me she was pregnant with William. I was so happy for her. At last she had found something to replace her love for art, a baby.

William was only two, I remember because I'd sent from England a beautiful little jacket for him which I'd saved up for months to buy. He was such a beautiful baby, all smiles and big eyes. The photos she sent me showed a little boy that had the perfect amount of the best features inherited from both parents.

SHE WROTE to tell me that she had been invited to Old Man Cullen's retirement party. I sensed that she was looking for validation of some sort - that she was clearly still viewed with appreciation and respect at Cullen, Jacob & Son and that they would probably wish to employ her again once her child reached school age.

I still remember when I read her letter, I had a feeling of foreboding. I'm not one for fanciful ideas of predicting the future. It wasn't something as mystical as that. I was afraid for her. I'd been glad to leave when I had, and the fact I hadn't insisted she leave at the same time and find employment in a less predatory environment has haunted me from that day until this.

JULIA WAS both shocked and intrigued reading the letter. There were pages and pages. She poured herself a wine, prepared a plate of crackers and cheese and settled herself in front of the fire and began to read further.

44

JACK

Jack had tried phoning his mother, but she didn't pick up, so he left a voice message and thought nothing more of it. He had plenty of homework to complete before he could return to the music room and continue with his piano practice.

The next evening when he'd still not received a text back from his mother, he tried calling again, but it rang out to voicemail. He then phoned Lizzie.

'Hi, Lizzie. It's me. Have you heard from Mum? I've been trying to get hold of her, but she's not picking up or returning my text messages. Do you think she's okay?'

'I haven't heard from her. But how about I try, and if I can't get through, I'll drive over to the cottage?'

'Would you? She's probably just busy with work. She's not had much time lately to talk to me. Lots of stuff on at work I think.'

'I'm sure she'll be fine. But I'll let you know.'

THE FOLLOWING AFTERNOON, Jack had his lesson with Mr Devlin. He felt out of sorts. He'd not heard back from Lizzie and nothing from his mother, and that was so unlike her.

He'd be glad when she finished whatever it was that she was working on. She was always so distracted at the weekends with work, and he'd been reluctant to interrupt even when he was dying to play her his latest piece.

'What's up, Jack? You're looking a bit solemn. Bad day at school?'

'No. It's Mum. I've been trying to get hold of her for days, but she's not answering my calls or text messages. She's just so busy with work she hasn't had time for me lately.'

'She's got a lot on. She certainly wouldn't mean to exclude you. Your mum's not like that. It was only recently you were complaining she spent too much time in your life.'

'You're right. I'm being a prat. I'll leave it until the weekend.'

Jack's lesson progressed well, with Mr Devlin setting him some additional tasks that were a lot harder than he'd tackled before, but this only excited him. He was finding these challenges Mr Devlin set him rewarding.

'You're my last pupil for the day, Jack. How about I drive you back to school?'

'That would be cool. Thank you.'

They chatted about music in the car and said their goodbyes at the school gate.

Jack felt relieved he'd raised his concerns about his mum to Mr Devlin. It was right of him to remind Jack that it hadn't been that long ago when he'd been complaining about her attention being an unwelcome intrusion in his life.

He was so wise, and Jack walked up to his dormitory settled and ready to start his evening homework.

45

PATRICK

Patrick left the studio and walked back to his apartment. He was looking forward to seeing Carrick and certainly intrigued about this property he owned in Lymington.

That had come as a complete surprise and made him realise there was so much about Carrick's life he didn't know - tonight would be the opportunity to rekindle the warm relationship he'd once shared with his brother.

EMPTY PLATES HAD BEEN PUSHED to the centre of the table along with one bottle of red wine now drained of its contents. Carrick was a good cook and Patrick had enjoyed the easy banter during their meal.

'Do you want another red, I've got plenty?'

'Why not, that last bottle was delightful.'

They retired to the lounge and sat opposite one another both taking a sip of the red wine Patrick had poured.

'You know when I went off to university – when I left home and left Katie behind. I thought my heart was going to break. It wasn't the departure I'd imagined. I was too immature to know how to fix it'.

273

Patrick looked across to Carrick expecting some response, but Carrick's face was blank, devoid of emotion.

'I used to think I'd seen her – Katie – in the street or sometimes even on campus. I wished so hard for it to be her, for her to have come and found me and to tell me everything would be alright – that the argument we had was a silly misunderstanding and she would wait for me. Wait until I returned from university. But that never happened and then it was all too late'.

Patrick dipped his head unable to control the sudden emotion that had welled up inside of him remembering back to a time that he'd spent years trying to erase.

'There were rumours – guys that had friends back in Baltimore. They said she was pregnant. Was that true?' He looked across to Carrick desperate now to learn of the truth.

'No. There was no truth in that rumour -and I didn't sleep with her either before you ask.'

'What did happen then. You may not want to go back to that time, but I need to know.'

'That's why I'm here Paddy. It's why I phoned. I want to find a way back to what we had and the only way that can happen is for you to know the truth'.

His voice sounded raw and edgy and Patrick steeled himself knowing what would come next may hurt even more.

'AFTER YOU LEFT and then didn't come back for the first university break, Katie believed it was over between the two of you. That you had used her. Led her on to believe she was the one and that your plans and dreams of escaping to London once you finished university had all been a lie. That you had only said all those things to get her to sleep with you.'

Carrick took a long sip of his wine. Patrick could see this was difficult for him, his mouth tightened, and his eyes held such sadness.

46

JULIA

T he fire was burning steadily. All Julia could hear was the sound of her heart beating rapidly and the crackling of the logs as she continued to read.

I WROTE BACK IMMEDIATELY WARNING her to be careful, but it was some months before I learned of what happened.

Your father wrote to me, the saddest letter I've ever received, and this is where the story, I'm afraid dear Julia, is going to break your heart.

You see, I don't want to go to my grave with you forever believing your mother didn't love you. She did, in her own damaged way. I use that term after deep consideration of the circumstances, because it was the harm inflicted on her that night that forced her to find comfort at the bottom of a bottle.

Your father hadn't been invited to the party. But he was shy, as I mentioned, and would probably have turned down an invitation, feeling inadequate in the presence of a crowd of egotistical lawyers so your mother attended alone.

I won't go into all the details, but as your mother was leaving, Old Man Cullen's youngest son, who I remember was a good looking but cocky young man, pulled her into his office. He raped her. She was left injured, humiliated and ashamed.

Your father went to the police. An investigation began but quickly fizzled out. That family were well-connected with influential people in the right places. They made public your mother's affair and dismissal from art college, and that question mark over her character was enough for the police to decide she'd encouraged the act. That what had taken place in that office had been consensual.

Shortly after, she realised she was pregnant and she knew, as only a woman can, that this pregnancy was the result of that assault and rape. She spoke to your father about an abortion, but it wasn't easy back then. It wasn't legal, and your father forbade it in fear for her safety should she visit one of those back-street establishments that existed for desperate women.

Your father, Julia, was a saint. A very special human being. He loved your mother unconditionally, something young people don't seem to understand these days. Your mother was inconsolable. She wrote to me of her pain, of her humiliation in her home town and for the growing baby inside her belly that so frightened her.

When you were born your mother had a bad case of the baby blues. It's now called postnatal depression, but in our day it was the baby blues and you were expected to just pull yourself together and run the household.

Well, she didn't and your father found himself mothering both you and William for months until I came back from England. I was so worried for my sister and for you and William that I willingly gave up my life over there and returned home to help as best I could.

Eventually the depression lifted, but she found a glass of sherry dulled her shame and helped her through the day. You know the rest. It didn't stop at sherry, or a glass.

Your father adored you, please believe that. He told me once that every time he looked into your eyes he saw his beautiful wife, because as I recall you have your mother's eyes, but you also bore a slight resemblance to your birth father, a daily reminder for your mother as to the act that conceived you.

Your mother told me once, when you were a baby, she couldn't bear to show you love, even though her heart was filled with it for you. She feared that to do so was an act of betrayal to her husband, that he may believe what the police had said, that it had been consensual, that she had willingly given her body to another man that terrible night.

She was so afraid he would stop loving her that she withheld any outward display of loving you whilst in her heart she longed to. The conflict drove her deep into despair - the demons of shame and guilt tormenting her until the day she died.

This may aid your understanding of why your decision to become a lawyer unknowingly rubbed salt in her wound, emulating her violator rather than her, the violated. Your father would write to me on occasion to tell me of these things relieving himself of the pressure of seeing and knowing so much and feeling powerless to do anything about it.

So, my dear niece, I fear you may never forgive me for burdening you with the truth. I've written to you because I've always believed you should know.

Your father forbade me to tell you and, to my eternal regret, following a heated exchange he banned me from their home and from ever seeing yourself or William again.

I tried to understand that he did not act out of malice, but to protect his wife. However, I cannot deny that it hurt me deeply, so I moved to Wellington, far away from their lives, and that is where I have stayed.

Now I'm an old woman preparing to meet my maker, and the bitterness I harboured for many years has dissipated with time.

I know what it is to love and be loved, but I never wished to be married. I didn't get to fulfil my dreams of completing my art conservation degree; that's what I was doing in England, but I have never regretted returning home for my sister. I loved her and regret that I was unable to help keep her from the dark place in which she found herself.

I've spent the remainder of my career at the Te Papa Museum and what a fine place to spend one's working life. I've been a lucky woman.

If I have a regret at all, It was not finding the courage to seek you out sooner but I loved your father the way one would love a brother and did not wish to be responsible for causing more pain if this secret was exposed while he was still alive.

I didn't know of his death until well after the funeral. I once would have found it difficult to forgive my sister for that unkindness, but I have chosen to let it go. Life is too short to squander it on wounded emotions; it really is.

I instructed my solicitors to send a copy of my Will, this letter, and the letters your mother wrote to you. She wrote quite a few and kept them hidden away. They only came to light after she died, and I was sent her personal effects as the next of kin listed on her hospital forms.

Don't think less of me for reading them. I did so in case any had been written in anger and wished only to prevent further unnecessary pain. Had that been the case, I would have burnt them without a moment's hesitation or one moment of remorse. However, as you will find, they are quite the opposite.

I must stop now, I'm tired and quite weak. I believe you have a right to know the truth that however awful your childhood was, and I believe that it was, beneath the humiliation and anger at her own circumstances, your mother loved you deeply.

I want to believe I've done the right thing in sharing this story with you. Don't people say that it is the height of selfishness to unburden yourself of the truth with no regard for the burden you thereby place upon the recipient? I

will have passed by the time you have this letter in your hands. My time has come but I have no fear of dying. I do, however, fear that you will find the revealing of this secret a burden and curse me for my selfishness. If that is so, please forgive my poor judgement.

Please go in peace and be gentle on yourself.

With love

Grace

47

———

PATRICK

It was difficult for Patrick to accept that Katie had so quickly given up on their relationship, content instead to think the worst of him.

'I realised when I got to know her better – not as a girlfriend – as a friend – that she was broken. She would never have gone to London with you. She would never have left her mother. I tried to convince her to leave to get away from Baltimore, go to Dublin, London – anywhere to get away from that awful bastard of a father.'

Patrick could feel his stomach knot at the mention of Katie's father and images of the bruises, her tears and her fear flashed before his eyes as though it were only yesterday.

'I gave her money – money I'd saved. It wasn't much, but I thought it would help get her a train fare to somewhere and enough for a month's rent if she took a room some place out of reach. Somewhere she could start a new life.'

'Did she take it?'

'Yes. She took it, whether she would have used it for what I'd intended, we will never know. We argued – Katie and I'.

Carrick stopped and lay his head back against the chair. Patrick noticed his hand was shaking, making the red wine tremble in his glass.

'What did you argue about – me or her father?'

'You. I was angry with her, furious in fact. She kept saying you had used her and dumped her like a worthless piece of meat.'

Patrick sat up, leaning forward his head down and his hands clenched in front of him.

'I told her that you'd never do that. That you loved her deeply. I knew you did, but by then I realised she would have been wrong for you. She'd have held you back.'

'Thank you for defending me. I would never use any woman in that way and especially not Katie. Why did she go out in that boat, why would she drown herself? She was a Catholic, whether she believed wholeheartedly in her religion or not, suicide was not something she would do.'

'When I gave her the money, I told her to go – to leave town and if she didn't there was nothing more I could do for her. It was cruel of me to be so harsh, but I couldn't stand hearing her denigrate you in the way she did. I realised she was not the girl I thought she was and not the girl I had foolishly fallen in love with.'

Carrick rose from his chair. 'I need the bathroom, back in a minute.'

As Patrick waited for his return, he reflected on what Carrick had told him. He was saddened to learn Katie had viewed him in such a disparaging way. It was not what he'd expected and he didn't know how to deal with the emotions that washed over him in waves as the story unfolded.

CARRICK RETURNED, sitting back down, he cradled his wine glass in both hands.

'A few days after I gave her the money, her father came home and ransacked the house looking for pennies to go back to the pub for another pint. He found the money I'd given her. Katie had hidden it in a shoebox in her wardrobe. There was no safe place to hide anything from that bastard.'

Carrick stopped and looked at Patrick. 'He beat her when she wouldn't tell him where she got it from, thought she'd been on the game.'

'Christ. Jesus and Mary. She would be the last girl in Baltimore to be on the game. He was a vicious sod. I'm glad he's dead.' Patrick said, his voice raw with pain.

'I SAW her running from the house towards the boat shed. She was a mess. I offered to take her to the doctor, but she wouldn't hear of it. All she kept saying was *"he's taken my money, all of it, there is no escaping now"*.

I stayed with her at the boat shed until late and then walked her back home. I should have done more. I should have found a way to get her out of there, but I didn't - the rest you know.'

Carrick took a deep breath before releasing a heavy sigh. 'She obviously felt drowning herself was the only way she could escape her life and for that I will be forever sorry that I didn't do more.'

Patrick waited as Carrick collected his thoughts.

'I saw her, the night she disappeared. I was walking home along the pier. I heard the sound of an outboard. If you knew the number of times I've revisited that moment – the moment when I could have run to our shed and taken out our boat. Stopped her. Saved her.' He dropped his head and cried, his shoulders shuddering with emotion.

PATRICK RESTED his glass on the table and walked across to Carrick. Carrick stood and they embraced.

'It's not your fault Carrick. None of it was. I'm sorry I misjudged you for all these years. I never gave you the opportunity to tell me what happened. I was content to believe the rumours and it was easy to blame you.'

Carrick gently eased himself away from the embrace wiping his hand across his face.

'It's TAKEN me a long time to acknowledge that music was my first love, still is and that Katie couldn't compete with that. She used to encourage me, and I believed she meant it. Now I look back and realise how naïve I was. It's what she thought she should say, what she thought she should think – it was not what was in her heart. We came from such a happy home. A loving childhood. How could either of us have imagined what her life was like. She was broken from the start and nothing either of us could do would have changed that. You must not blame yourself Carrick for any of this. We have to let it go now, both of us.'

THE TWO SAT up until late reminiscing, sometimes shedding tears and sometimes laughing uproariously remembering their silly antics as young boys.

The evening had been cathartic for both men and they could now move forward with their lives, rekindling their love for each other and making new memories.

48

JULIA

Julia lay face down on the floor in front of the fire, numbed. She'd run the gamut of screaming, crying, and raging and now lay spent, realising her entire childhood had been a lie. *A great fucking lie!*

Her phone had been ringing and beeping to confirm messages had been left, but she couldn't face speaking to anyone.

THE NEXT MORNING Julia woke with an aching body and a blinding headache. She phoned Maria to say she was ill and wouldn't be in. The call was short and blunt.

She did not want a prolonged conversation with Maria about the state of her health. She then went back to bed and lay there contemplating what she now knew of her family.

The bastard child of a rape victim. *It doesn't get much worse than that.* Her eyes filled with fast, sharp tears. She was yet to read her mother's letters.

They lay spread out on the kitchen table like a poker hand. The fact that they had passed Grace's censorship didn't take away the feeling of trepidation. Right now she sure wasn't feeling too lucky.

By mid-morning, she'd visited the toilet three times and vomited up everything she'd recently eaten, including bits she was certain she hadn't.

A knock on the door made her sit up in bed too quickly, causing a pain like she'd been stabbed in the eye. She decided to ignore the door. Probably Mormons calling to preach and hand her the *Kingdom of God* pamphlet so she could be saved from evil.

'Well, too bloody late,' she muttered to herself.

She wondered what they would say if she announced, 'I've just discovered my father is not my real father and I'm the child of a rape victim. How does your God deal with that one?'

The knocking continued until finally she climbed out of bed, pulled her dressing gown around her, and went downstairs. Lizzie was standing outside, looking agitated and freezing cold.

'God, you look awful. So you are sick, then?'

'Looks like it. Come in.'

Lizzie walked directly through to the lounge and stood in front of the fire, warming her tiny frame.

'I've been calling you and getting no response. I called the office and Maria said you were sick. I thought I'd check in case you wanted me to get you anything. Julia, are you okay?'

Julia stood in the doorway, tears streaming down her face.

'What's the matter? What's happened?'

She handed Lizzie her aunt's letter and left the room to use the bathroom and shower. She felt unclean in more ways than one.

When she finished showering, she dressed quickly. Coming back down, she found Lizzie standing in the kitchen, waiting for her.

'I don't know what to say. This is an enormous shock.'

Julia brushed past her and went back into the lounge and sat down.

'As if that isn't enough, there is more. The letters, I haven't read them yet.'

'Do you want to, while I'm here? It might be easier with someone to talk to.'

Julia ignored the question. 'How am I going to tell Jack that the person I believed to be my father, his grandfather, is a fraud? It was all a big lie.'

'Stop that, Julia. That's ridiculous. Your father loved you more than you could have dreamed of. Whether he was biological or not is irrelevant. He taught you how to love, and that's why you're such a great mother. It was his parenting. I remember how he was, don't forget that. I was there, I saw how he adored you, and think how amazing that is now that you know what you know. He's still *Julia's dad* to me, and so he should be to you.'

Julia began to cry again. She wondered how one body could keep producing so many tears, just when she thought she was all cried out.

'Come on, let's read them together. You've always tackled problems head on, and I'm here, right by your side.'

Lizzie hugged Julia. The two sat holding each other before Julia went to the kitchen and retrieved the letters. There were six in total.

By early evening, Julia and Lizzie had read all six letters, one for every year up until age six. She realised that was when her mother had begun to drink to excess, and the violence and rages had taken over from the undemonstrative but gentle mother.

'How do you feel now that you've read them all?'

'Numb. I don't know, too many emotions to list. I guess I have to work through this until I come out the other side.'

'I think you will need to see someone, Julia. This is huge. It's not something you can handle on your own. I know you thought you didn't need counselling after Nick, but I've always believed you did, and now I'm going to insist you see someone.'

'Maybe you're right. I'll think about it. Do you want something to eat or is Michael waiting for you?'

Julia wished to change the subject. Psychologists, counsellors, whatever—how could she possibly sit down with some unknown person and divulge such personal information?

'No. He's got late surgery tonight. How about I see what you have in the fridge, which, knowing you on a weekday, will be nothing? I'll see what I can rustle up from nothing, shall I?'

But Julia wasn't listening, lost in jumbled thoughts and unanswered questions.

49

PATRICK

It was Friday night and the band were playing at the club up in London. He'd heard nothing further from Jack so assumed he'd managed to get in touch with his mother, but the conversation with Jack earlier in the week had bothered Patrick.

It wasn't like Julia to ignore her son. Something big must be happening at work and that was occupying every spare minute of her time?

The band opened with a Christian Willisohn version of a blues number called "Blues in My Bottle". The club was full, with only a few tables left. They'd drawn a great crowd.

It was near the end of the first set when they were performing an old blues song -"The Sky is Crying" that he saw Julia in the audience. She looked pale and tired, her face showing the strain of long hours at work, he thought, but he was thrilled to see her sitting there.

He finished the song and noticed her hand raised to her cheek as though she were brushing something away.

She was alone, filling her glass from the bottle of wine on the table, she wasn't looking at the stage. Instead, she appeared consumed with her own private thoughts.

They started the next song by Gary Moore, "The Hurt Inside." As he sang the lyrics, he watched her face change, twisting into a grimace as the words he was singing appeared to resonate at a primal level with her.

All those nights so lonely, the tears that you cry, you can't hide from the hurt inside.

As he reached the end of the song, he watched with dismay as she pushed back her chair, took her bag, and headed towards the door, squeezing between tables as she went.

With the last melancholy chord still fading, he signalled to the band he needed to take a break. He quickly unfastened his guitar and almost ran from the stage, out and up the stairs, catching her just as she was about to disappear into the night.

'Julia. Julia, stop! What's wrong? What's happened?'

She turned to him, and he could see she was crying, her body shaking. He went to her, pulling her into his chest, holding her head against his heart and stroking her hair.

'It's okay. I'm here. You'll be okay. Please don't go. I've only two more songs and we're finished for the night.'

'I can't go back in. I'm a mess.'

'It's fine. You don't have to. Come with me. There's a room out the back that's private. You'll be safe in there until I'm finished.'

He led her backstage to a small room, making sure she was comfortable, finding a glass and filling it with water. The heating was on and the room was dimly lit and cosy. She'd be fine there until he came back.

'Promise me you won't leave until I'm back? I don't want you going home like this.'

'Thank you. I'll wait. Promise.' She looked up at him through her tears and smudged mascara.

Patrick rejoined the band on stage, and they struck up the George Benson song "This Masquerade."

The crowd applauded, enjoying the slow tempo. Their last number for the night was Santana's "Love of My Life," at the conclusion of which the band left the stage to a standing ovation. Patrick excused himself, almost running to the back room.

He was half expecting that she had gone. He was relieved when he saw her sitting there in the dim light, her eyes closed. When he went across the room to her, she stood, looking embarrassed.

'My car is out back. I think I should get you home,' he said.

'Thank you. I'd appreciate you driving me. I've had too much to drink and I don't fancy catching a train in this state.'

It wasn't until they were out of the London traffic and on the M4 back to Berkshire that Patrick glanced across at her. She had a dazed look on her face as she stared ahead.

'Do you want to talk, tell me what's wrong?'

'I don't normally drink very much. Lizzie will tell you I can't handle my booze; she'd be right. I'm not like my mother.'

Patrick had no idea what her mother had to do with it, but he'd shut up and listen.

'I don't know where to start or even if I should start.'

'Okay. If you want to sit and relax, that's fine. Either way, I'm here for you.'

She looked across at him, her face a portrait of pain and sorrow, making Patrick choke with emotion. He couldn't bear to see her like this. Whatever it was, it was big, and he only hoped she would trust him enough to talk.

When they pulled up outside the cottage, he saw her inside.

'Would you like a coffee?' she asked.

'That would be lovely, if you don't mind?'

'It's the least I can do to thank you for bringing me home safely.'

They sat up most of the night, talking. She cried like a wounded animal, and it took all Patrick's emotional strength not to cry with her.

By morning she was all cried out and sleeping peacefully on the sofa. He'd found a blanket upstairs to cover her. Putting more wood on the fire, he stretched out on the other sofa and sleep soon overtook him.

· · ·

HE WOKE to the smell of fresh coffee. After pulling himself up and stretching, he padded out to the kitchen.

She was standing with her back to him. She'd changed and showered as her hair was still wet and had been pulled up into a ponytail. She was wearing tight jeans and a long pink jumper that came down over her slim hips.

'Good morning.'

She turned, startled, her face reflecting her wretchedness as she attempted a smile. He wanted to stride across the kitchen, pull her into his arms, and kiss that beautiful mouth.

'Are you hungry? I've made porridge,' Julia asked, turning back to the stove to continue stirring.

'Starving, and I love porridge. I'll have to give you my culinary review. See if it's as good as my mammy makes,' he said, trying to lighten the moment.

They sat at the table together, eating in companionable silence. After pouring coffee for them both, she spoke.

'Thank you for rescuing me last night. For listening, for everything.'

'My pleasure. I can't imagine what a shock all of this must be for you. But you'll get through. You're strong and you are surrounded by people who care for you and love you.'

'Would you be one of those people?'

'What? A person who cares for you, or...is that what you're asking?'

'Yes. That's exactly what I'm asking.'

She stood, and Patrick pulled his chair back and closed the gap between them. He took her in his arms and kissed her tenderly at first before he was overcome by the months of longing for her and his kiss became passionate. He traced his fingers across her lips where his own had just been, cementing his love.

He ran his fingers through her hair, releasing it from the ponytail and letting it fall to her shoulders, he kissed her neck, her face and heard her moan with pleasure

'Yes. I do love you, more than you can possibly imagine.'

50

JULIA

Easter was early the year of 2005. Julia had booked flights to New Zealand for herself and Jack. St Julian's had a month of holiday including the Easter break so it was the perfect time to head away. It was late March, early autumn in New Zealand and still warm she hoped.

As they taxied down the runway she looked across at Jack who was busy trying to figure out how his headphones worked. They would be gone three weeks. He would miss his music, but the excitement of an overseas trip had in part, made up for not having his instruments to hand.

It had been a big decision – a scary decision for Julia to return to New Zealand. She'd not been back since she left with Jack. All those years ago - waving goodbye to Nick at Christchurch airport – now he was her ex-husband.

Little did she know back then it would take six months before

Nick would join herself and Jack in England and her world would be changed forever.

Lizzie had wanted to accompany her, but she'd declined the offer much to Lizzie's annoyance. It was important she do this with Jack. It was their time. Time to return to the place of their birth and bury the skeletons from the past that had prevented Julia from venturing anywhere near her country of birth.

Jack had been pensive at first, afraid she would suggest that he visit his father who had now returned to live in New Zealand after years in Tokyo. That was never on the agenda as far as Julia was concerned.

They would be flying into Wellington. After that she knew what she had to do. What she wanted to do. There was a grave to find and words to be spoken.

Lizzie would look after Chino and check on the cottage weekly. It was Patrick who filled her thoughts as their plane rose, banking steeply away from the terminal.

He had been wonderful since that night he'd brought her home from the club. She couldn't fault his tenderness - his kindness and she knew he loved her – but was she ready for a relationship?

She loved him, of that she was sure, but living together - that was a different matter. Right now she had to focus on finalising her aunt's affairs. Selling the apartment. Deciding what to do with the items she'd been bequeathed. There was a lot to consider.

Malcolm Braithwaite was tall and lean. He wore a bright pink shirt beneath a beautifully cut expensive suit. A purple silk square sat perfectly straight in the pocket of his jacket. His blonde hair was cut short and neatly combed to one side and his eyes were blue. Gentle, kind eyes that matched the sound of his voice. Julia could appreciate why her aunt had put so much trust in Malcolm.

SINCE THE TIME Julia had received the news of her aunt's death she had been in contact with Malcolm on a regular basis. Despite George handling the legal matters, Malcolm had made a point of contacting Julia personally. *"Just checking in"*. He would say. *"It's what Grace would have wanted me to do"*.

She understood why. It had been soothing for Julia to hear Malcolm's calm measured voice over the phone. He reminded her of William and now standing in front of him she could see why. He looked nothing like her big brother, but it was obvious he was gay as William had been.

THE EARLY ARRIVAL and busy morning were having an effect on both Julia and Jack. It was difficult to stay awake in Malcolm's car as he drove them to her aunt's apartment in Oriental Bay. They would stay there. Malcolm had insisted it is what Grace would have wanted. Cleaners would come in after they left and then the property would be listed for sale.

After Malcolm had shown them around, Julia and Jack headed for bed. It was late afternoon and Julia knew they really ought to try and stay awake until at least early evening to avoid the worst effects of jetlag but neither of them could keep their eyes open a moment longer.

JULIA THOUGHT it might be odd, almost creepy sleeping in a deceased person's bed, but the whole apartment felt like a luxury hotel. Malcolm had made sure of that. Photos and other personal items had been packed away and all that remained were the essentials for a short stay.

When Julia woke it was after 7 p.m. Jack was still fast asleep and she debated whether to wake him or not. She decided to leave him for another half hour and explore the apartment on her own.

There had been a lot to take in when Malcolm had shown them around earlier. She could now study the furniture and paintings her aunt Grace had bequeathed in her own time and in the quiet comfort of her own thoughts.

The items of furniture were beautiful and the art breathtaking, particularly the Tom Esplin. Julia had always loved his work but never dreamed she'd own an original.

She decided she'd keep it all and have it shipped back to the UK.

Malcolm had stored her aunt's jewellery, photographs and other mementoes in a safe in his office. They would also be shipped back along with her aunt's ashes.

Just where she would scatter them, she didn't know, but believed when the time was right she would know in her heart where to go.

She looked out through the stacker doors to Oriental Bay. The night had drawn in, but the night lights sparkled and glimmered across the water. It was a beautiful view and she could appreciate why Grace had loved living here.

They spent several days exploring Wellington. Visiting Te Papa where Grace had worked for many years and meeting staff who remembered Grace and were able to share stories with Julia and Jack painting a picture of the aunt Julia barely remembered.

JULIA HAD BOOKED flights to Kerikeri after talking with Malcolm who had kindly given her the keys to his holiday house which he insisted they use. She would hire a car when they arrived so they could explore easily.

Malcolm's idea of a *little holiday place* was quite the opposite. The property was large, elevated with private water access.

The views were glorious and Jack had quickly unpacked, changed and as she watched from the balcony, strapped on a lifejacket and carried the kayak down to the water. 'Be careful.' Julia called, 'you're not used to kayaking.'

Jack looked back at her, his arm up to his face to shield the sun. 'I learnt at school, remember?'

'Oh, of course you did. Sorry, silly me.'

She smiled back at him feeling relaxed in a way she hadn't in a very long time. Coming back to New Zealand had been a far better experience that she could have imagined.

All those years she's spent haunted by a past she wanted to forget - now she was here seemed silly and overly emotional. It was different being in the North Island and she was aware she may have differing feelings had she been forced to go back to the South Island.

THEY SPENT days on the water kayaking and Julia even tried her hand at paddle boarding, although spent more time in the water than on the board.

They took a tour to Cape Brett and the *Hole* in the *Rock* on Piercy Island. Jack learned more about the history of his country of birth and relished giving Julia a history lesson over dinner each evening.

The weeks had passed quickly, and it was now time to travel to Russell. Julia had been bracing herself for this visit.

SHE'D LEARNED from Malcolm that her mother's ashes had been buried at the Russell cemetery. Grace had shared with him childhood memories of wonderful holidays in the Bay of Islands. It was a place her sister had always longed to revisit.

Grace had only learned of her sister's wishes after she died when Grace received her personal effects. There had been no money in the estate so Grace had paid what was necessary to ensure her dead sister's wishes could be fulfilled.

Malcolm had accompanied Grace to Russell where they buried the ashes of Julia's mother and erected a small tombstone in her honour. *"It was a sad day"*, Malcolm had recalled. *"Grace was quite distressed. She still felt guilty for having not protected your mother. She carried that guilt to her grave"*.

.   .   .

Julia believed she could have been entering a cemetery in an English country hamlet as she pushed the gate open. Its tiny white church, manicured grounds, neat and lovingly kept graves sitting at the top of the ridge overlooking Long Beach was stunningly beautiful as much as it was peaceful.

The sun was directly overhead and warm on Julia's face without being too hot. A soft breeze brushed against her bare arms. As she read the words engraved on her mother's tombstone a feeling of peace settled over her heart.

'Look mum', Jack said.

Julia glanced up and saw a fantail perched on the top of the tombstone. It fluttered its wings but made no move to fly away. Julia stepped back and placed the flowers she'd bought in an old glass jar Jack had found stacked to one side of the church.

'Hello Mum. I've brought flowers, I think they're the sort you liked. What I remember Dad bringing in from the garden for you. My son Jack, your grandson is here with me. You would be proud of him. He's a wonderful musician. I remember you loved music once'.

She hesitated for a moment before carrying on. 'I've come to say goodbye and to wish you peace at long last. I also wanted to tell you that I love you'.

Her voice shook as she stumbled over the last words. Jack took her hand, his head down saying his own little prayer to a grandmother he never knew. They stood in silence for some time each lost in their own thoughts.

As they walked away the fantail fluttered above their heads until they reached the gate. Julia turned and watched it fly back to her mother's tombstone. *She has company. I remember she loved fantails.*

EPILOGUE

~

Two years later, Julia, Lizzie, Michael, Maria, Carrick Devlin, and Susan Neeson were seated together in the club in London. Michael opened several bottles of champagne, and as he filled everyone's glass, the band walked out on stage.

'Tonight, ladies and gentlemen, we have Mr Hamish Neeson on drums and a guest artist performing on sax. Please stand and give a warm welcome to Mr Jack Davis.'

Jack walked out on stage, his saxophone under one arm, raising his free hand to acknowledge the audience. He locked eyes with his mother, exchanging a look only a mother and son knew the true meaning of.

'This song has been arranged by Jack especially for tonight's performance. "Lily Was Here," first performed by Candy Dulfer and Dave Stewart.'

Hamish opened with the drum section, quickly followed by Phil on keyboards and Johnny on bass guitar.

On cue, Patrick picked out the ringing notes of the melody on lead guitar before Jack, watching him intently, lifted his instrument and responded with the beautiful sound of the saxophone.

Patrick and Jack played facing each other, close and comfortable, the way their relationship had developed. The love they shared for each other and music was evident in the way they performed together.

OVER THE PAST TWO YEARS, Julia had accepted help on the sofa of a wonderful psychotherapist.

She'd learned to deal with the break-up of her marriage, the domestic violence she'd been subjected to at the hands of her ex-husband, and Jack's traumatic sexual abuse.

She'd then worked with the psychotherapist to come to terms with the reality of her childhood and who she was.

There would always be scars, she knew this—some things just couldn't be mended—but she had learned techniques to deal with the memories and the triggers that brought them to the surface.

Loving Patrick and trusting him to share her secrets and pain had been the balm to heal her emotional wounds.

Occasionally when she was out walking in the woods a fantail would flutter overhead following her footsteps before disappearing into the trees - until the next time.

JACK CONTINUED to astound with his musical ability and would apply for Juilliard School of Music in America when he graduated from St Julian's.

THE END

～

ACKNOWLEDGMENTS

Music as a therapy is becoming more widely used around the world and I believe passionately in the power of music to make the most of people's potential, overcoming obstacles such as disability, trauma and mental illness. Music is a constant reminder of where we've come from, where we are and where we wish to be. It serves as a life diary - taking us back to a time and place or propelling us forward into a brand-new world of discovery.

The list of music referred to and which influenced the writing of this novel, is listed on Page 307 together with the link to the Spotify Play List.

My deepest thanks are owed to many people who gave of themselves repeatedly and unselfishly during the period it took to write this novel.

To my husband for his amazing editing skills across multiple drafts. His sage advice, patience and love and the person who keeps me going when I have moments of self-doubt.

To Andy and Xadi - two professional musicians who unselfishly shared their knowledge and advice regarding the technical aspects of music, instruments and how we play them. Forever grateful for your valuable input.

To Cheryl and Jane for taking the time to read my completed manuscript, provide feedback and respond to my many emails!! You're amazing.

And finally, I want to thank you my readers, you have bought a copy of this book - I am eternally grateful for your continuing support.

MUSIC REFERENCES

Adriana's Playlist on Spotify – link below (cut and paste into your browser to listen) – songs are in order as they appear in the novel

- https://open.spotify.com/ playlist/1r2QET5ColSbpVWTnz9HdE

- Ventures - *Walk don't Run*
- Sting – *Fragile*
- Mary Black – *Vanities*
- Maura O'Connell – *Summerfly*
- Sharon Shannon – *Blackbird*
- Grover Washington Junior - *Just the Two of Us*
- Aretha Franklin – *You Send Me*
- John Williams – *Cavatina*
- The Beatles – *Blackbird*
- Dave Brubeck's - *Take Five*
- Kenny G - *The Girl from Ipanema*
- Beethoven - *Für Elise*
- Diana Krall – *Just the way you are*
- Christian Willisohn – *Blues in my Bottle*

- Gary BB Coleman – *The Sky is Crying*
- https://www.youtube.com/watch?v=71Gt46aX9Z4
- Gary Moore – *The Hurt Inside*
- George Benson – This *Masquerade*
- Santana – *Love of My Life*
- Candy Dulfer & Dave Stewart – *Lily was here*
- Ambrosia – *Biggest Part of Me*
- George Benson - *Breezin*
- Chris Rea – *Shine, Shine, Shine*
- Chris Rea - *Blue Café*
- Chris Rea - *Josephine*
- Chris Rea - *Sweet Summer Day*

Can we ever really escape our past?

New Zealand expat, Julia Davis, arrives in England hoping for a new beginning. It's a chance for her son Jack to heal, and for Julia to finally rid herself of the guilt that torments her daily thoughts.

The arrival of her husband Nick should complete Julia's family. But as Jack runs into trouble at school and Julia and Nick's frayed relationship begins to unravel, secrets are exposed with devastating consequences.

Can Julia cling on to her fragile happiness – and all she holds dear?

Consequences is a novel about the ties of motherhood and marriage, about confronting the past and finding the courage to face the future.

Reviews:

Consequences is phenomenal, so eloquent and powerful. **Dr Lucinda Molan (Australia)**

Not just a story for women, men need to read this too -What a lovely story that lifts you, bangs you down hard, and picks you up again - I was completely immersed in it! Not only will this particularly touch the emotions of anyone who has witnessed violence or abuse, but it shines a light as to how we have choices and responsibilities whatever the path we take. Enjoyment apart, I learned things from this story that as a husband and father I ought to have known, but didn't, so this is a book that deserves a place on many couple's reading list.

Al Richard (Australia)

Consequences gripped me from the first page. A lovely story and a powerful message.

Karen Copper (UK)

An easy, organic and relatable read. Adriana's writings made it easy to form vivid pictures of the characters & their surroundings. I'm not much of a reader yet I looked forward to returning to this story each evening. I look forward to more material from Adriana Guyton. **Stella (USA)**

From the prologue to the last page I loved every word of it. Along with the characters, I felt I was "living" in the book. **Amazon Customer (USA)**

I really enjoyed reading this book. I didn't know what to expect and was pleasantly surprised. I'd highly recommend it. **Capstar68 (USA)**

WHERE TO GET HELP

If you find yourself in need of support, please contact one or more of the organisations listed below:

- **Domestic Violence - Domestic Shelters** - https://www. domesticshelters.org/resources/national-global-organizations/international-organizations
- https://www.2shine.org.nz/get-help/helpline
- https://www.rape-dvservices.org.au/Contact-Us
- **International Suicide Prevention** -
- https://www.supportisp.org/
- https://www.lifeline.org.nz/services/suicide-crisis-helpline
- https://www.lifeline.org.au/
- **Rape Crisis Network** - https://www.rcne.com/links/international-organisations/
- http://www.rapecrisisnz.org.nz/
- https://www.rape-dvservices.org.au/Contact-Us
- **The International Society for Prevention of Child Abuse and Neglect (ISPCAN)** - https://www.who.int/violenceprevention/about/participants/ispcan/en/

- https://www.msd.govt.nz/about-msd-and-our-work/work-programmes/initiatives/family-and-sexual-violence/specialist-services/helpline.html
- https://www.healthdirect.gov.au/sexual-assault-and-abuse-helplines